Phoenix

Mya R. Lampley

To Ann:

Hope you enjoy it!

Mya Lampley ♡

ISBN-10: 1546412409
ISBN-13: 978-1546412403

DEDICATION

This book is dedicated to my parents
Katie and Vince Lampley
for being my motivators.

CONTENTS

ACKNOWLEDGMENTS

Thank you to my friends for fueling my imagination.

Part 1

Prologue

We're what you would call Beasts. Or as the Agency says, genetically improved human beings (GIH). Normal people only assume we're demons. I'm no demon that's for sure, but they don't know that…

1

I woke up to find thousands of eyes peering down at me. I looked around to see...People, real people for the first time. The only people I'd ever seen always wore gloves and these strange suits when they were around me.

"Thank goodness he's not dead," said a man's voice.

I looked up. Three men in army camouflage looked at me and one of them stared at me as if he were interested in something about me. I was quite pleased because no one had ever looked at me like that before.

One of the men nodded and spoke in a loud voice.

"I see potential in this kid. What do you think?" He looked up at thousands of boys who pounded on the rails of stairs and balconies above.

"What's your name?" Another man asked through the noise. I thought for a moment.

"If you want you can pick a new one but choose carefully, some names stick," he added. So I went back to thinking. I knew I couldn't use my old name, it was just a bunch of numbers and seemed stupid.

"Phoenix," I smiled, and the pounding suddenly halted.

"Well, everyone welcome… Phoenix to MJD," said the man.

Everybody from up above suddenly poured from the balconies to the floor and crowded around me. I was still confused but lost in the happiness of everyone else.

"Great initiation!" One boy said talking to another.

"Great name Phoenix!" One boy came and grabbed my arm and helped me to my feet.

2

I walked down a hall of closed doors that night while staring down at the paper the three men had given me:

PHOENIX
ROOM: 256

Classes:
Magic Abilities
Magic Control
Weaponry
Lunch
Magic Training

I opened the door and stepped inside without a word.

Three boys sat around the room sharpening weapons, and trying to see who had more muscle than who.

"I'm your bunkmate, I'm sleeping on the bottom so you're up top. I'm Rufus by the way," said one of the boys.

"Oh, right. I'm Behn, and this is Lucas. He does nothing but practice magic during his spare time," said another boy.

"I do not! I only do it so I don't get expelled. They have very harsh rating systems at this school," groused the third, upside down dangling off his bed with a book in his hands.

"And who are you again?" Rufus asked.

"I'm Phoenix," I said climbing up the ladder to the top bunk.

"What did your parents do to you giving you a name like that?" Lucas said, face in his book.

"Well I… I don't remember. But I do have… Guardians if you want to call them that."

"Dude, are you adopted?" Lucas asked.

"Or a run away or something?" asked Behn.

"Call it whatever you want but, what does MJD mean?" I asked trying to change the subject.

"It stands for Magical Juvenile Delinquents. It's a school for rebellious boys. Most of us have magic abilities," Rufus scoffed.

"Speaking of which, got any of your own?" Lucas asked again.

"Me? No," I shook my head. They seemed a little disappointed and I wanted to tell them my secret.

3

I woke up early around dawn, I looked behind me at the large blue wings that sprouted from my back, and draped down over the side of the bed, an inch away from Rufus' face. I pulled a small potion jar from my satchel, it was almost empty, I wouldn't have enough for tomorrow. I used as little as possible as I covered every inch of my wings, until they shimmered from the sparkling gel. I waited for a few moments, and watched as my wings began to disappear. At least my wings would be hidden for the day, at least, I hoped they would.

First class I was caught sleeping, it was hard to fall asleep the night before.

For the rest of the day I was quiet, it wasn't normal for me to be tired, but today I was. I grabbed an apple and stood in the corner of the lunchroom. My roommates came to join me. Lunch was silent, and no matter how many times they tried to talk to me I wouldn't say anything; I just leaned against the wall and closed my eyes.

"Phoenix. Phoenix wake up," I looked up at one of the teachers. He seemed pretty cross.

"What happened?!" I jumped up in shock, I couldn't seem to remember anything. I found myself in another class that looked exactly the same.

"Don't worry, everything's okay. I just wanted to talk to you one on one. You seem really sick and we thought that this was a good time to pull you aside and get a chance to talk about this. We just wanted to hear about where you're from, just a bit of background information, if there are any medications you might have taken in the past."

"Oh okay," I nodded, and remembered Ferdinand's made up lie that I was supposed to use. "Well...I'm from the city, pretty close to here. My parents sent me here for disciplinary issues."

"I don't see why, you seem like a very nice boy," the man smiled.

The questions seemed to go on forever.

What is your parent or parental guardian's name?
What kind of disciplinary issues do you need to work on?
Are these issues things we can address?...

And I answered them all, then they started to ask me about my "sickness". I just said that it had been a lot of traveling because my family didn't have a car and they were going to work the day I left to come to the school. I said that we lived close to the woods and that the shortest route was right through it. Of course I had to add in the harsh adventure through the woods and that I walked off the hidden path. It took at least another two days to find my way there. The surprising part, was that this man actually believed my story.

4

Classes resumed in the morning. During weaponry, they made us go through a simulator. I wasn't too worried, since I'd practiced with them before. Inside there were needles connected to cords that hung from the ceiling. Pain shot through my back as the needles zapped my body and I yelped and tried to jerk away.

"You are going through the simulator that can make things real. If you need to stop just say so. Remember these are only your fears, but some can bring emotional and physical pain," said the professor through the speaker.

It was a room, like a kid's bedroom. There was a rug on the floor in the shape of a spaceship, the walls were painted blue with stars and galaxies on it. There was a bed in the corner and a shelf attached to the wall next to it. Two old books sitting there.

There was a boy in the corner sitting on the rug, about my age. At first I found it unreal, until he stared right at me.

"Go away. I don't know what you are, or why you're here but believe me...We are never going to be friends," the boy snarled, and I was so confused, I said nothing.

"I said get out!" The boy lunged at me with a dagger in his hand.

The simulation disappeared...

I got off the floor and ripped the needles out of my skin. I had earned first rank.

Next was fighting with magic, and the kid I was sparing with was Saube, and for some reason, he was really mad at me, but I didn't understand why.

"...I wanted first rank!" He shouted. He lunged at me and I dodged just in time.

"Then just get one," I shrugged.

"It's not that easy! That's our one way ticket out of here! You blew it for me, I was so close!" Saube gritted his teeth and lunged for me again.

"Really? How long have you been here?" I asked, grabbing him in a chokehold.

"Two years, six months, and seven days. Seven hundred ninety eight days to be exact," he managed to grab me and flip me over himself and onto the ground with full force.

"Well sorry, geez, I didn't know," I tried to explain but he wouldn't have any of it. He flung the dagger down at my chest and I gripped the blade with my hand to slow the attack. I felt the blood run down my hand and I cringed in pain but didn't let go. I suddenly felt the blade snap, and it clattered to the ground.

Finally, there was our free period, and by then I was so exhausted I climbed onto my bed and fell asleep without even meaning to. When I woke up Lucas was studying, Behn was with his computer - studying...I think - and Rufus...Well Rufus was ripping up books.

"Rufus is trying to quit school so he can go home, so he's burning his study books," Behn explained, not even looking up from his computer.

"Phoenix I know you just woke up but can you help me burn my books?" Rufus asked.

"Yeah sure," I lit a flame in my hand and everyone stopped.

"What?" I asked.

"Dude you lied! You can get in huge trouble for lying about powers. I heard that the last kid who lied about his abilities, got thrown out. What a lucky guy," Lucas shook his head.

"I thought the whole point was to not get thrown out," I wondered why all these people kept talking about wanting to escape...But all the while get good rankings.

"The whole point is to make it to the next level. That's where they help you develop your abilities and use them for the right things, teach you how to use them. The only problem is that most of us here, won't make it. We either just won't step up in our rankings, or just can't do it physically. Out of the four of us here, only two have a chance. That's you and Rufus," Behn explained.

5

The next day rumors spread that the headmasters of the institute had brought in two new students to be evaluated for the school. Just after our last class the rumors were confirmed. The new students were introduced to everyone.

"...I hope that everyone will treat Dox and Rogue as if they are your brothers and sisters. It'll take time to get used to… because your bunk arrangements are going to be changed," one of the men explained. Everyone began to complain but I couldn't tear my eyes off of the boy, who had a sly smile on his face.

Dox and Rogue were added to our bunk, Lucas and Behn had been kicked out and switched to another room.

"So why are you here?" Rufus asked Dox.

"Nothing, honestly. I'm a messenger, Ferdinand sent me to fetch you two," he looked at Rogue and then at me. "I bring you back to headquarters, I get my reward, and Ferdinand gets what she wants."

"I thought we weren't supposed to say anything!" I snapped, we were never allowed to tell anyone about the Agency, most consequences were either severe pain, or death.

"Don't worry, if he told anyone he'd sound like a lunatic," Dox snickered.

"Can't we stay a little while? It looks like fun here, and it's my first time outside," Rogue pleaded.

"Wait, you're new?" I asked, and she nodded.

"I can't, I'm under strict orders to take you back immediately, so don't get too comfortable we're leaving soon enough," Dox shook his head.

"Oh you're too serious. I want to have a little fun," she had a sort of happy personality about her, I liked it, and she was much better than Dox because she was right, he was pretty serious.

Dox sighed, "We're leaving at dawn, and Phoenix, whatever happens, she's not going home with me." I nodded, I knew Dox pretty well, and I knew the second I saw him here that he was here for the money. Ferdinand payed him for things like this. And so when dawn came Dox, Rogue, and I were ready to leave, but so was

Rufus.

"Please take me with you. I won't follow you I promise, I just want to go back to my house in the city," Rufus pleaded.

"We have to leave you here. You'll cover for us when we leave," Dox added. Rufus sadly agreed.

Dox, Rogue, Rufus, and I all stood around in the small bedroom. I swiped my hand over where my wings should've been, and slowly they appeared. Rogue had wings herself, but she had been hiding them under a sweatshirt, even though it wasn't that cold out.

"Ready?" Dox looked at Rogue and I, "I can't be late or I'll miss my payment." He looked at me suddenly, with a more stern look, " Since I can't fly I'll expect you to get me there, and I have to be there on time no matter what. So there's no 'take your time', got it? You better not mess up or I'll double your payments 'til you die."

"Okay, okay. We'll get there," I promised.

6

Rogue, Dox and I turned back one last time, looking toward the balcony where Rufus stood, waving goodbye. Dox, sitting on my back, turned towards the Woods.

"Let's go, I won't waste any time on goodbyes," he said.

We flew for hours on end. "That's it," I said looking down at a vast ocean of skyscrapers, buildings, and houses. Roads connecting it all. We landed on the rooftop of the building, when an alarm triggered and guards burst onto the roof.

"Put your hands in the air," the guards shouted. Rogue's hands shot up, and I followed, Dox stood with his arms crossed. "That means you too kid," the guard barked.

"I'm just doing my job," Dox shrugged, and showed the guard a tattoo on his arm.

They led us into the building and through the winding hallways up to two metal doors. The doors opened and a woman sitting at the table stood with a sly smile.

"I'm surprised by your performance 208. I was worried you wouldn't be able to succeed," Ferdinand nodded at Dox, "Excellent work." She tossed him a tiny bag tied with a string. He opened it up with a huge grin on his face.

"Will this do?" she asked. He was speechless but nodded, he spun into a black wolf with sparkling gold eyes. With a sudden flash he was gone.

"Phoenix, I thought you didn't want to come back," she said.

"I still don't, but I like to know what you're up to," I snapped.

"What do you want with us anyway?" Rogue groused.

"Not much, really. All I ask is the knowledge you've found and your skills of adaptation," The woman said pacing back and forth.

"You're leaving something out of this, like you always do. I'm not falling for this again." The woman looked down at her long blackish-purple nails. I lunged for her, and she took a step back as two guards pulled me back. They began to drag me towards the door as I held Rogue's worried gaze.

"Don't worry sweetheart, he'll be fine. Come with me now," the woman said seeing the fear in Rogue's eyes.

The guards pulled me down a winding hallway. One of them held my arms while the other unlocked a metal bolted door. They shoved me in and locked the door behind me.

I found myself in a pitch black room. I lit a flame in the palm of my hand. Its glow was dim. It vanished instantly. Then I tried again, and again. Every time the flame went out as soon as it appeared. I was going to try it one more time.....

"Don't bother, it won't work anyway," Rogue stood quietly with the woman behind a glass wall. "None of your abilities will work in here."

I walked up to the wall. "Don't try it Phoenix," The woman glared, "even Rogue tried to break it when we put her in here. It doesn't-"

BANG!

"-break," breathed the woman. I stared at the hole.

"I thought you said it couldn't break," I said tapping at the glass. I punched the glass, cracking it. The more I punched it the easier it was to break. One more blow and it would shatter. I heard the doors open behind me. I turned, my hand was almost to the wall when I was pulled back. Guards pushed me to the ground and held me still. I struggled to break their grip.

"PHOENIX!" Rogue ran up but was held back by Ferdinand. I pulled myself up tossing the two guards holding my arms, flying into the desk. A guard held an injection in his hand. I leapt onto him and knocked him down.

"Phoenix, behind you." A guard gagged Rouge with a cloth. I turned and kicked the injection out of his hand. The guard behind me grabbed me, and held me down.

"NOW!" the guard yelled. The guard stabbed me in the shoulder with the needle. I immediately lost consciousness and fell to the ground.

7

I woke up on a bed in a metal chamber.

Two guards came in and stood with their backs against the wall.

"Hey Phoenix; welcome home," said one of the guards. It was Laurence, my caregiver when I was younger, and before I was released.

"This is not my home," I snapped.

"Just let us do this and we'll take you to Ferdinand for an examination. That's all it is."

"No!" I barked. I used all my strength to take me phoenix form but my body changed right back. I yelped and dropped to the floor.

"More pain's gonna follow. Worse than this, so you're going to obey?"

I tried to pull myself up but buckled to my knees. I bowed my head to my leader.

I tried again and was able to transform. They brought me to Ferdinand who stood next to an examination table. I climbed up and glared at Ferdinand, who smiled slyly.

"What have you learned so far about the human society, Phoenix?" She asked.

"They're perfectly normal people and we don't need any more of them to die," I growled. I felt a flash of pain in my neck.

"Tell us the truth Phoenix. This injection holds you back from lying. Start to tell lies and you'll feel pain immediately. What do you know about them?" Ferdinand barked.

"Fine. They're normal people, and they...," I squinted my eyes shut, pricks stinging my body. "They'll put up a fight if they need to."

"Have you told them anything about the Agency or about you? You know the consequences by now."

"I didn't..," I yelped and fell back on the table.

"Did you tell, Phoenix?" The woman paused, waiting for my answer.

"I told them I don't have parents, and all that."

"Anything else?"

"N-Please, please, make it stop," I cried.

"Will you tell the truth?" She asked.

"Yes!" I yelped.

"I can't guarantee that you will though can I. From what I know about you I know you can't keep your word. Can you prove me wrong?"

I panted, staring into her eyes. "I-I can't."

The guards brought me back to my chambers for the night. Ferdinand stood alone in the examination room.

"It's sad, I really thought they could start it, but I guess I was wrong," she pressed a button and spoke into a speaker clipped to her jacket, "Tomorrow morning prepare them both for release."

8

The guards grabbed us by the arms and pulled us down the hallway and up the stairs and onto the roof. Guards stood around in a big group with guns in their hands.

"Phoenix what's going on?" Rogue seemed frightened.

"Probably release or execution. The second one seems more likely with these kind of people," I scoffed.

"Oh calm down. It's release not execution. To Ms. Ferdinand you're worthless, you didn't meet her standards," a guard said.

"Of course we didn't," I laughed.

They stood us at the edge of the roof looking straight down at moving cars on a highway. We flew off into the distance toward the Morse.

After a bit of flying we landed at the gate of thorns.

"How do we get through?" Rogue asked, confused.

"You walk right through. They listen to me here. They reject intruders, but don't worry, it'll let you pass. No problem," I started walking through the walls of thorns. They stayed open until Rogue and I passed through, then they closed behind us.

"I'm positive you're going to like it here."

Shadows fell overhead and Rogue tensed, looking up.

"Are those. . .?"

"No. Nothing else lives here. It's just me and you from now on."

"Where do you sleep and find food? It seems hard living out here to me."

"You sleep in the willow trees. Food, we have to steal it from a nearby town. I need to keep this place safe, it's all I have," I explained.

"You mean we'll have to keep it safe," Rogue smiled, leaning on my shoulder as we walked into the Morse.

"Where are we going?" Rogue asked.

"Somewhere special," I said, picking her up and flying over the pond in the center of the fence of thorns. We landed in the tallest willow tree overlooking the woods.

"Close your eyes," I said moving Rogue up the steps. At the top I looked around.

"Open them," I smiled and Rogue gasped, a wide smile across

her face.

"Wow!" She breathed, "It's beautiful."

"This'll be your new home. Thought I would show you the best of it."

Rogue was hypnotized by the jagged cliffs, and ponds below. "You live out here all alone," Rogue seemed sorry for me being by myself.

"I'm not alone anymore, I have you. There isn't anything that lives here, but I have a few....friends."

9

Rogue stayed at the Morse while I went and got what I needed for my so called "friends". Then I took her with me to a tunnel, deep in the Woods. We made it through...wolves. The wolves here were known as Traders. Give them what they want, you'll get what you need.

"What do you got for us this week Phoenix?" Dox asked.

"We tried our best, Dox," I shrugged.

"You know them!" Rogue's eyes went wide.

"You don't remember me?" Dox asked, but apparently she hadn't. He suddenly transformed into the student back at the institute with the same sly grin. Rogue relaxed, "They're not going to kill us," she said to herself breathing a sigh of relief.

"We rarely ever kill, don't worry. So what do you got?"

I pulled out a roll of money from my pocket and passed them the bag of food. They rummaged through the bag and took the money.

"Not enough, Wednesday to Sunday only," he nodded.

"What?!" I couldn't believe it, I'd given them the same amount the week before and they said Monday to Sunday. I knew better than to use their own word against them though. The Traders were dangerous people and would do anything to get what they wanted. We stepped outside just as someone came running in at top speed and slammed right into me knocking us both to the ground.

"Watch it!" I groaned. I was still in a bad mood from the meeting.

"Sorry. I need help," he was breathing heavily and partially wheezing from exhaustion. But I couldn't take my eyes off of his silver wings.

"With what?" I asked still dazed from our collision.

"I was attacked by a Trader, I need a place to stay," he explained.

10

By dawn I had checked the thorn wall for the fifth time. I stood at the edge of the wall, but nothing came. So I flew back to the Willow, and watched the sunrise.

An hour later, Rogue climbed the ladder, and found me half-asleep in the branches of the willow tree.

"Have you been up all night?" Rogue smiled.

"I have to patrol until Wednesday when they'll protect us," I yawned, sitting next to Rogue. She put her wing around my shoulder.

"Just promise me, you'll get some rest tonight."

"Alright," I said drifting off to sleep.

I woke up and Rogue was still there in the same position from before.

"Where's Kalo?" I asked.

"I sent him to go look around the Morse. He promised he would come back so we could talk," Rogue explained.

The three of us got together in the marshes near the cliff side. We talked for a while and Kalo said he came from a different Agency base. There were Agency bases everywhere and they held more phoenixes. I was surprised, I hadn't known of any other bases besides the one I had come from, and I guess it was the same for Kalo. I guessed there would be phoneixes from the base where I came from, more of them that we could save. "They're in underground tunnels deep below each and every base," he explained

"Let's split up. Rogue, take Kalo with you. We have to go find them. We'll group back together at dawn. If I'm not back by then I should be by tomorrow," I explained.

We separated, and I flew back to the Agency. I landed on the roof but the alarm didn't trigger. I hovered off and landed on the edge of a window sill. I wedged open the window with my fangs and slipped into an office. On the computer was an alarm system. A red light flashing in one of the quarters. "There, the underground system." I rushed off down the empty hallways. I came to the end of a tunnel where I found a huge hallway of cells.

"Help us please!" they begged. Girls and boys bigger, smaller, younger, older.

"No problem, but we have to move fast," I said unlocking the cells. Once they were all released older boys and girls carried younger ones, and flew them out, as alarms went off everyone was out and I flew off last. Guards right on me, just out of reach.

I sent them back to the Morse and searched around for other agencies but found none nearby.

Rogue and Kalo returned with phoenixes behind them. We settled them in the willows and by midnight Rogue and I relaxed watching fires in the distance flare.

"I can't believe how many we found... Phoenix, they're all calling you Leader," Rogue smiled, her eyes bright.

"And what about you? What do they call you?"

"Queen. They think we're going to be like kings and queens."

I had the older phoenixes do patrol with me each night and I could see them having fun together, like an actual family. After patrolling the Wall we would take groups into the nearby town to find food. At the end of the week Rogue and I made one last run for food and money for the Traders.

I patrolled one last time. Then I would stop near the Willows to be sure everyone was asleep, before going to the Traders. I had checked the last willow, where a boy slept on his own. I had heard about him, he was one of the youngest, Tommy. I looked around at the things he'd built. Wind chimes out of beautiful jewels he'd stolen. This kid was a master thief, but so much more. Taking things and making them better. It was the most amazing thing I'd ever seen. I was just about to leave for the tunnels when I heard the boy stir awake.

“Leader?" I turned, the boy was sitting up in bed. "What are you doing?”

"Uh... Nothing, just go back to sleep."

"But I want to go with you."

I knew I couldn't leave him alone, but I knew it wouldn't be safe for me to bring him.

"Look I have to go..."

"Why aren't you with your Queen?"

"Go back to sleep. This is none of your business," I hissed looking off into the distance.

The boy slid back in bed and watched me fly off over the Wall.

I flew off with bags of food and money, and walked from the Wall to the Tunnels. I heard Dox howl from inside the Tunnels, and ran ahead.

"You're late, what took you so long?! We're starving!" Dox growled at me.

"Nothing, just...business," I shrugged.

"Yeah well this business goes after us on your to-do list," he snapped.

I tossed them the sack and slapped the roll of money into Dox's hand.

"Honestly, we'll take anything, but we need to know about this 'business' thing of yours. You're acting real suspicious Phoenix, and we can't help you if we don't trust you."

"Fine. We freed some others from the underground tunnels in Agency. We need as much as we can get, and without you I'm making double the rounds to protect people. I need your help," I explained.

"One month. But keep them away from us. If any of them interfere with us they're our next meal whether you like it or not. We've got people to feed too you know. And they're twice as big as your little friends," Dox barked.

11

"Phoenix, what are they doing in the willows?" Rogue hissed.

"We made a bargain, protection for a month, in exchange for a willow tree in the Morse, and a share of the food, it's not that bad."

"Fine. But just keep an eye on them, I think this was a bad idea."

"Rogue they'll be gone all day, but if it makes you feel better than I will, alright?"

"Alright, 'cause I'm watching the little ones and being sure everyone's settled in. I need your help now."

"Alright. Tomorrow I'll go into town and get some supplies."

The next morning I slipped on my black cloak. At the edge of the city, I saw wanted posters of the new phoenixes from the Morse. We were still unknown, so we had to be careful not to show our faces. I walked through town slipping through store windows into closets stealing blankets, and clothes. I shoved them into the sack and kept moving.

"Hey you!" A man shouted, I turned. "What do you have in the sack?" A guard walked up to me.

"None of your business," I said pushing past.

"I saw you not too long ago with an empty sack, but I never saw you pay for anything. So what do you want to tell me?"

"That I'm leaving," I snapped. I pulled something from my pocket and threw it on the ground. It exploded with a plume of smoke and the guard coughed, as I ran off into the woods.

"I almost got caught, thank goodness I stole these."

"What are those?" Rogue asked.

"I... don't know. I asked the man behind the counter, he said they just blew up with smoke but they're not dangerous, just a distraction."

Rogue snatched one from me and slammed it on the branch of the Willow. It popped with a plume of smoke. We coughed and laughed.

"Cool!" Rogue grabbed the rest from my satchel and began

popping them open one by one.

Suddenly I heard Dox's howls and rushed to the Wall, Rogue flew, behind me.

"SURRENDER, OR THE MORSE WILL BE DESTROYED!" We stood in front of an army of government troops, weapons drawn.

"YOU'RE GOING TO DESTROY IT EITHER WAY!" I barked back.

"THEN YOU CAN WATCH IT BURN!" The soldier yelled. Suddenly screams erupted from inside the Wall.

"Stay here, Rogue-" But Rogue was already after the others.

"Rogue!" I snapped, and chased after the others.

The older kids took the little ones, but couldn't carry them off.

"Where's Tommy?" I looked around and flew off to his willow tree. Fire surrounded the tree and Tommy sat in the branches, scared.

"Help! Help me!" He croaked. I dropped, swooped in and grabbed Tommy, who clutched to me, shaking. Rogue carried two small children, the others behind her.

"Is that everyone?" I asked looking back at the blazing flames.

"Yeah," Rogue stared at the two children in her arms and the larger group behind us.

We flew the group over the thorn wall.

"TAKE THEM DOWN!" the guards yelled. Arrows shot in the air, the others fell to the ground. I felt an arrow sliced my wing, but I did my best to keep flying. Another arrow hit me and I fell from the sky. I just happened to get Tommy wrapped in my wings before my impact with the ground.

"Are you okay?" I asked, more worried about him than about myself.

"I'm fine, what about you?" He looked at me worriedly.

"Fine, just a bit shaken," I nodded with a grin, trying to keep him hopeful. He stood and went to join the others and when he couldn't see me anymore, I spread my wings.

One wing was fully extended, the other bent, and twisted. So I wasn't really in the best shape, but it wouldn't matter, as long as no one worried.

Dox and the wolves ran up, panting.

"The Morse is gone, burnt to ashes. Phoenix, you need to get them moving. They are putting out the fire, and chopping down the burnt willows, you have some time." Dox had something in his eyes

I'd never seen before... Sadness, worry, fear.

"Everyone get up! Run for woods!" I yelled and they followed the orders quickly, and ran carrying the little ones. We got moving quickly and after a few minutes we stopped running.

Dox howled twice, loud and warning.

"We need to go," I said to myself staring in the direction of Dox's howls. "KEEP MOVING!" I shouted, and we got walking. We walked for as long as the group could stand it, then, for the night we slept in the trees above. While they slept I stole some food and supplies from a group of campers.

12

"Why can't we fly instead of walk?" The phoenixes groaned.

"Walking will be easier when we're not dead!" I barked, "Trust me, this is worth it in the end."

"Can we rest for a while?" Another pleaded.

"Fine," I scoffed, staring back at the others. I climbed the nearest and watched as the others climbed in for rest. Rogue climbed up after me.

"Phoenix, your wing," Rogue gasped.

"I know, it's okay, I'll let it heal on its own. I can't let the others know, they'll be horrified," I nodded.

"Fine, but take it easy, you're working too hard," Rogue sighed.

"I know, I'll try," I nodded, and soon fell asleep.

The next morning we got moving at dawn. Carrying the little ones who were still asleep, with blankets over our shoulders. We met the wolves, tired, injured, and starved. I talked with Dox, trying to help heal him with Rogue.

"Are you okay?" I asked.

"Barely. I've never had that rough of a time with humans. They've got at least eight of my men, but other than that we're fine. Your group here is our priority, and we'll get the job done. But I can't risk the lives of any more of my own, or there won't be enough," Dox explained.

"We just need you to keep the group moving. They beg and plead with me to stop and rest or find food. I don't own them, I lead them. If you could even get the group moving that would be helpful."

"No problem. Scarring and bribing people is what we do best," Dox shrugged.

The wolves lashed teeth and growled, and snarled. Frightening the phoenixes and grouping together.

"Don't be alarmed, they're here to keep you moving," I said walking ahead.

They kept up, worried to be eaten alive. They stopped complaining, pleading, begging, just gasps and quivers of fear. Dox and the wolves, moved in, growing louder.

"Dox, I told you I'll find you something," I said not looking back.

"Better get it soon, or your friends are already gone," he said looking at Kalo carrying Tommy, who was trying his best to stay awake.

After walking for another eight hours I told the others "Let's take a break," sitting on the ground where they joined me. Sitting in a circle we discussed where we should go. Kalo laid out his map.

"Where did you get this map, Kalo?" I said looking down at the parchment.

"I stole it from Ferdinand's office, before my release, they said it was fine to take it, since it was worthless."

"Where should we go? We have to make a decision fast," I said staring at the picture of lines and dots

"Leader, the Nut Groves," he pointed at a spot on the map, "That's a good spot, it's surrounded by cliffs, near a waterfall. They have willow trees with fruit and nuts. We could stay there until we find a forever place," said Kalo drawing an X on the map, with the dirt.

For days we walked, stopping only at night and doing our best not to be eaten alive by wolves. "This is it," said Kalo, looking down a tunnel of trees I made a wall of flames in front of the entrance. I walked halfway through and stopped.

"What?" I looked at them, each with wide eyes.

"You're walking through a wall of flames. How?" Tommy gasped.

"It'll come in time. Walk through," Rogue walked through, with ease, and no pain at all.

"Tommy, you trust me, walk through," I said holding out my hand, through the flames.

"Stop, how do we know this isn't a trick," said a voice in the back. To me the voice seemed familiar. I walked to him. A stranger in one our black cloaks.

"What are you doing here?" I asked pulling back the stranger's hood. Saube stared back at me.

"Well, I had to follow you," Saube smiled.

"How could you follow me?"

"My mother's an old friend of yours. Ferdinand isn't it?"

I grabbed him up and stared into his eyes.

"What are you here for?" I said through clenched teeth.

"None of your concern."

"Leader, take these," said Kalo handing me a pair of titanium cuffs. "I stole those too." Saube tried to break from the cuffs. "You have less of a chance to get out of those than I did so don't even try."

Saube tried again and again, until he was out of breath. I groaned tying him up to a tree.

"I'm already cuffed why do I need to be tied to a tree," Saube glared.

"If you can be out of breath trying to get them off, the next thing you'll probably do will be slamming yourself against a rock or something. Just so you won't do anything stupid I guess," I shrugged.

13

I tossed Saube a mango from the trees, and went to find Rogue, who sat by the flaming wall, making a new fire when the old one went out. She was staring out at the wolves who were patrolling the new area.

"What are we going to do with Saube?" Rogue asked.

"Get him to talk, then send him back to Ferdinand. If he doesn't talk we'll give him to Dox's wolves. They haven't had blood in years."

"Dox! I've got an offer-" Dox was already in front of me, towering over me the second I said "offer".

"I might let you eat him," I shrugged.

"I'd like that. But you have to keep him shielded from heat, we like fresh meat better," Dox gave me a toothy grin. Suddenly someone slammed into me and I looked behind me to see Saube, in handcuffs but untied from the tree.

"You know I might just eat you myself. Never had blood before," I said glaring down him, I grabbed him by the collar of his shirt. "So what can you tell me?" I hissed baring my fangs.

Saube didn't speak. I tossed him into berry bush and screeched angrily.

"Phoenix leave it alone he won't talk, "Rogue said pulling Saube from the bush.

"He will if I toss him into that tree," I scoffed.

"Nice try Rogue... But Phoenix hates me and I hate him," Saube glared at me breathing heavily.

I screeched showing fangs.

"What does that mean?" Saube asked.

"He's saying he's gonna tear your heart out and stuff like that," the wolves laughed.

"Phoenix don't!" Rogue tried to pull me back, but I jumped on Saube, turning into a phoenix. Saube jolted back. I picked him up off the ground, shirt in my fangs, hovering fifty feet over the ground.

"Wow, dude, you're seriously going to drop me?" Saube eyes went wide.

"Why's that a question?" I said through clenched teeth, then dropped him. Rogue, on the ground pulled out a blue whistle, and blew hard. I heard it, pain whizzing through my ears, and flew down to grab him. I snatched him up in my claws, and brought him to the ground. Rogue blew the whistle and I screeched, and landed at her feet, panting. I stood glaring into her angry eyes.

"Are you crazy?!" she exclaimed.

"He's Ferdinand son!" I barked back, "I want to kill him now as much as Ferdinand."

"Well you don't need to drop him fifty feet in the air. That's stupid."

"Rogue, he's a part of the agency that wants me dead. I would rather try to kill most of them then die myself."

Rogue blew into the whistle and I buckled to my knees. She grabbed Saube and walked off.

"What was that?" the wolves seemed interested about the whistle. "It didn't hurt us at all."

"That's my whistle. I'm commanded to follow its orders. If the whistle is blown and you don't obey it can really hurt. That's why loud noises hurt me."

14

"Phoenix! Our whistles!" Rogue clutched me by the collar of my shirt.

"Okay, okay, calm down. Where did we last have it? Yours was in my pocket when I was making a new fire line around the groves."

"Yours was in my pocket when I was here in the tree. I was watching the new burning fire through the trees, before falling asleep. They just disappeared."

"That's impossible. Someone must have-" I stopped short and flew off.

"Where are you going?" Rogue yelled and after me and flew off behind me.

"I'm going to let you travel with us but you better not lie to me," I said unlocking his cuffs. I shoved him against a tree.

"Where are they?" I barked, but Saube stared at me innocently.

"Who?"

"You mean, what? Where are the whistles?"

"I don't know?!"

"You know! Don't play dirty with me anymore," I growled. "Where are they!?" I barked again, slamming him into the tree, and holding him by the neck.

"Al... alright," he choked. I loosened my grip and Saube gasped for air. He quickly pulled from his pocket a red whistle.

"Don't!" I began to choke him again and he pulled out the other one.

"Phoenix don't do it!" Rogue flew over.

"All for love Rogue," Saube smiled slyly and cracked the whistle. Its screaming pitch in my ears. Rogue pounced for Saube but he cracked her whistle and she fell, pain blasting through her. He blew through my whistle and I yelped, looking up at him, ready to follow his commands, my purple eyes now marble-black.

Suddenly helicopters flew over the nut groves. Somehow Saube must have gotten word to Ferdinand. The phoenixes eyes were black too following their leaders. We were under Saube's command. Our group was caged and muzzled, and carried off.

"Good work son," said Ferdinand, as Saube put the cracked, wooden whistles in her hands, "Who knew all it took were command whistles."

Saube stared off into distance, smiling with his mother.

15

Muzzled, and weak I woke up. The whistle screams were gone. I looked up at Ferdinand who stood in front of me. A dagger in her hand, her eyes full of rage her face full of guilt, mind haunted. The dagger was glowing gold.

"Believe it or not I hate to do this, but you leave me no choice. Ever since creation you were a rebel, I knew you would lead a rebellion to take me down. I have to take precautions. I'm not going to kill you, this will just tear you up inside. You know, once the leader is down the others are lost."

I backed up against a chamber wall. I breathed heavily staring at the dagger in her hand. She suddenly grabbed me by the neck and pushed me to the ground. "Don't take this personally," she sighed guiltily, then stabbed me in between my wings. I yelped and cried in pain. I wrestled and flapped my wings. Ferdinand put her hand on my back to keep me steady. I wrestled some more and tried to break free, pain bolting through me. I yelped again as she pushed the dagger deeper.

"I know it hurts, I know," she said still holding me. "Almost done, hold on."

My eyes fell softly and my body weakened. She pulled the dagger out, and I hit the floor. I balled up on the floor, shivering as pain zapped my body. I pulled myself up a bit, as Ferdinand walked out and guards moved in. They brought me to the simulator, in a metal room. The glass wall Rogue and I broke, now fixed. They connected me to the machine and I fell into a memory. I was in my body, as a human, staring at my master.

"DO IT!" he barked, looking ahead at someone, blindfold removed, gag gone. It was Rogue, staring back at me, tears in her eyes. I ran up to her, and stopped short, standing face to face. I kissed her on the lips and she faded away. I turned back, my master's angry eyes stared through me. A bundle of rope, in one hand, a knife in the other. He gave me a command, but I didn't listen, and he slashed my chest with the knife. Every time he slashed me it hurt even more, but I refused to buckle. Suddenly the man faded and Rogue appeared, rope and knife in hand.

"Bow down!" she barked. I stayed standing. She grabbed me by the neck, and slammed me to the ground. She changed into a phoenix, and tossed me against the wall. I felt my arm snap, and I yelped, trying to get up. I tried to transform, but I could only flash between man and beast. Rogue grabbed me and hovered, then she dropped me and I hit the floor. My wings broke, and I screamed. Rogue formed into a human, and sank her fangs into my shoulder. I yelped and clawed her in the face. She stumbled back, we fought back and forth until it all disappeared.

I bolted up and ripped the simulation tubes from my skin. Rogue was next to me in a second simulator, bloody, and barely breathing. I unhooked her quickly, and made my eyes glow gold to heal her. She gasped, clawing for breath. She looked me over, tattered and bloody. She clutched me tight, and cried.

"I'm so sorry," I whispered into her ear, holding her tight.

"I'm sorry too," she said breathing heavily, scared to let go.

Guards burst in guns loaded and pointed at us. Saube walked in wearing a white suit, their logo printed on the pocket of his jacket. I turned, wings spread to guard Rogue, who lay helplessly on the ground. Saube spoke into a speaker clipped to his jacket. "Turn it on, level 1," he said, staring at me. Suddenly, I felt dizzy and weak, and dropped to my knees. I felt sick, like the world was spinning. I tried to fight it, but stumbled, breathing heavily. I kept my wings spread trying to cover Rogue. She felt for my hand and squeezed it tightly.

"We can save her, and your group. All you need to do is give in. Unlike my mother, I don't lie to my creations."

"We're not creations, we're alive."

"Are you sure? I saw you as one of the first creations, you know. When I was six, I wandered into the lab. Unlike real children, you experiments don't cry. That's a sign of life," he said, turning to the speaker, "Level 2 please."

Pain zapped through me. I weakened, the sickness getting worse. I yelped and fell to the ground. I panted, my mouth was bleeding, drops of blood falling to the floor.

"You want to give in?" Saube stared, I looked back at Rogue.

"I give in," I panted, more blood spilling from my mouth.

"Stop, the injection," Saube spoke into the speaker. Suddenly the pain decreased, and I fell to the ground. Doctors, and nurses rushed over, they crowded around me putting an oxygen mask to my mouth.

They pulled me onto a stretcher and moved me into the lab. Voices yelled and people moved about.

"Hang in there okay?" a nurse said, staring into my eyes, worry in her face. She held the mask to my face. They shot me with injections, and tested my blood. I growled, voices yelling, beeping noises, angrily I tried pulling myself up from the table, but chains pulled me back. I flapped my wings angrily.

"He's awake, let's move!" a doctor yelled. They all loomed over me feeling my body, trying to hold me down. I tried flaming up but it didn't work, probably an injection. They unchained me and I screeched bolting up on all four.

"Easy, Phoenix, you're still a little-" said a nurse, but I tackled her, and ripped off the mask.

"WHERE IS SHE?" I barked.

The doctors pushed me onto the bed, and chained my wrist.

"Rogue is resting Phoenix. You should be too," said a doctor.

"No! I won't calm down until I see her and know that she is safe!" I said pulling as hard as I could at the chains, suddenly I felt weak, and hung my head.

"Lie down okay," said a nurse pushing me back. I didn't resist.

16

I woke up, Rogue sat near me.

“Rogue?” I croaked, weary and sick. Rogue turned and rushed over.

“Phoenix! Thank goodness!” she said pulling me close, kissing me on the top of my head.

“What’s going on?”

“Saube let us go free after treatment. He said if we upset them one more time, it’s over, and that we know what’s coming. The others are here too. You need to tell them you're okay.”

“I will, I will. I’m just still weak from the injections,” I said sitting up.

“Alright,” she said, then she blew through a brown painted whistle. The wolves howled, and the Groves erupted with cheers.

“What’s that?”

“It’s a whistle for the wolves, you can communicate with them. I told them to tell the others that you're okay,” she said handing me a whistle. I blew through it, and the wolves howled back.

For the first time in about a year, I felt safe.

I pulled a mango from one of the trees and felt the juice roll down my chin. I screeched and the older phoenixes joined me for a meeting.

"Do you have a plan for a new home?" I asked.

The phoenixes looked at each other and nodded.

"We’re thinking right here," said Kalo.

"I think it's perfect. We have all our needed resources and we're hidden away. We don't have to steal anymore. We can get what we need. This is home,” I agreed.

I went to make a new fire around the groves.

"Phoenix," I turned as the wolves came up, “Phoenix we're going back to the Tunnels."

"What? No you can't, you’re family."

"Yeah, and unlike you guys, we can leave our families. Who are we family to anyways? The group is frightened by us. You only need us for protection. Who are we family to?"

"To me! You found me in a tree when I ran off. I had no idea where I was!"

"We helped you get to your feet. We can't be family. We're wolves, we're creations like you."

"No, you're not, you're people. You're only a failed experiment that went wrong but you're still human."

"Phoenix we need to-"

"No-"

Dox howled and pushed me off but I came back. I jumped on his back, but he grabbed me by the wrist and flipped me over leaving a huge gash on my arm. Dox looked at me afraid, and ran, the others following behind him.

Rogue flew over hearing the howls.

"Phoenix! Are you okay!?"

"Yeah, I'm fine," I said breathing heavily staring at my wrist, bloody and red.

"HELP! HELP ME!" I flew over the Wall. It was Kalo and another boy pulling three boys, bloody and dying.

"No," I breathed, heart beating. I grabbed a boy and set him down in the Willow. Kalo and the other phoenix flew them over after us.

"Who are these people?" Rogue gasped.

"It's Dox, and his wolves," I told her before my eyes glowed.

"Phoenix, what are you-" Rogue's eyes went wide, and my eyes glowed again. I felt slightly sick but I knew I had to save them all, they were family.

The wolves looked at each other bloody and ragged. They screamed staring at their new bodies.

"What did you do?" Dox stared at me wide eyed.

"The phoenixes found you in the woods," I said breathing heavily, "Do you remember what happened?"

"Yeah, you ruining our bodies!" another groused.

"No! Not that! The other thing," I snapped.

"Oh, yeah something came out of the shadows that we couldn't see, it tackled us and fought us, but it jabbed us with something, and then it all went black. Whatever it was it turned us human," Dox explained.

"Who are these two?" I asked.

"These are my brothers, Mori, and Edgar. They never wanted

people to know their names, since they sound more human-like."

Howls erupted from outside the Wall.

"What's happening?' Rogue seemed frightened.

"Their looking for me, their noticing the change too," said Dox staring out at the fire blazing through the tree. The ground erupted, with loud footsteps. Ragged people, parted the Wall and burst in. They howled, barked, snarled, and growled, scaring off the phoenixes. Our groups fought back, roaring and screeching in their faces. Boys and girls, fighting, sinking their fangs into each other.

Rogue and I screeched and Dox and his brothers howled, and the fighting halted.

"YOU IDIOTS! WE'RE HUMAN NOW!" Dox lashed.

"NOBODY FIGHTS ANYMORE, NOBODY STEALS!" I barked. "FROM NOW ON WE SHARE THE TREES, THE FOOD, ALL OF IT WITH OUR NEW GUESTS!" I ordered.

"What! They're savage animals!" one of the phoenixes yelled.

"Well at least we're not based off of chemicals and injections," a wolf spat. They suddenly went at each other and I dropped down in between them, and grabbed them both. I looked at the phoenix.

"You follow orders from your leader," I said gripping him tighter, then turned to the wolf.

"The same goes for you, so tell your group not to double cross me."

"Why would I listen to you?" he croaked.

"'Cause I saved your leader," I hissed, and dropped them, then flew back up to the tree.

"Your wolves are idiots," I scoffed.

"Your phoenixes can't listen, that makes sense though. They can't listen because their leader is the same way. Looks like it's true that the group is like the leader. No wonder they can't listen," Dox growled.

I turned my back to Dox and stared out at the two groups colliding, trying to work together. This was going to take a while.

"See just like their leaders, both crazy and stubborn idiots," Rogue lashed.

"What do you know about us?" Dox turned.

"That wolves are as stupid as they are as humans," Rogue scoffed, staring at the ground, "And people like Phoenix can't listen."

"You know nothing about me, you know about as little as your lunatic boyfriend," Dox barked.

"Oh what? So just because I think of you as family I'm a lunatic. I ran off when I was seven, and you gave me shelter. That's family, but how would you know since you never had one. How would you know after you've been covered by rage and anger because you don't know what family is, what love is."

"I did love someone, I lost them to hunters. How would you know if you've never lost the people you loved?" Dox grabbed me by the neck and pushed me to the branches. "I told you, you know nothing about me," he said growling, tears in his eyes.

"I do. That you try to fight the fact that you're actually human." Dox threw me to the ground. "I know the truth that you've tried to throw away, but it'll only come back until you accept it," I pleaded.

"NO! Phoenix you don't know me!" Dox howled, "You don't," he whispered in my ear, eyes wide.

17

"Dox your wolves are starting riots, get them under control! More and more of my people are getting hurt!" I shouted at him.

"Actually my wolves are perfectly fine, they're happy. Isn't that what you want for your people?"

Of course, but you always need to have control or it leads to chaos. "

"No, we've already met chaos, now we're standing face to face with it," Rogue said at the top of the tree overlooking the battle between the two sides.

"Get control of them Dox, or I will," I growled.

"What would you do then, kill them? You can't kill even if you tried. You're afraid it'll mean another memory you can't escape. You're scared inside but you just won't say," Dox lashed out standing face to face with me.

"Not again," Rogue sighed, turning to Mori and Edgar. "You deal with it this time." Rogue glared at the brothers.

"No way, Dox is not someone who likes to be pulled away from a fight," Mori stood wide eyed and shook his head. Edgar pointed at Mori.

"I've dealt with our brother, not the friendliest."

"It's not too pretty with my boyfriend either," Rogue stared.

"Dox you need to get them under control, and fast," I glared at him angrily.

"Phoenix, I'm their leader and what I say goes. I'm a leader and I don't need help," Dox growled.

"I saved your life, you should at least consider my help," I flared.

He hesitated a bit, I knew I'd gotten his attention. "Fine, but I tell my wolves what to do," he said pushing past me. "Don't expect me to always follow orders, Phoenix," he said before climbing down the tree.

The next morning Dox climbed the tree, clearly angry, and grabbed me. I bolted awake from my sleep.

"What did you tell them!?" Dox barked.

"What?!" I said, sleepily.

"Your people attacked us last night. What did you order them to do?"

"Nothing, I swear!" I choked.

"Don't you lie to me, Phoenix," he said clutching me tighter. I sank my fangs into his wrist, and he shoved me off.

"You bit me!" he glared at me in shock.

"Like you've never bit someone before," I groused.

"It was an accident, you were annoying me," he exclaimed. "At least your girlfriend is somewhat nice to me," Rogue screeched and landed in the Willow.

"You idiots!" She barked, "You're fighting over things that happened in the past when there's a real war going on! Get out here, or I'll shove you both out into the woods for the night!"

"Yeah, that's my girlfriend," I sighed flying out of the tree.

The phoenixes were on one side, lashing fangs, screeching, and batting their wings. On the other side were the wolves, howling, showing off their sharp fangs, and growling. In the middle of it all was one wolf and one phoenix battling each other. I swooped down between them, wings spread. The two girls in the middle stopped their fight. One bowed down to me the other stayed standing.

"NEXT PERSON TO START A FIGHT, DIES! UNDERSTOOD!?" I roared, and everyone backed away. With my finger I made a line of fire that split the Groves in half, "Where you are now, that's your side. If you see anyone cross to your side, you bring them to me." I glared at both sides, as they trailed back to the willows. Rogue landed next me, looking at the line. The flames disappeared, leaving only a trace of black ashes.

"Good idea, do you think it'll hold?" Rogue asked, staring at ashes.

"I hope so, they're rough, and fierce, they don't listen, but it's possible."

"I'm sure it'll be fine," she scoffed.

"I worry you're being a bit too optimistic about this one," I sighed.

I heard an angry howl from the Willow and sighed.

"Don't get involved, alright?"

"What, why?"

"Dox and I have a really rough past, and he hasn't forgotten, so he won't stop until he gets the fight he's looking for."

"I thought you said there would be no fight."

"Yeah, but that's what he wants, and if it'll get him off my back, I'll do it."

"Fine, but be safe, Dox isn't too friendly from what I've heard from his brothers."

"It was worse for me. His brothers had to watch me suffer from his wrath," I said, showing her scars on my back and chest. Dox howled louder. "I need to go," I said before rushing off toward the marshes.

"What do you want from me Dox?" I glared.

"Only that you leave me and my people be. You act as if we're more dangerous than when we were wolves. We're still getting used to this. My people are still waking up scared, forgetting they're human now. Just leave us be, care about your own people. My people already have a leader, me."

"I'm just trying to help you."

"Yeah, and we don't need your help."

"What's up with you? You're not the same as before," I said, wondering what was wrong.

"None of your business, you're too nosy."

"Well I want to help you!" I begged him.

"Leave me alone, I don't need you to help fix my past."

"Well you can't get rid of me. What happened to you?"

"Nothing!" Dox barked.

"Something must be wrong."

"Nothing!" Dox glared.

"Tell me and I can help you."

"Phoenix!"

"Don't you care about me?"

"Yes, but."

"And I care about you, so trust me."

"LEAVE ME ALONE!" Dox howled at me, "Phoenix, I'm now half wolf but that means I'm still independent, I care about you but I can't support someone, I can't have a family."

"Then why are your brothers with you?" I said a sly smile on my face. Dox's brothers tackled him and wrestled with him.

"Quit it!" Dox yelled, being bit and scratched by Mori and Edgar.

Rogue stood behind me smiling.

"That's so sweet," she sighed.

"Also no fight. Walked away not even hurt," I laughed, "Well he might just get hurt wrestling with his brothers."

18

Screeches erupted from the gate that morning. I stirred awake and rushed over. The phoenixes held down two boys, both of them dirty and in shredded clothes.

"Phoenix!" the boys pleaded with me to help them.

"Leave them be," I said staring at the two boys. As I approached I realized it was Behn and Lucas, from the school. "Go back to your homes." I ordered the phoenixes, who slunk back away from the boys.

"Where are we?" Lucas asked looking dazed.

"Welcome to the Groves, don't get too comfortable you won't be staying long," I said looking around, to be sure no one spotted them. "What are you guys doing here?"

"What's up with you Phoenix? You seem... different," said Behn staring at me oddly, as they climbed to their feet and followed me to the Willow Forest.

"Let's just say that over the past year, we've made some improvement," I said. Shadows flew over their heads and they looked up into the trees.

"Are those?" Lucas seemed dazed and awestruck.

"Every last one, that is on this side," I said glaring at the black line on the ground.

"If they own this side who owns the other side?" Behn asked looking at the other side covered by the shadows.

"Wolves. My friend and his wolves enjoy the blood that's why I want you gone, by tonight. His people need meat they can't just live off the fruit and nuts from the trees. They find out you're here and I can't protect you. Their leader won't listen to me."

"If what's his name is the leader over there then who's the-'"Behn was cut off when Kalo landed in front of me."

"Leader, Dox needs meat now, they're threatening the phoenixes closer to the Line."

"Alright I'll talk to him, you just move them into another willow tree. Also I need you to find me a cave for these two. You can't tell anyone they're here. Find me a cave in the marshes."

"You're their leader?" Lucas breathed.

"Yeah, but I don't let it go to my head. All I ask is that they follow my orders. Rogue and I freed them from the Agency," I said standing in front of a dark cave. Kalo stood at my side,

"It's far away from the Willow Forest, and the Line. The phoenixes don't like the shadows; so they can stay here and no one will find them. The wolves wouldn't even dare come over here, it's too far from their side," Kalo stared at the cave etched into the cliffside.

"Good work Kalo, have some of the people stay near the Line. If I don't get food for Dox's people, we can expect some dangerous threats."

Kalo flew off and I started walking into the cave.

"Follow me."

"I don't think you have a very good ideas on what to call home," said Lucas staring into the mouth of the cave.

"I know it looks bad but it'll keep you safe," I said turning toward them. "My friend won't be too happy if he finds out you're here. Especially since he's half wolf. Don't worry I'll come check on you every now and then, but you two might not last long here. Nobody really cares where I go during the day so I can visit and no one will care."

"What about me?" I turned to Rogue who didn't seem so happy.

"Rogue go back, please, Dox might-"

I heard Dox from the Willow, enraged and furious.

"He's starving I bet," I stared off into the distance, before flying off to find Dox.

"Phoenix, why do I smell *human*, on your side of the Groves?" Dox growled.

"Dox we're all half human, are you sure you're okay?"

"Oh, I'm fine and you're lying to me!" He yelled before pressing me against the tree.

"How do you know? You might just be sick from no protein that can really mess with your senses." I choked as Dox gripped tighter.

"Phoenix, I know I'm not sick. You're hiding them, you know how much I hate humans!" Dox growled.

"Yeah, but if you give them a chance they're not so bad. They're actually really nice once you get to know them."

"Phoenix, they're not all that nice. Especially the one that wants you dead!" Dox barked, staring into my eyes. He was angry for sure, but he seemed… worried, like this was all a bad idea. Like Behn and Lucas and their kind would turn on us all in the end. "Look, Phoenix, those two can stay but you better keep an eye on them, they seem nice and trustworthy one minute, until they turn on you; until they turn on all of us, and we're captured, and used like we don't even matter."

"Alright, but let's make a bargain. I keep watch of the two boys, if your people help us with something?"

"Seems fair to me, but what?"

"How would you like to taste real blood again?"

Dox paused and thought, but it didn't take long at all. "You have my attention."

"With our numbers, I say we storm the Agency. If we have our sides come together, we could take it down. My phoenixes and your wolves. We'll have the Agency taken down in no time, and you will get more meat than you could ever imagine."

"Alright but what about Saube and Ferdinand? I don't think killing them quickly is a good idea. I say we kill them last, but outside."

"Outside, why?"

"I thought it would be nice of us to have them watch as their work all falls apart, then we kill them. I want to kill Ferdinand as much as you so I say we kill her together. We were both her first experiments. The two of us killing her would make it special."

"I couldn't agree more, but we should also kill Leader too. I hated him, more than Ferdinand."

Dox and I sat in the grass planning everything out that night. I went home and told Rogue that in a week we'd storm the Agency, and watch the it shatter to pieces. Rogue decided that tomorrow we would tell the two sides, but it might not work.

19

The phoenixes and the wolves agreed to our decision, and we prepared, quickly. We all knew we wouldn't need weapons, or anything like that. We sent travel groups to go into towns and steal some things. I went out with Dox, Rogue, and Kalo. I slipped into a store, wings uncovered this time. I went underneath a table, and got some good things. I pocketed people for money and then bought things with it. I bought smoke crackers, and grenades and rushed back to the Groves. Now we were ready.

We lined ourselves up against the building, pockets full of trinkets. We signaled the first group. Dox and I slipped through an open window. The halls were empty, and Dox and I rushed ahead. We climbed the wall and hung upside down from the metal ceilings.

"Nice job on the magnets," I whispered to him.

"No problem," Dox smiled.

We slipped into the control room. The guards were gone, and we sent a signal. Then footsteps burst through the doors, tackling and biting guards. Dox tackled Ferdinand and I dropped down behind him, grabbing Saube by the neck.

"Back again, I see," Saube choked. Dox handed Ferdinand to me and slipped out the window, I hovered over the ground and landed outside the Agency. Dox grabbed Ferdinand again and squeezed tightly.

"Stop don't kill him please. Kill me and let him go free," Ferdinand whispered, barely breathing from my friend's grip.

"Oh we're not going to kill him, we'll only have him watch with you as this place shatters to pieces," I laughed.

"Phoenix, let Saube go. He won't do anything once this place is gone," Ferdinand pleaded.

"I just want to be safe, I'm alive after all," I said before staring into his scared eyes. "'Cause if I wasn't alive I couldn't kill you myself." I sank my fangs into his neck and dropped him. He didn't move. "If I wasn't alive I couldn't know how to kill," I said staring down at Saube angrily.

"NO!" Ferdinand screamed, and Dox let her go. Suddenly red

lights flashed in the windows of the buildings. Everyone ran out.

"That's all of us," said Rogue before staring down at Saube, lifeless, "Did, you really?"

"I did... But we're safe now." Suddenly the building exploded shattering to pieces. Glass from the windows rained down from the sky. "Wings up!" I shouted out to my phoenixes. With everyone's wings spread, we were a shield for the wolves, and let the glass clatter onto our wings like ginormous raindrops. The building crumbled from where it stood, waves of dust from the crumbling cement crashed into us. Finally when the dust cleared, the Agency's crumbled down form stood before us.

AFTER

During the explosions, Ferdinand disappeared off into the woods. No one has seen her since. Dox and the wolves left us two months later and every now and then I can hear his howls from a mile away. Behn and Lucas just disappeared somewhere, but it doesn't matter where. When we were eighteen, Rogue gave birth to a boy, half phoenix. Dox was married to another half wolf named Kareen, and she gave birth to two children, and they visited sometimes.

Part 2

Prologue

“Dox!” I ran up and hugged Dox, who starred behind him.

“Get off me, Vess,” Dox stared back at a boy clutching his leg. He turned to me. “I have a family now, my son Vess is the quiet one, who likes to hide behind me,” Dox barked. Vess ran off toward Kareen, holding him in her arms, with another little one holding her hand.

“He’s your son you know,” said Kareen, glaring at Dox.

“The kid’s like a blood sucking leech on my leg. That's not good,” Dox snapped back.

“It’ll get better if you play with him I can only deal with one at a time,” Kareen sighed, holding Vess in her arms with Ex at her side.

“Fine, he can ride on my back on the way home,” he turned to me. “So how’s your life been?”

"Well, I have one kid and our group is thriving, that's for sure."

"The wolves at home idolize our family, but I don't know why."

"Same with our family, everyone loves the kids."

Rogue came up behind me.

"Where is he?" Rogue glared.

“I thought you had him!" I snapped back.

"Look out!" I looked up a second too late and was toppled to the ground.

"So this is your son," said Dox, "Why am I not surprised."

"I got you this time!" Fangs said still on top of me.

"Get off!" I roared and Fangs climbed off me and stood up. "I told you, I’ll teach you soon. Not now.”

"Phoenix, I can't wait that long,” Fangs groaned.

“Later. Now go play,” I sighed before he went running off to join Rogue.

"You don't make him call you dad?"

"No way, dad just sounds weird. How about you, what do Vess and Ex call you?"

"Nothing yet, he's shy so he usually hides behind me. He doesn't talk a lot either. They're little so it makes some sense. Ex calls me by my name too. You get used to it."

"Come on, why don't we leave the kids to their moms for a bit."

"That would be-"

Kareen yelled behind him, and Vess grabbed him by the leg,

almost tripping him.

"What now?!" Dox groaned. Vess pointed a shaking finger at Kalo.

"That's Kalo, Vess. He's not going to hurt you," I laughed," Your kid is nothing like you."

"Three, two,…," Dox growled and Vess hurried off in the other direction. “Alright we can go now," Dox sighed. We walked through the marshes, covered by the trees, casting shadows all over.

1

Rogue, our son Fangs, and I sat on the cliff side, watching the sunset. Fangs was eight years old, with black hair, blue eyes, and ghostly pale skin. Rogue and I continued to look eighteen years, since all phoenixes stop aging at eighteen, and we couldn't have been happier.

"I finally got the family I always wanted," I said, kissing Rogue on the cheek. She leaned her head on my shoulder.

"I finally got my true love, the one I used to dream of," Rogue sighed, as she grabbed Fangs into her arms, and stared into his eyes. Fangs was a calm boy. He didn't run off anywhere without us. The other phoenixes adored Fangs, and played with him when we couldn't. More and more of them were found and settled all over the Groves. Our species was thriving. Growing more and more. I couldn't be happier. Every now and then I thought about the attack on the Agency. That one moment where I did something I thought I could never do. I also couldn't help but think, what if I could've done it better than that. Had I listened to Ferdinand's offer, I wouldn't be thinking of it now. I heard Dox's howls, and my troubles faded away. I screeched and he howled back. Rogue screeched for Kareen who howled back with joy.

Fangs rushed off to his cave in the marshes every day. I made him a space where he could have fun, thinking he could do whatever he wanted with his childhood, unlike mine. Every now and then he'd ask questions about when I was his age, but I had to lie to him, thinking telling him the truth would be too much to handle.

"Phoenix, what was your life like?"

"I had a really good life, but I wanted you to have a better one," I said.

"Where are you from?" Fangs questioned.

"I'm from..." I paused thinking if I should lie or change the subject. "You know it doesn't matter where I'm from. What are you doing in there, Fangs?" I asked, staring down the darkened tunnels. Fangs got up and tapped at something on the wall of the cave. Lights flickered on one by one as Fangs held my hand, dragging me through the tunnel. We came to an open space. A big flat rock was covered by wires, nails, shards of glass, and books of all kinds.

"You've been building thing in here?"

"Yeah, I built this," Fangs held up a clip.

"What is it?"

"I've been hearing those howls from off in the distance and-" Fangs paused to think for a moment. "Why do you and Rogue screech back to them?" He asked confused, but interested at the same time.

"You wouldn't remember him, but he was my friend, we've been through a lot together, just me and him." I couldn't answer his next questions about what we'd all been through and things like that. Fangs was so interested, but I could never make him understand, or know what had happened before he was born. I heard a howl from far away. I screeched and it echoed off the cave walls. Suddenly roars, and howls erupted from the gates, and Fangs hid behind me. I grabbed him in my arms and flew to the gates. Rogue stood with Kareen who held her two children by the hand.

"Phoenix!" Dox waved from below and howled. I swooped down and put Fangs on the ground who looked up at Dox and hid behind me.

"This my son, Fangs," I said looking into Fangs scared eyes. I was puzzled looking around at three wolves spread out around us. "What's with the guards? My people aren't threatening you again I hope."

"No this is for my older son Ex, he's seven years old and can get a little wild. He too hasn't accepted that he's half human." We turned to see Fangs, Vess, and Ex, playing tug a war, with one of Ex chew toys. Vess and Ex stood on one side, while Fangs stood on the other, flapping hard, dragging Vess and Ex.

"Well, he does get the strength from his father," Dox laughed.

"Your kids get that fierceness from you I'm guessing," I smiled. Fangs was spinning the other two around in a circle, and sent them flying. Dox dashed after them and caught them both in his fangs. He bolted back and dropped them panting.

"This has been my daily routine, for the past week," he panted.

"Fangs be careful, please," I groaned.

"What!? That was awesome, let's do it again," Fangs laughed.

"NO!" I snapped.

"Well at least your kid can listen," Dox glared, at Vess and Ex.

"Actually it slipped my mind that we haven't fought in two years. It feels… good, I guess."

"Finally no more rivalries."

"You two used to fight each other?" Fangs seemed eager to know.

"Was it epic?" Ex asked harshly.

"He's really into things that deal with pain, apparently," Dox shrugged.

"I can see that," I nodded staring creepily at Ex.

"What happened?!" Fangs moaned.

"Let's just say we used to not get along very well."

Rogue and Kareen glared at us. "Don't lie to them, you two hated each other," Kareen sighed.

"You two loved to wrestle and toss each other out of trees too," Rogue added.

"Awesome! Don't stop, keep talking," Ex definitely enjoyed hearing about his father and me fighting.

"Yeah, I guess what they're saying is true," I shrugged.

"Every last word," Dox sighed.

"Shut it Dox!" I snapped, pulling him in. "I don't want them to know."

"I know they won't care about knowing if we fought back then. Don't worry, Kareen doesn't want me telling the kids about the past either."

"Okay, but why?" Fangs seemed confused in the point of fighting for no reason.

"He ruled his people, I ruled my people but we both hated the way each of us did it."

"You're people never listened, and hated me."

"Well 'cause you're not their leader. Your wolves on the other hand, started riots, and you said they were happy?"

"What?! They were happy, having fun, doing what they wanted, when they wanted."

"So your people enjoy, killing, blood, threats, and meat."

"Definitely meat, but we're also independent, that's why I never wanted your help."

"So that's why you tossed me out of a tree, and broke my wrist," I glared.

“I told you years ago it was an accident. You and your people drive me crazy.”

” So you enjoy being wild more than being half human.”

“Exactly. Oh I almost forgot,” Dox handed me a silver chain, with a gold key in the middle. “When Fangs is old enough to understand, you can show him. It unlocks the lab. I gave two more chains to my sons. Ex’s chain unlock the simulation room, and Vess’ unlocks the chamber room I used to be in.”

“I don’t think I ever could. Not after what I’ve done,” I stared at the grass.

“You don’t need to share everything, only some things so he knows. Who knows, maybe you could find Ferdinand. She disappeared off into the woods, who knows where she is now,” Dox stared ahead, at the woods.

“If she is alive she’s coming back for me. I killed her son, now she might just kill mine.”

“I won’t let that happen. Plus I almost killed her so she’ll be coming back for both of us. If you need protection, it’s on me this time.”

2

I put the chain around Fangs' neck. He stared down at it, fingering at the gold key. "Now can I know what this is for?" he asked.

"You'll see when you're older, for now I can't say. Dox gave his sons the same key, but they unlock different things," I said as we walked through the woods.

"But I am older, I'm eight, I should get to know by now," Fangs whimpered. "I've had the chain for two months, Phoenix, when can you answer my questions?"

"You mean you lost the key twice and I had to go find it," I corrected him and he shrugged.

"Same thing," he scoffed. So I screeched and called for Dox.

"What's going on?" Dox panted running up, "Honestly Phoenix, do you have to run me all me over the place."

"Fangs wants to see it." I gave Fangs a quick glance.

"Now?"

"Yeah, he says he's ready."

"I was hoping he wasn't, Ex wants to see and he's nine, but he won't go anywhere without Vess."

"Let's get this over with," I sighed before flying off. Dox and his sons ran below. After a bit of traveling we came to an old building, windows busted, and shattered, big holes through the roof, and walls.

"This is it," said Dox, pain, and fear in his eyes. "Phoenix, you okay?" Dox stopped short, turning back to me. I stood in front of Saube's corpse, bloody, and decaying. "I'm fine," I said stepping over him. We walked through the halls, scattered with the dead bodies of guards. Glass shards, covered the floor. We came to the lab first. Fangs passed me the key, and I unlocked the doors and pushed them open.

"My wolves hit here first, they were an easy target and a good source of food. We took every last one of them," Dox breathed, looking up at dangling, wired lights. Glass shards were scattered all over the floor, blood stains over the examination tables.

"What is this place?" Fangs turned to me, spooked.

"This is where Dox and I are from, well, before we blew it up," I shrugged.

"You killed all these people," Vess seem afraid of Dox.

"No, Vess, we did something good, even though it looks bad," Dox gave him weak smile.

"Dox! That's not how you approach things!" I snapped.

"What?! I'm bad at this whole parenting thing, I'm just starting," Dox shrugged.

"It is bad, our fathers are killers," Ex stared at his father.

"What about Rogue and Kareen? Did Rogue kill anyone?" Fangs growled.

"Fangs-" I tried to explain as calmly as possible.

"No, I get it…You're a killer. You kill people for no reason!" he yelled at me angrily.

"Fangs don't-" Dox tried to calm him.

"Dox stay out of this!" I barked. "Fangs I'm no killer."

"Then why are we here?"

"To show you the truth. I knew the truth would be too dangerous for you."

"How do you know that?"

"Because-" I stopped short, "Follow me." I walked into the simulator room. The needles dangled from the ceiling.

"Stand right here," I said placing Fangs in front of the simulator, and the needless suddenly shot him in the back. Suddenly the simulator turned on. We watched him through the monitor. When it was over Fangs ripped out the needles, and collapsed to the floor.

"You know nothing about me." I stared at him angrily, and we stood face to face.

"Well I do know you've lied to me my entire life."

"Because I knew you'd be frightened by what you saw. You said you were ready though, so I let you see."

"Well you could've told me you killed a boy."

"He tried to kill me five times in school. Then his mother stabbed me in the back, with a dagger. He also claimed I'm not alive. If I wasn't alive, I wouldn't know how to kill."

"But how?"

"I won't ever say how, what I've shown you today is enough." Suddenly an alarm went off and we covered our ears.

"What's going on?" Fangs stared at me worriedly.

"It's an alarm for the lab, something's wrong."

We rushed over. Everything was the same.

“Phoenix, look. They're still alive," Dox stared into two water chambers. Inside was a phoenix, and in the other was a wolf. The wolf's fur was black and white, and the phoenix's wings were black and white too. My eyes automatically turned black, and I saw a vision of who it was. I collapsed to the floor, and my eyes were their normal color.

“Phoenix," Dox crouched down in front of me.

“I'm not their leader," I stared into his eyes.

“What are you talking about?"

“Dox, I'm not their leader, he is," I said pointing at the boy, “And she's yours,” I pointed at the girl but Dox just shook his head.

“No way, I am not going to be bowing down to a girl," Dox scoffed.

“Their wings and fur is different than ours, that means, they're the Alphas," Fangs said looking through a pocket book. "This is it," he said pointing to a picture of both of them, holding hands. Suddenly the two animals started moving, trying to free themselves. I pressed a button on the wall and the water chambers opened splashing water everywhere. The creatures were twice our size, and out of nowhere they tackled the boys and they screeched and howled.

“Fangs run!" I yelled as I jumped on its back. The creature's spade-like tail coiled around me and threw me against the wall and I blacked out.

3

"Where is it?!" I bolted awake and grabbed Dox by the collar of his shirt. "Where is he?"

"Calm down they're gone, and he's at home with Rogue. We were about to be attacked but the animals retreated to..." Dox stopped.

"Who?" I barked back.

"Ferdinand. She's alive. She said that she created them after we stormed them. She said she returned to get them. That our friends would soon become our enemies or something like that."

I gaped at him, my stomach sank. "Behn and Lucas. They know that I killed Saube and they told the school. They're coming for me. Ferdinand was running in the direction of the school the day she disappeared. She must have turned them on us. We can't get help from them anymore."

"Well, lucky for you I'm a solitary animal. Also wild."

"Thank goodness I have you." We laughed as I stood up and we walked back to the Groves.

The girls, grabbed us and didn't let go. Rogue cried into my shoulder, Fangs hugged me too.

"I was so scared. You promised me," she cried.

"I know, I'm so sorry, I put Fangs in danger too," I whispered in her ear, holding her close.

"He told me you saved him, I can't be mad at you for that," Rogue looked up, her eyes red. She laughed a little trying to brighten up from her fear.

"I won't take him back there again. He said he wanted to go, and he felt so strongly about it, I couldn't say no." Rogue clutched me tighter, and turned to Fangs.

"I can't blame you for your curiosity but, the truth is you know nothing about Phoenix and you know nothing about me," Rogue growled.

"I put him through the simulator. He knows now." I stared at my son. Rogue calmed down, and kissed Fangs who wouldn't let go of her. Dox and Kareen were quiet. Kareen wouldn't stop checking him for bleeds and gashes.

"Kareen I promise you I'm fine," Dox laughed.

“I’m sorry but you scared me half to death. Don't do that Dox, please don't leave me."

“I won't, I promise," Dox pulled her close.

Rogue and Kareen finally let us be. We talked with the council, and they agreed to stay there, but they weren’t all that happy about it. No one would leave the Groves. When Rogue and Kareen found out about the Alphas they wouldn't let the boys out of their sights. Dox and I watched the Line. I made a wall of thorns like from the Morse. I put rocks and boulders in front of the Wall. The girls wanted the Groves to be entirely protected. Kalo made groups do shifts on watching the grounds below. For weeks nothing came. Dox and his family stayed in a cave in the meadows. Dox and I soon became a threat to everyone around us. Our eyes turned black, and we couldn’t control our own bodies. We ran off into the woods during the day and ended up coming home, scratched, and bloody.

“What happened to you two?” Rogue asked looking me over for bleeding.

“When we’re in the woods we don’t hurt anyone but each other. Neither of us can tell what we’re doing, and by the end everything in the past is a blur.”

“Well either way you two fight tough.”

“I bet I could fight Phoenix and Dox at the same time,” Fangs gloated.

“Don’t gloat, once their eyes turn black, you’re a goner,” Rogue snapped.

“I-” My eyes were black and I stared at him, and Fangs backed up frightened, they were suddenly their normal color, and I stepped back from my family. I flew off to find Dox, who howled from below me. When I landed, he was scared and speechless, just like me.

“We need to stay away from our families, I scared Fangs, now he's terrified of me."

“Your problem isn't too hard to deal with, but I don't think Kareen will ever let me around her again," Dox hung his head.

“What happened?" I breathed.

“I bit her."

“Maybe we should camp out. Then when our eyes go back to normal we can stay out in the woods."

"Alright, I'm worried about Kareen though," said Dox staring back toward the cave.

“You really do love her? You said you didn't belong to anyone."

"If I didn’t love her, I wouldn’t have married her," Dox snapped and turned into a wolf and sprinted for the woods. I flew after him.

4

Dox and I woke up lying on the ground, beat and scratched. The sky was still dark, and covered with stars, but I was wide awake.

"Anything broken?" Dox said checking himself.

"No, how about you?" I said looking up at him.

"I'm fine."

"I want to see her so badly, but I'm afraid. I'm a threat to them now," I said staring at the wall of thorns and stones.

"I want to see them too, but Kareen will keep them from me. She's afraid of me now. I told you… I'm wild, I can't have a family," Dox had his head in his hands.

"We're only dealing with the depression of being away from our families. We can't fight it,-whatever this is- we're being controlled. It might control our emotions too."

"Alright, let's get prepared for the next change-." Dox stopped, hearing howls and screeches from far away. I screeched back, and heard Fangs' screeches, and I screeched louder. Dox howled to his family.

"That's better," he smiled.

"It feels good to hear from family," I sighed-.

I yelped and fell to the ground, my eyes were black. Dox stared back at me, growling deeply, his eyes were black too. I lashed my fangs, and screeched before tackling him to the ground. He clawed me in the face and I lifted him off the ground.

"Phoenix don't!" I heard Rogue scream.

"Dox!" Kareen stood frozen.

Dox bit my leg and we both went down. I punched him and he flipped me over on my back. He jumped on me and sank his fangs into my neck, and I pushed him off, bleeding. I felt at my neck, my hand was quickly covered red. I grabbed him and tossed him into the trees.

"Stop! Phoenix, stop!" Dox put his hands out. I dropped to the ground, back to my normal self. I looked up at him. Dox felt at his leg, bruised, and weak.

"My leg… I think it's broken," Dox looked up at me breathing heavily,. "Your neck."

"Its fine, it'll heal," I said staring at my hand covered in blood.

My eyes changed red and back to their normal color. "It's not broken, it's just bruised," I said staring down at him.

"How do you know?"

"Ever since the Agency was destroyed I got more abilities, I think you have it too. X-Ray vision, you can see the bones, and veins in someone's body."

Dox's eyes did the same thing.

"That's amazing," he smiled.

Our families rushed out of the Groves. Rogue ran up to me, injections in her hands. She pushed me to the ground and injected it into the cut. I yelped and pushed her off, panting.

"What was that?!"

"Injection it'll help you heal faster," Dox yelped and fell back as Kareen injected him in his leg. The girls left minutes later. Fangs and the other boys wouldn't see us, terrified. The girls handed us packets of the injection, telling us to inject ourselves after every fight.

After three weeks, our eyes stopped changing, and we got to go home. Fangs still stayed away, hiding in his cave.

"Fangs, come out please. I've missed you so much, and you know I would never hurt you," I said standing at the mouth of the cave.

"You scared me. You didn't look like yourself, you looked... wild. How would I know you'd never hurt me," he said from inside the cave. I screeched and it echoed into the cave.

"Stop that! It really hurts my ears," Fangs shouted from inside. I screeched again and again. "Stop, Phoenix," he groaned.

"I won't stop until you come out."

"Fine but you won't hurt me?" Fangs sighed, I could hear the worry in his voice as it echoed from inside the cave.

"I won't."

"Do you promise?" Fangs stood at the end of the tunnel, scared.

"I promise," I said in a reassuring voice. Fangs ran up and hugged me.

"I missed you so much," he sobbed.

"I missed you too. I know I scared you, but that's not me."

"Then who was it?"

"People who I thought I could trust, but I can't. It wasn't me. This is me."

"I know it's not you."

I met with Dox in the woods at dawn.

"They understand. How about your son?" Dox said calmly.

"I think Fangs understands too. Did Kareen forgive you?"

"Of course. She can't stay mad at me for long," Dox laughed. Two minutes later Dox had me up against a tree. I sank my fangs into his wrist, and threw him into the mud. We punched, scratched, and clawed at each other. Dox grabbed me in between my wings, and I struggled. He slammed my back into a tree, and pain shot through my wings. Dox, pushed me to the ground, I kicked him and our eyes flashed to color. I yelped, and fell to the ground, flapping helplessly.

"Phoenix!" Dox helped me up. "Your wing, did I?"

"Its fine it'll heal," I yelped, knocking myself against the tree. Dox howled loudly, and I covered my ears.

"What are you doing?"

"Getting Rogue," he turned and howled again, when Rogue screeched and swooped down.

"Phoenix!" Rogue ran up, about to use her last bit of magic.

"Rogue don't waste it!" I snapped. She grabbed an injection and tossed it to me. I injected myself and outstretched my wings. I swooped down pushing Dox to the ground, my eyes black. Dox's eyes changed color and he scratched me. This time the fight was longer. Dox slammed me to the ground. I kicked him off and he stumbled back. I lifted him off the ground and tossed him into the trees. My eyes were their normal color, and I fell, my body tired and weak.

"Phoenix!" Dox looked up and caught me by my shirt in his fangs, and laid me down. I sat up and injected myself for the tenth time that day. The fights continued, coming and going, we barely slept at all. By the end of it we were tired and barely got time to inject ourselves, as the fights got longer and longer.

5

We came back home for a while, it had been two months since we'd seen them.

"You're okay, thank goodness," Rogue ran up hugging me. "What happened. We didn't hear any noises from outside the Wall?"

"No we were still fighting," I laughed, " We were fighting the whole time. Some of our fights lasted overnight."

"I'm just happy you're home."

"Rogue we're not staying. The switches happen at different times and we don't know when it will happen again."

Kareen screamed, Dox on her, his eyes black. I screeched and pulled him off. He stared into my eyes. "Phoenix run," Rogue whispered. Dox lunged for me and I ran for the woods, as he chased after me. My eyes turned black and I toppled him to the ground, he kicked me off. Our eyes were normal. The girls ran through the Wall, the boys stayed close to it.

"Get out of here," Dox lashed.

"It was an accident, that's all," Kareen shrugged.

"We don't want to hurt anyone, just go home," I growled.

"We're not going to leave you this time, we all miss you," Rogue growled back.

"We don't need your help!" Dox barked.

"Go back home!" I screeched and they backed away. Dox howled fiercely and they ran. We didn't fight that day, but we stayed in the woods. Days passed and nothing happened. The girls, and the kids stayed away.

"We need to stop this," Dox groaned.

"First we need to find Ferdinand, I think I know where."

"Where is that?"

"MJD, Magical Juvenile Delinquents. You're not going to like these people. They are rough, crazy, and stupid at all times."

"Won't matter to me, sounds just like my wolves," he laughed.

"They think we're murderers, so we better be careful."

"No problem," just like that Dox sprinted off, and I flew off right behind him. After hours we got there. "Follow me." We slipped inside, no guards were around.

"They're having spare time, no one will be around for a while."

"Alright let's find Ferdinand."

"No, we find Behn and Lucas. Ferdinand created the Alphas, Behn and Lucas own them, they know a lot about me, so they'll use it against me. Ferdinand knows everything about you too, and she'll tell them," I whispered.

"Fine, but who do I hurt," Dox growled with a nasty grin.

"No one!" I snapped, "I know their room, let's go."

We slipped up the stairs and into the room.

"They're not here?" Dox seemed puzzled.

"No we're here, we all are." Behn slammed the door shut, with a sly smile. Hands grabbed me, and pulled me to the floor. I grabbed Lucas by his shirt, and slammed him to the ground. I snatched the muzzle from his hands and muzzled him instead.

"You know for a second there I thought I'd be the one being muzzled, Well now you can know what it's like to be treated that way," I sneered, tightening the straps.

"More like they'll be the ones to confess and we'll be the ones to walk back to our families and not get hurt," Dox had Behn and Ferdinand choking on his grip.

"How about Lucas hands over the duct tape he has in his pocket and I won't snap his wrist," I barked using my X-Ray vision. Lucas slipped it from his pocket and handed it to me in the blink of an eye.

"Good kid, you know if he doesn't try to kill me I might just let him walk away."

Dox and I taped them to the wall nice and tight.

"Where are the Alphas, Ferdinand?" I asked.

Ferdinand just glared at me and yelped when Dox sank his fangs into her shoulder. "I told all of you the truth, and you'll tell the truth to me."

"All three of you will tell the truth until we get the information we need," Dox barked. "Ferdinand answer the question."

"I couldn't complete the process when your armies attacked the building. So instead I had them sent to the water chambers so they could still function. But I didn't get to go back and finish it, so I came here. Now everyone knows the truth, that you killed them. Everyone! Innocent guards, who had families to go home to. And most importantly, my son," she explained.

“Oh come on!" Dox groaned, staring at Lucas and Behn. "Are you seriously going to believe her? Everything she is telling you is a lie. She tells you she'll make you a good life, she tells you that you are loved. She tells you that you're not a monster, and then she makes you a weapon. She makes you a killer, a murderer and then she tries to kill you herself!" Dox barked.

"Oh, no that was a prediction. You weren’t meant to have good life. You were meant to be soldiers. But apparently I trained you too young. When you still had minds of your own,” Ferdinand shrugged, “But either way, it’ll be pure justice. It'll be justice, revenge, and the victory my son and I desired. The ones that turn on you will turn back, begging for mercy."

“No. It won't be justice if my son dies for it. It won't be justice if his sons will die for it, if our families die for it," I yelled, then I turned to Dox. “Get Lucas and Behn, and let's go," I snapped. Minutes later I had Dox on my back and we were headed home with the two hostages.

6

"Why do we have to chain our roommates to the Wall?" Rogue stared at Behn and Lucas who glared at me.

"Cause they're not our roommates if they're going to kill our son," I explained and Rogue nodded in agreement.

"Wait?! You have...a son?" Behn looked at me wide-eyed.

"Well, yeah. Isn't that obvious?" I scoffed.

"Anyway, why would you tie us to a wall made of thorns and rocks, it gives us more of an advantage of escaping, don't you think?" Lucas seemed puzzled.

"Yeah it would, unless you were eaten," Rogue shrugged.

"What?!" Behn was now frightened, staring at Rogue wide eyed.

"That's our warning," I nodded. "Nothing survives a night in the Woods, one night you're alive, the morning you're gone." Rogue took off and I went after her.

"Wait stop! Don't leave us, please!" Lucas and Behn pleaded, and shouted frantically, not wanting to be left there all alone.

"On one condition," I said flying back to them, Rogue went back to the Willow. "You tell us how to destroy the Alphas."

"They're human, all you need to do is rescue them from their animal bodies and they're done. They're not in their right minds," Lucas cried, confessing everything, "Please don't leave us here to die!" he whined.

"Behn, if you don't have anything to confess, you'll stay here," I said untying Lucas' wrists.

"Only that I do believe Ferdinand, you did kill Saube. She showed me… he's dead, because of you. You killed him, you're a murderer! You're, a monster! Admit it still haunts you, you freak!" he barked. I stopped short and pressed him against the Wall, by his neck.

"Say it again, I'll kill you like I killed him," I whispered, furiously.

"You killed him, just because he's the son of your enemy. That's no reason to murder someone," he hissed, "You're a freak! No wonder they put you in the institute. Could've put you in a circus, and you'd still fit in."

I cut his chains, and pushed him to the ground.

"You think you have a miserable life. I'm still haunted by mine."

"That's the truth, you're scared, and you're haunted. You don't fight it. Your memories are stronger than you are," Behn lashed out. I grabbed him and choked him, in my grip.

"I'm no killer, I'm no freak, and especially not a murderer," I snapped.

"If you're not then you'd know better than to kill me," he choked.

"You're right, so I'll kill you differently." I stumbled backwards, my eyes turned black. Suddenly something swooped in, overhead. It landed and my eyes were normal. The Alpha of my kind stood in front of me. I walked up, and it screeched, and I screeched back. It grabbed me up, by my wings, and flew up into the air. It pulled harder, breaking my wings, and I yelped, struggling. It dropped me and I didn't move, I didn't even scream. I fell breathing calmly. Suddenly something grabbed me and pushed me to the ground. A warm tongue licked my face and I looked up at Dox heaving for breath. Dox tried to fend it off but it knocked him out. I couldn't move, it grabbed me and tossed me into the trees. I hit my head and blacked out.

7

Rogue hovered over me, tears in her eyes, watching me when I woke up. I sat up, dazed.

"Am I dead?" I asked, Rogue grabbed me, and cried some more.

"You were out for days. The Alpha flew off thinking you were dead," she whispered softly.

Where is he?" I bolted to my feet, worried.

"Who?" Fangs looked down at me from the top of the tree, and I breathed a sigh of relief. He was safe. For a moment I thought he had been captured.

"How long have I been out?" I sat back down to catch my breath.

"About a week. Also, you can't fly," Fangs explained.

"WHAT?!"

"Your wings are broken, remember?"

"No, my wings are fine."

"Phoenix don't do it!"

I hovered a bit and luckily, grabbed a branch, before falling to the ground. Rogue hovered over me.

"You can't fly," Rogue repeated what Fangs had said, "But you will soon"

"…Not good definitely not good," I told myself. I had begun to pace back and forth, my thoughts rushing, "Ferdinand's alive, the female is roaming everywhere! Behn and Lucas aren't at my side anymore, and neither is Rufus. Rufus is gone too, and people will get hurt, and, that means Fangs gets hurt and…-"

"Who's going to hurt me?"

"Nothing, Fangs," I sighed turning toward the Woods.

"Don't lie to me! Stop saying nothing's wrong!" He urged.

"I don't want you to worry about it," I snapped.

"Tell me!" He yelled.

"Fangs I'm-" Fangs' body flamed a blue fire, and I flamed up too. He lunged for me and knocked me over.

"Tell me and I won't hurt you," he growled. Half my body leaning over the edge.

"Oh like you'd hurt me at all," I glared, tossing Fangs head over heels out of the tree. He flapped his wings, hovering in the air staring face to face with me. " Like father like son," Rogue mumbled from the Willow.

8

"TELL ME!" Fangs roared, " Who's going to hurt me, who are they?!"

"Again, not going to tell you," I hissed," I don't want to keep you up all night knowing there's someone who wants to hurt you. All I'm trying to do is be a good parent, and I'm not doing a very good job, but at least I try to be," I groaned.

"So you're a liar, and a murderer," Fangs didn't seem surprised.

"No. Only that I don't want to frighten you."

"You already have. Men and women stabbing you in the back, you were forced to kill children," Fangs said, tears in his eyes, and he screeched before jumped on me pushing me to the ground.

"Fangs don't!" I yelled as he pushed me down harder. I transformed, grabbing him in my claws. I dropped him on the ground changing into a human, panting heavily.

"Fine. Her name is Ferdinand Blanch, I killed her son. Now she's after you, she wants revenge on me, by hurting the people I love. So it's your average revenge plot, shouldn't be too bad...I think" I stared into Fangs' eyes, ashamed I hadn't told him.

"You'll have the phoenixes protect me though, won't you?" Fangs seemed scared and worried.

"I'm going to protect you myself, and send the phoenixes to fight. I can protect you on my own," I stared off into the woods toward MJD.

"What's so special about some...? Woman?" Fangs shrugged.

"She's not some woman," I scoffed, my face changed and I growled. "She's someone who should deserve to be alone, hated, locked up.... To be treated like an animal, like a monster... Like a freak!" I roared angrily staring at the ground.

"What do you mean? I never learned anything like that from the simulator... Is this a lie too?"

"I would call it fifty-fifty," I shrugged, "I showed you everything from school until now and nothing from the beginning."

"I'll leave it be this time," Fangs growled. "But at least tell me what you mean by being treated like a freak."

"Like I said before, Ferdinand will tell you something, make you trust her, then she doesn't need you anymore and she throws you out.

She told me when I was younger, that I'd get what I wanted then she just made me into the opposite. She made me a murderer, a monster, a weapon."

"What did you want, exactly?" Fangs was calm again, his flames gone.

"When you're in a place like that, at that age, what more could you want than to be loved? To have a family, to not be locked up, chained to a wall, or forced to follow orders."

"Wouldn't those people be like you're family. What about your trainer?"

"I had to obey whatever he said. I would never call him family after what he's done to me. Behn and Lucas believe Ferdinand about me killing her son and now they think I'm a killer. They will stop at nothing until I'm gone." That seemed to satisfy him, for now that is, until there was more I'd have to explain.

9

The next day Rogue showed me the damage the Alpha had caused. "Leader! Queen!" A group of phoenixes stood in a circle peering down at a boy, a dagger laid next to him. A phoenix girl leaned over him trying to heal him.

"Is it alive?"

"He," one of the phoenixes corrected me.

"Still an it," I snapped giving the final word.

I stared down at the phoenix girl, looking over the boy. She looked up at me sadly and shook her head.

"Who killed it?" I said glaring at the ground, "WHO KILLED THE BOY!" I roared.

"Dox killed the Alpha wolf, I killed the boy." One of them raised their hands in the back of the group. It was Kalo, he picked up the dagger and handed it to me. I felt at the dagger, and screeched furiously. I glared at Kalo.

"Your orders were to keep the boy alive," I growled.

"You said to kill it, so I did," Kalo snapped.

"I said to kill the Alpha, and that frees the boy. I wanted the boy alive," I hissed.

"The boy's a part of the Alpha, he'll destroy us all!" Kalo glared, "I did the right thing. I killed the boy, he would destroy the Groves, and overthrow you. I saved you!"

"ENOUGH!" I roared, "The boy is dead, we're not entirely sure-" I stopped short and took a step toward the boy. The girl healing them stepped back and my eyes glowed bright red. I saw the inside of his body, he was out cold, but still alive, his heart beating.

"You didn't kill him Kalo, he's still alive. If you try to kill him, I give you to Dox."

"That's not a threat," Kalo scoffed.

"Well, we're the more social kind, we're in groups. So the other side… that would be the independent, the wild. Meaning the wolves, and they'll take whatever they can get," I growled.

"Yeah right," Kalo scoffed, "Dox's wolves don't hunt people, or phoenixes anymore."

"Oh they will. They've been putting the meat aside for a few years, and they'd just love one of our own. They come across something and whatever it is it's already gone." Kalo stormed off and I stared at the boy, now breathing, but asleep. The phoenixes carried him off so he could be treated. Kalo was one of my closest allies, but I didn't know if he is anymore. He might just be another enemy. Fangs landed next to me.

"That was awesome!" Fangs smiled, "You totally fought with him, and you won! It was like a total stare down, and-" I put my hand over his mouth, and Fangs stopped talking. "It was threat wasn't it?" Fangs stared up at me worriedly.

"I trusted Kalo. He went against my orders. Either he wants to overthrow me, or he'll turn into an enemy."

"Well an enemy, yes, but there is no way he'll overthrow you. You're my father, you're Rogue husband, and a thriving leader. They call you leader, isn't that what you want to keep?"

"I don't take it to my head, and you shouldn't either. When you're old enough you'll help me rule the group. If they turn on me, you'll still have control."

"WHAT?! I can't lead a group! You're experienced, I haven't had any training," Fangs stressed.

"Don't worry, I'll give you tips when you're ready to start lead our people," Fangs breathed a sigh of relief, "To start you can do patrols with me. I could use some help."

"Where did the thorns come from?"

"Potions. I stole millions of them," Rogue landed and kissed me on the cheek. Fangs, covered his eyes entirely disgusted, and we laughed.

"I'm so glad the Alpha's gone," Rogue sighed, I turned away, angrily. "Phoenix what's wrong?" she seemed worried.

"Phoenix got into a threat fight with… Kalo," Fangs whispered.

"But Kalo's like your best friend," Rogue put her hand on my shoulder. I kissed her, and held her close.

"Dox is my best friend, I know I can trust him, Kalo disobeyed my orders. He'll overthrow me now. He killed the Alpha, which freed the boy, but Kalo almost killed him. He was knocked out, so the phoenixes took him for treatment-" I heard screeches from the Willow Forest and smiled, screeching back. "He's awake, he's going to be okay."

The boy struggled, trying to break the chains. The phoenixes had chained him to the tree.

"Let me go!" the boy said through clenched teeth.

"Not until we can trust, you won't hurt anyone," I glared at him.

"Fine," he groaned turning his head.

"Leader, this boy… is human," one of the phoenixes stared at him, "What do we do?"

"Once he can fend for himself, we let him go," I turned and flew off.

"Wait!" the boy yelled. I turned staring at him.

"Wait…" he paused staring into my eyes, "Phoenix?" the boy's eyes went wide, as I landed in the tree.

"Johnny," I stood face to face with him.

"Long time no see buddy!" Johnny thrust out his arms as if he were expecting a huge hug from me.

"Not your buddy. Now tell me what you, have to do with the Alpha," I asked, backing him up against the edge of the tree.

"Phoenix!" Rogue swooped down and ran up. "Phoenix let him go!" Rogue tried to pull him off.

"No way! Johnny should be held hostage," I growled back.

"Johnny? You know him!?" Rogue's eyes went wide.

"Yeah, and he's someone who will destroy us! He hates me anyways," I glared at Johnny, and loosened my grip.

"Yeah, but you don't know that for sure. Please don't kill him, it'll just spread more rumors around with the humans," Rogue tried to reason with me and she had a good point.

"She's your sister?" Johnny guessed.

"Not important right now," I groaned.

"Right. So what is important is me finding myself a place to stay, in this haven of yours," Johnny pushed past me and I grabbed him by his shirt and turned him toward the woods.

"Actually you should leave," I said pushing him towards the edge.

"I couldn't agree more. He's actually quite annoying," Rogue groused.

"Fine, but you'll regret it. You need me," Johnny exclaimed, "Ferdinand put me in the Alpha for a reason," he said walking away.

"Yeah right," I scoffed, and flew after him. I wanted to be absolutely sure that he left.

10

"See, Phoenix I could've killed him! You threw him out anyways. I could've killed him and you wouldn't have cared! Neither would your queen," Kalo lashed.

"I didn't know who he was, he knew me," I snapped, "My orders were not to kill him. I let him go. He won't hurt us, he'll thank us for freeing him."

Kalo growled and walked away.

"He's still mad at you?" Fangs walked up to me.

"Why do you care about what goes on between the two of us?"

"You two are really nice, now I'm seeing the other side."

"This isn't the other side of me Fangs, this just…" I sighed thinking about what happened before he was born.

"Well either way, I want to help. It might help if I resolve people's problems. When I'm a leader with you, I can help,"

"You don't want to get in the middle of a fight, Fangs. We're a little tough, on each other."

"I can take it, Phoenix let me help."

"Alright," I sighed, and called Kalo back to the tree. He landed on the ground, started between me and Fangs.

"So you want to kill him right?"

"Well humans shouldn't be here. That boy will tell Ferdinand. She'll attack and we'll all be imprisoned. I don't want to go back there and neither do the others. We all want to be free," Kalo stood, his face was calm, but his shoulders tense.

" I'm sorry I didn't know I needed the opinion of the council before letting go of human, who would destroy us if we kept him," I lashed.

"Well you could've at least been sure he was trusted, that's just poor leadership," Kalo shot back.

"Come on guys, we're all friends here," Fangs out stretched his arms standing in between us.

"Your father was my friend, not any more. Just 'cause I don't follow his orders, I'm his enemy. Yeah right, I forgot he rules over me," Kalo scoffed.

"All I want is to keep the group under control so it doesn't lead to chaos," I growled, Fangs pushed me back, and I moved him aside, standing face to face with Kalo.

"Alright, let's settle this… Form fight."

"Fair enough. If I win you stand down."

"Fine, but what's in it for me?"

"Patrol guard. Should be a simple task, since you care about the safety of the group. You, me and Fangs patrol at night."

"Fair," Kalo stared back at me, his scales shimmering in the morning sun. My blue scales were darker in the deep shadows.

"WHAT?!" Fangs stood in between us as we hovered off the ground. We fought back and forth, clawing each other. Fangs flapped, chasing after us, left and right. I had Kalo in my claws, and he flamed up, and I bolted back, blazing flames. Our flames lit the sky, brighter than the sun. We clashed, and clawed each other. I grabbed him up and tossed Kalo to the ground. His form flashed back, scratched and bleeding, he gasped for air coughing, and wheezing. Fangs landed next to me.

"You're not going to finish him off?"

"No," I panted staring at Kalo. "He's done, he'll stand down. If you win a form fight you have to obey the trade. I thought you were supposed to stop the fight?"

"Yeah, I think I'll leave stopping fights to you," he gave me weak smile.

"If you threaten them, they stand down, that's my tip for you," I heard Rogue screech angrily, she landed, glancing between me and Kalo.

"I'm too late aren't I?" Rogue moaned.

All morning I'd been up, listening to Dox's howls. He and his family had gone home to the group, and I hadn't heard from him in a month. Out of nowhere, his howls got louder and louder.

"Is that Dox?" Rogue asked climbed up the branches.

"Yeah, he seems… frightened. He's been howling since dawn-" I heard Kareen start howling too, and now they're howls erupted over the woods, waking the group. My eyes went wide of worry.

"What's wrong?" Rogue yawned.

"Ex and Vess are… gone."

"What! No, surely they would've found them by now," Rogue tried to cover her worry. Dox howled, and fell silent.

Later on that morning Dox and Kareen met us the Wall.

"We couldn't follow their scent, whoever took them, covered the ground with water. Now I can't find them," Dox was worried, and looked over at Kareen crying, while Rogue tried to soothe her.

"I'm so sorry. Fangs is upset too, that he lost his friends. He's out looking in the woods," I tried to be cheerful. I knew this would be hard for Dox. He loved his kids more than anything.

"You should call him back, we checked the woods, they weren't there."

"I tried he's not coming home."

"The wolves are lost. Ex and Vess were supposed to rule the group together, to be the next ruling leaders. Without them the wolves won't cooperate. Everyone's worried."

"Yeah, now I know this is the worst part of parenthood, I thought being sure they didn't get hurt was enough," I laughed.

"I thought trying to keep them out of trouble is enough. Ex always got Vess to help him make mischief," Dox laughed too. I heard Fangs, his screeches faded.

"No," I groaned.

"What-" Rogue screeched, flapping above the Wall, she landed next to me. "You heard that too right?" she asked, as if she thought she was going crazy.

"Yeah, it sounded like he was being gagged. Someone has him, I think I know who."

"Don't be serious, Behn flew off on the Alpha, Lucas is afraid of us-" Rogue smiled slyly.

"What?" Dox seemed puzzled.

"I'm so going to capture him. He'll be an easy target," Rogue and I smiled slyly.

"What?" Dox still had no idea.

"You want your sons back?" I stared at Dox, Dox stared back at me like I was stupid.

"We're capturing Lucas aren't we?" Dox sighed, he changed his form and sprinted off into the woods.

11

I glared at Lucas who tried to talk over the cloth around his mouth. Dox slipped it down around his neck, and Lucas panted.

"What did I do to deserve this?" Lucas asked breathing heavily.

"Nothing, you just assumed that we'd capture you?" I laughed hysterically.

"Yes…" Lucas mumbled softly.

"Tell us Lucas, where are our kids," I growled, and staring into his eyes.

"I don't know!" Lucas cried, struggling to break himself free from my grip. I gripped tighter, and Lucas choked.

"Easy Phoenix, we don't want to hurt him if he can help," Dox ushered.

"I need to find my son. He's a part of my life, Rogue will be heartbroken without him, and I want her to be happy. She's my love, and I'll do anything for her. I have to find my son!" I roared, gripping tighter.

"Phoenix…" Lucas choked, his face ghostly pale, I let go, and he fell to the ground coughing.

"Where are they Lucas?" Dox stood over him.

"I'm telling you the truth, I don't know," Lucas begged for mercy, Dox had him pressed against a tree. Dox growled showing his fangs, ready to sink them into his skin. Lucas flinched, frightened.

"Don't forget Lucas, he's still wild, and so am I," I said watching.

"Fine! MJD has them. That psychopathic woman, told the whole school you killed Saube. Now MJD isn't a school anymore. That crazy woman took over, making the students, troops. They're going to storm the woods, and capture all half creatures, your people will be slaves," Lucas sobbed. Dox stopped, and gagged Lucas. I snatched him up and we flew off to MJD.

"GIVE US THE BOYS, OR YOUR FRIEND HERE IS DONE FOR!" Dox roared.

"Bring out the boys," Ferdinand stood on a balcony glaring at us. Dox put Lucas down, who ran down the steps, and into the swarm of troops. Troops dragged the kids in nets, muzzled and roped growling fiercely. I dropped down flaming up, and troops stepped back. I burned the ropes to ashes, and Fangs hugged me.

"You're okay, thank goodness," I said hugging him, Fangs cried into my shirt embracing me.

"Can we go home now?" he sobbed.

"Of course," I looked over at Dox embracing his children.

"Actually let's make a bargain," I landed on the edge of the balcony, glaring at Ferdinand, who stared back at me, slyly.

"Anything, only that the children go free," I said holding her gaze.

"Alright. The children go, Phoenix and Dox stay," Ferdinand proposed.

"NO!" the boys yelled. Suddenly a net pushed me to the ground and troops surrounded. A boy held a rock in his hand. "Knock him out!" the boys yelled, and the boy hit me over the head with the rock. The last thing I saw was my son, flying off with Vess and Ex. They would go home and be safe.

I woke up in an empty chamber, my arms and legs roped. My wings bound, my muzzle was metal…I sank my fangs into it and flinched, titanium. The door opened, and a voice laughed.

"Look at you, so helpless. All it takes is family, I guess. All it takes is love to soften even the wildest of hearts," Ferdinand lifted my head staring into my dark violet eyes. I lashed my fangs trying to bite. "You won't get anywhere with those binds," she laughed. I outstretched my wings trying to snap the rope. I groaned, helplessly. I screeched, and Ferdinand covered her ears. I screeched and growled louder and louder, until I was out of breath. I heard Dox howl back to chambers down. He howled, but it stopped short and fell silent. I heard boots clamp into the room.

"He's still a little restless. You can shoot him," Ferdinand walked out, "Teach him a lesson not to bite." It was Johnny and Behn. They unlocked the muzzle and held my mouth open, shooting and injection spray, into my mouth. I lashed my fangs and the boy jolted back. My mouth fell numb, and lied my head on the ground.

"Still wild," Behn scoffed.

"Not surprised," Johnny laughed. I couldn't bite the binds, and lied there for hours. Then Ferdinand walked in.

"Missed me?" she laughed, and small pocket knife in her hands.

"Not at all. What did you to me?" I growled.

"I numbed your mouth so you can't bite me, isn't that obvious?" she grabbed me by my chin and looked in my mouth at my fangs. "If you hold still it won't hurt," she smiled slyly. Suddenly I felt the edge of the knife, cut at my gums, slipping underneath the tooth. I screeched, struggling, and Ferdinand gripped hard, her ice cold skin freezing against mine, blazing hot. The knife suddenly slipped underneath my tooth, and she pulled up, pulling it from my mouth. I screeched and pulled back, the gap filled with a normal tooth. She cut out my other three, all replaced with normal teeth.

Weak and helpless, they cut me loose knowing I was too helpless to get out. Ferdinand left for a second, and came back.

"Thought you be lonely so I brought you a friend." The troops slammed a net to the ground and cut Dox loose. He growled and stopped. He knew he was done, the guards left and so did Ferdinand.

"Phoenix?" Dox looked at me worried, "We're done for aren't we?"

"Look at us, Dox. We've never been weaker, more helpless. We're done. They're going to kill us, and our families too," I sighed.

"At least I'm not alone."

"I thought you said you wanted to be?"

"I was just angry." Troops came in, shoving us into nets. They dragged us outside of the school, and chained us against the river. They pushed us into the river, water rushing up my nose and mouth. Overnight the river roared, cutting the chains and we were pushed off down the river. Knocked out, water clogging our throats, scales and fur soaked.

12

"Phoenix?! Phoenix?!" It was Rogue's voice, and I slowly opened my eyes, coughing up water. My wings and scales were drenched.

"Dox?" I croaked. I turned and Kareen was looking down at Dox drowned and sick. He opened his eyes and looked up at Kareen, black eyes gleaming. I looked up at Rogue, holding my head in her lap. "You'll be okay, you'll be okay," she smiled, and my eyelids, heavy fell closed.

I woke up weak, and Rogue gasped rushing over.

"Don't you dare close your eyes again. You almost gave me a heart attack, I thought you were dead," Rogue breathed a sigh of relief.

"I won't I promise. See, I'm okay-" I fell back the ground trying to pick myself up. My arm burned, pain blasting through it. I looked at it, bandaged.

"You're not okay, your arm is broken. Your form is done."

"What are you talking about?" I said changing into a phoenix. My body flashed in between phoenix and human. I changed back to a human, panting. "I can't lose my form."

"You didn't, but you're so weak you can't hold it long enough. Dox can't form either."

"I can't lose all my powers, my fangs are enough."

"What happened to your fangs?" Rogue glared, she opened my mouth and gasped. "How?"

"Ferdinand. She cut underneath it. It removes the fangs permanently. Dox's were removed too."

"No," Rogue breathed.

"Where's Fangs?"

"He's in his cave, he was scared of that place. Whatever they did it scared him."

"Ropes, he's never been bound before. I'm so sorry Rogue, I tried to keep him from that and-"

"Shh.., I know, just rest."

For days Dox and I lied down, weakened by the gushing river. Fangs stayed his cave only coming out to eat. He didn't speak when he joined Rogue to steal with the group.

I woke up and Rogue was gone I picked myself up, and walked through the marshes to Dox's cave. Dox growled, staying still, he was still weak.

"Dox it's me," I said softly.

"Phoenix?" Dox wasn't in his form, he seemed thinner, and he limped over to me. He lied his head on my shoulder, shutting his eyes.

"What's wrong with me?" he sighed, his eyes shut.

"Well we did get blasted by a river at twenty miles an hour," I groaned.

"I feel...Weaker. I've never felt that way before."

"Here." I passed him a basket of food. "Rogue left the basket near me, but you need it more."

I saw the group was back. I heard Rogue screech and Kareen howled. Dox was too weak, I screeched twice, and two minutes later the girls, Ex Vess and Fangs found us at the mouth of the cave.

"He's going to be fine. I gave him the basket, he was starved."

"You care a bit too much sometimes," Rogue mumbled, "But at least your caring for others. Here." Rogue put a piece of bread into my hand. I tore it into the pieces and ate it quickly. Fangs came over to hug me, but wrenched away angrily, as if he didn't want to anymore.

"What are you mad at me for?"

"You said we'd both go home. You left me."

" Only because Ferdinand wouldn't let both of us go. She wouldn't be left with nothing. Plus she wants me more than you, she hates me."

"Well you scared me. I saw you on the riverbank. I thought you were gone forever!"

"What did they do to you?" Rogue asked, "I had to cut you out of nets."

"They shoved us into rope nets, and chained us to the side of the riverbank. They tried to suffocate us. Overnight the river was so strong it broke the chains and we were drowning, the water was strong, and the rocks in the water were slippery, it was probably how I broke my arm, I can't remember." I stared out at the rushing river, reliving being swallowed by the waves. Of course though, I couldn't remember how I broke my arm.

Dox woke up the next morning and we walked along the cliffside, looking down at the Willow Forest. No one was awake yet and the sun rays sparkled through the branches of the trees.

"I never want to do that again," Dox groaned feeling at his teeth. "They ripped out yours too?"

"Yeah. They take a while to grow back, but now they're gone forever."

"I guess so."

We walked to the edge of the cliffs looking down over the meadows. I saw Fangs disappear into the tunnels carved in the side of the cliff. Suddenly an arrow whizzed past me.

"Phoenix look out!" Dox reached out to grab me, but I slipped, falling.

I flapped up changing form. Dox jumped up climbing on my back.

"Wait, don't!" I couldn't hold form much longer and I fell to the ground with Dox on my back.

"I think you just broke my wing," I croaked and spat dirt out of my mouth.

"Sorry man." Dox climbed off me and I flew off to find Fangs. I swooped down, snatched him up, and dropped him up in the Willow Forest. Arrows slipped past me, as I spun left and right. At the edge of the barrier. Troops in white uniforms stood around the Groves, bows loaded with arrows. In the middle of the army was a woman in a black leather jacket, a white shirt and black skirt. She rode the Alpha wolf a dagger in her hand. Ferdinand stared into my eyes with a sly smile.

"SHOOT HIM DOWN!" Ferdinand commanded. I dodged arrows, zigzagging left and right, one shot through my wing. I fell on my back, my wrist like a blazing fire. Troops flamed the Wall, with daggers and swords they cut their way through the massive thorns. Charging in setting the trees aflame, the group flew off frightened, troops grabbed them, lassoing them with chains, pulling them to the ground. The Alpha scaled up the cliffside climbing to the top. Ferdinand jumped off and pet the wolf slyly.

"Do whatever you want to me just don't hurt him, or his family," I begged.

"I like you begging, do it again?" Ferdinand glared.

"I beg you," I begged holding her gaze.

"Alright. Your families will go unharmed." Ferdinand turned to the wolf that howled and roared. I heard Dox yelp and howl and he fell silent. The wolf snatched me up and threw over the cliffside.

"Wait! I can't-" I yelled before it tossed me over and I fell into a net. Troops closed it up, and I wrestled trying to break free. The troops started to beat me with a bat and something new happened. My freely faded in the place of fangs. I growled, and screeched lashing my fangs, and they hit me over the head.

13

"Not again," I groaned, staring at the muzzle around my face. The door squeaked open, and Ferdinand, and two troops walked in, Ferdinand held a dagger. The troops cut me from the net, and put chains around my neck, and limbs. With the chains they attached them the wall. I growled, lashing my fangs while tugging on the chains.

"Take it easy Phoenix. You won't need to do this anymore once it's over. You know the consequences, you've disobeyed long enough." Ferdinand loomed over me staring into my frightened eyes. "I'll let you have one more visit, before your leadership is gone." She snapped her fingered and troops pushed Rogue in, her wings bound and chains around her wrists.

"Phoenix! You're okay." She breathed a sigh of relief, and I hugged her. But the troops returned as quickly as they came. "No-" Rogue was pulled back, her screeches muffled. Ferdinand stepped back into the room, a sly smile across her face. She cut the binds on my wings, and pushed me to floor. Her hand shook, as she struggled to keep me to the floor. I panted and felt the edge to the dagger touch my wings, I flapped, trying to push off-. I yelped and fell to the floor. Ferdinand stood over me, my dark midnight wings lying on the floor, cut from my back.

"Serves you right. You should've suffered the consequences ages ago," Ferdinand glared down at me angrily. She picked up my wings and troops put a chain around my neck again.

"Let the ceremony begin," Ferdinand walked out talking into the speaker clipped to her jacket, and the troops followed dragging me. I stumbled and fell, they dragged me into a net. Ferdinand stood in front of the troops each holding phoenix or wolf by a chain.

"Today will be the day these wild beasts, fall!" Ferdinand yelled to the troops, who stomped their feet in unison. "Today these beasts shall rue the day they stepped foot on our land, stealing our food, and supplies, killing innocent people. They kill because they're wild. Today we will rid them of their power, of their control! Starting with their leaders!" The troops dragged Dox and I, chained. The groups gasped, and cried, knowing their time was up, if the leaders were dead.

"Let's start with you, Phoenix." She pushed me to the ground and I didn't fight back. She held the dagger to my throat, and I growled deeply. "This is my revenge for my son." She stabbed me to side of my chest, away from my heart and I fell back. "I'll spare your life, I guess I owe you one," she whispered. She crouched down, and I pulled the dagger from my body painfully, and sliced her throat.

"You owe me ten," I growled, before falling back, shutting my eyes. Suddenly wings formed on my back, white and black like the Alpha.

"I thought you were dead!" Rogue screamed at me.

"I'm sorry okay, I didn't think she'd take it that far!" I yelled back, not noticing Fangs land in the Willow.

"I almost thought I'd have to take care of our son by myself! I thought you left me!" Rogue pushed me against the trunk of the tree-
.

"You're alive… How?" Fangs stared into my eyes, "You're dead! You were stabbed, I watched you die!"

"Easy, Fangs. She spared my life," I showed him the gash on my chest. "Said she owed me one, she owes me more than that," I put my hand on his shoulder, "I'm right here."

"You say you're here, that everything is fine! You scared us all!" Rogue shouted.

"She didn't kill me, she spared my life!"

"For what!? You're rivals, why would she spare you?" Rogue whispered standing face to face with me.

"Nothing, she spared me because she owes me her life," I growled back.

"Tell me the truth Phoenix! I know that's a lie. You'd lie to me, only to protect me, I know that. What did she spare you for? She doesn't have a speck of goodness in her heart, she would never let you go!"

"She spared me only to watch us die in the future," I growled, grabbing her by her shoulders.

"You can't just tell the truth, can you?" Rogue mumbled.

"I do it to protect you, to protect both of you."

"Just don't…Don't scare me like that. I thought I lost you forever."

Days passed and my wound healed. I walked around the barrier with Fangs every day.

"Will the wolves ever come back?" Fangs missed hanging out with Ex and Vess.

"I'm sure they will, they might be busy, I don't know."

"We haven't been attacked in a while it feels nice."

"You know, why we don't do an observation test."

"What's that?"

"We'll go into town for the day. See if they're friendly or not. If they're people are stable for living."

"Are we moving?"

"Al I know is Ferdinand is dead but her relatives will know soon enough. She must have more family. Once they find out she's gone, and our people killed her, we'll need to go into hiding."

"What if someone catches us?" Fangs thought of being put in jail, for execution.

"Tip for when you go into the city. No one ever looks up." Fangs looked at me puzzled.

We landed on the roof of a house.

"You jump from roof to roof. The buildings here are close enough for an easy jump."

"Are you sure this is safe?"

"Are you with an adult right now?"

"Yeah, you're my dad."

"I think you'll be fine." I pushed him over to the next roof.

"Wait!-" Fangs shouted and I grabbed him but his hand slipped and he fell to the ground.

"You're supposed to jump," I told him jumping onto the ground, "Follow me." I led Fags down a narrow path, we climbed over a fence and Fangs grabbed me and shook me by my shoulders.

"Are you insane? We are not stealing from someone!" he whispered.

"And we won't," I whispered back, "All we're doing is sneaking in and stealing their daggers, swords, weapons."

"That is stealing, Phoenix!"

"Oh who cares? We'll be in and out, and back home in no time."

"I care! I don't want to be a criminal!" Fangs replied.

"Fine, you wait here. I don't care what happens, you stay here."

"Thank you," Fangs smiled.

I spread my wings and flew off, but Fangs sprang up after me, not wanting to be left alone. We landed at the gates of a large house.

"You can steal food but not weapons. Phoenix this is a bad idea."

"Yeah, right," I scoffed, "that Richie won't even notice they're gone."

"Richie, what do you mean?"

"Last time I stole something from the mayor, I got caught, he let me go with what I stole. He suspected I was poor, and let me take. He wouldn't even care if it was gone. He's a Richie, which means if you steal something from him, he'll just get more of it. He has enough money to buy another kingdom, if he wanted," I growled.

"Maybe it was the clothes you were wearing back then, or-"

"Are you defending him?" I growled, Fangs backed up and bumped into a tree, cornered.

"No, I just…well he's human and-" Fangs stammered.

"Exactly they're Richies, all of them."

"They're not all bad. You told me about another city. They were poor." Fangs began to stand his ground.

"That's the poor side of the woods. That's where I grew up," I grabbed him pressing him to the tree. "I worked for the wolves, when I was seven. I went out and stole things for them. Every day when I'd steal I was caught and attacked. One tried to cut my wings with a knife as I flew off." I showed him a scar on my black and white wings, still there.

"Never defend a human Fangs. When I was young, I defended Ferdinand once. Look at where it got me!" I put him down.

"Look I know, I'm sorry."

"You're just a kid. I don't want you to ever defend them. Because when you do… this'll happen." I fingered at the scar on my chest.

"Alright. I mean they've been so nice to me. If I got caught they'd let me go."

"They probably think you're an orphan. But you're a kid, that's why no one wants to hurt you. You're too young for them to hurt."

I dropped the sack at Rogue's feet, and she sighed angrily.

"You idiot, why would you steal from that huge house?"

"I got away with it," I scoffed.

"You stole weapons, they're useless to us," she groaned.

"Someone took our home once, Rogue. I won't let this one be destroyed, not again."

"Phoenix, they'll hunt us. I was in one of the houses, they had phoenix wings, in a case," Fangs gawped, worriedly.

"They won't catch us. I escaped out of a house once that even bigger than that with a sack full jewels. How did the wolves become boss? By me, I made them wealthy, and rich!" I barked.

"Yeah, then you tried to run off with your pockets full, you cheat." I turned to Dox who glared at me with a smile, "We're lucky we caught you before you ran off."

"Oh come on. I made you rulers of the woods, I made you rich beyond your wildest dreams," I hissed.

"True. We were rich but you stole it back from us. Just to get a job. You fool, no one would hire you, you were too young, plus who would hire someone with wings? I saved you from being locked up, you were lucky."

"Yeah, I get it I was dumb then. I didn't rob you I needed it."

"Well you should've robbed us then. We were robbed last night. Hunters are storming the woods, I forgot to tell you. It's hunting season."

14

"You can stay here. Far down in the Groves there's an open prairie, miles wide. It's surrounded by trees, and the barrier, so you're still safe." I walked with Dox along the cliffside like we'd done before.

"Thanks. Did you seriously steal all those weapons?"

"It was a piece of a cake. I snuck in and out, punched some people, simple really," I shrugged.

"Did you bring me anything?"

"You bet." I slapped a fish in his hand. He slipped it in a satchel over his shoulder.

"What kind is it?" Dox sniffed at the satchel.

"You can't tell? Come on it's your favorite, remember?" Dox kept sniffing at the bag. He sat down at the edge of the cliffside, depressed.

"Dox, you can't smell, can you?" Dox sighed.

"They knocked me out, and injected me with something. When I woke up, I couldn't smell," Dox groaned, hanging his head.

"I don't know how to help you, I wish I could."

"You don't have to, I'm leaving."

"What?! You'd leave your family."

"I can't protect them anymore, Phoenix. Without scent I'm confused, I'm vulnerable, and I can't protect them if I can't even tell who the enemy is."

"Dox you can't leave them. You can't leave me, you're like a brother to me."

"Phoenix, I'm done for, my sons will take over, and Kareen..," he stopped.

"What about her, you'd leave her heartbroken?"

"Well what will I do?"

"You'll heal, and get better. You'll be stronger than before once you're healed."

"I can't wait that long. If I can't tell when a hunter is near… I'll be more vulnerable than a rabbit. I eat rabbit, Phoenix."

"Don't worry, I'll give you protection this time. I can send the phoenixes for border checks around the clock. You and the wolves will be safe, I promise."

Dox howled and footsteps rumbled in the woods. The barrier opened up and boys and girls rambled, knocking into phoenixes. Hugging and embracing each other. A wolf howled to Dox from below, and scaled up the cliffs.

"Phoenix this is Wane, her twin sister Rafe is in your group. I wouldn't let her cross the woods by herself. She's looked for her sister," I screeched and Rafe landed.

"Rafe?!"

"Wane?!" The twins embraced each other. I couldn't believe it. They were both from different groups. One with wings, one with fur. They turned to us smiling. They had the same black hair and green, emerald eyes, everything about them was the same.

"If they were human how would tell them apart?" I asked.

"We have different tattoos." They each had tattoos on the side of their necks. "We got them done in town. We stole a little money and got tattoos of our animals." Rafe's tattoo was of a bird, and Wane's was a wolf.

"Do you have it?" Dox looked at Wane who nodded and pulled

A strange ball from her pocket, It was silver and shimmered in the sun.

"I found it in the Caverns, near the Tunnels. It can harness two different powers. Ferdinand said when I was old enough I would find Rafe and we would use it together. It's extremely powerfully, so we agreed not to use it. Instead, we thought we'd burry it, here in the Groves, if we're going to be together now."

"Seems valuable, I thought it would be safer here," Dox looked at me, and I agreed. We sent them on their way.

"Burry it in the caves! In the meadow?! You're crazy!" Rafe and Wane stood arguing the next day.

"No one would think about it being there!"

Dox and I pulled them aside.

"What's going on here?" I asked.

"We're figuring it out. The orb isn't buried yet, we need more time. We just can't agree on a place," Rafe snapped.

"Just put it someplace else, for all I care," Dox groaned, "Just get it buried, I don't want to hear about this again."

"This was a bad idea, never let the leader help with your problems," Wane scoffed.

"Alright Wane, I've had enough of you and your twin's ridiculous fights!" Dox barked.

"You don't seem to of much help! Neither of you!" Wane howled. Dox grabbed her up, and she screamed. Dox was different... he was more wild. He lashed his fangs, gripping Wane tighter. She choked and couldn't breathe.

"Yeah, well you're not of much help to me either! I'm doing the best I can, but I've got a lot of things on my hands right now!" Dox hissed. Wane didn't reply barely breathing. I snuck up behind him and sank my fangs into his shoulder, pulling him back. Dox yelped and punched me in the face. Rafe sat next to Wane lifeless in the grass. Suddenly Wane glowed gold and faded away. I stood bleeding, Dox held his hand over his shoulder.

"You idiot, don't grab me like that. I couldn't tell who you were!" Dox yelled.

"She's dead because of you!" I growled back.

"Serves her right to question me like that."

"You killed her! You promised them!"

Dox growled, stressed. "I can't control my anger, Phoenix that's what I told you. I should've left and stayed away," Dox rested his head against a tree breathing heavily.

"You didn't need to leave-"

"Leave me be! You can't fix me!" Dox grabbed me by my wings and flipped me to the ground.

"Dude, you have serious problems," I groaned, feeling at my wings.

"I'm losing my sense of smell by the day. I can't even tell who you are from a foot away!"

"It's alright, you still need to heal, trust me-"

"ENOUGH!" Dox roared, and grabbed me up, choking me. "Phoenix you can't fix me. You will never fix-" he pushed me to the ground, growling. Dox was different his yellow eyes became darker, his pupils wider. He formed into a black wolf and growled. I flew close to the ground and he sprinted after me. Dox caught up with again, he jumped and pulled me to the ground. I punched him in the gut, he fell back, panting. He was back to normal. I had scratches all down my back my wings were split at the edges. Kareen and Rogue came up noticing our fight.

"How many times are you going to hurt yourself," she groaned tending to my wings.

"You don't need to heal me, I'll be fine," I smiled.

"Don't hit me this time."

"What are you doing?"

"Hold still." I flapped my wings and she shot the injection in my back.

"Right, that."

15

"Don't do this to me, Phoenix," Dox growled, "You know I'm sensitive to chains."

"I don't want you to get hurt. Like you said its hunting season, if you run into hunters in the woods they'll shoot you. I'm keeping you safe."

"Are you my enemy, or my family?"

"I'm your family, but I want you safe."

"Let me go Phoenix." Dox pulled at the chains, binding him. I stepped toward him, face to face. He grabbed me and I punched him in the face.

"What did you… do?" Dox felt as his nose, dripping blood. Rogue came up behind me, I turned away, about to leave the cave.

"Don't you dare walk out on me boy?" Dox hissed.

"I'm no boy to you. I'm the same as you, no more, no less." I kept my back turned. "You just think I'd never hit you like that, that I'm that weak, you thought wrong." I walked out and Rogue stayed.

"Rogue tell him! Let me go!" Dox yelled, and I turned back to him, growling fiercely.

"You don't force her to do anything. She has her freedom, I'm putting you here for your own good." Dox punched me back and, blood dripping from my mouth. Rogue screeched, and took my hand dragging me away from him. She pulled me into the meadow under an oak, and we sat down.

"What's wrong with you two?!"

"He can't control his instincts it's not his fault!"

"You punched him didn't' you? Phoenix, what's happening?"

"He grabbed me and I fought back."

"You've never done something like that before, though. I'm worried about you."

"I'm sorry Rogue, I wasn't thinking." I had my head in my hands pacing back and forth.

"Just apologize to him." Rogue wrapped her arms around me and lied her head on my shoulder.

"He'll never forgive me, it haunts us forever. Once he gets out of those chains he'll come for me."

"He won't get out there, and he won't hurt you 'cause he'll have to go through me." Rogue smiled, shutting her eyes.

"He's stronger than you think, he's stronger than me or you. I don't want you to get involved with it. Just take care of Fangs for me, keep him away from Ex and Vess. Dox tries to steer his family away when we're in a fight. I want to do the same, it'll keep the family safe."

"You're fighting again?" Fangs sat down with us.

"Yeah, don't get involved alright. You can't fix this one."

"You're bleeding." I looked at my hand covered in dark red blood. "What happened?" Fangs didn't seemed surprised.

"He punched me. Dox is pretty tough on me, but that's how he is."

"Are you guys brothers?"

"We owe each other our lives, we've been together for years. Blood is only half the story." I showed him the scars on my neck.

"He did that?!" Fangs stepped back.

"You need to stay away from his sons."

"Oh come on! Just because you're in a fight I can't see my friends?"

"Dox will keep them away from you too, until this over."

"Fine. I'll be back before dawn, I'm starting to work with potions and I'm almost finished."

"You're lying, you're smart enough to know not to work with potions in a cave, it reflects off the walls," I stood with my arms crossed, "You're going to see them aren't you?"

"Yeah. You're always in a fight with someone so I can't have fun. It's fair to you but it's not fair for me," Fangs hung his head.

"It'll keep you safe Fangs, I won't be able to watch the group, that's where you and Rogue step in."

"Alright. How long will this take?"

"Not long. Dox and I are still going to be friends by the end of it."

"Fine. But, why do you need to fight, isn't he chained up?"

"He'll break out of there by dawn. Phoenixes aren't nocturnal so that'll give him some time."

"Why did you come back?" Dox snarled, chains still around his wrists.

"I'm surprised you didn't come find me."

"I know you'd never hit me like that, you care too much."

"Because I've known you my entire life."

"Stop saying that. We've fought each other most of our lives."

"It's true though."

"You idiot. When are you going to let me go?" Dox sighed.

"Not until I know for sure that you won't go behind my back and leave me forever."

"I wouldn't leave forever. Just for a while, until I'm healed."

"You're lying to me, instinct," I shrugged.

"How do you know your instincts are right?" Dox hissed.

"Are you asking me?"

"I can't trust mine, now I know. Never trust your instincts, they're wrong."

"You're still lying, but not me."

"Then who would I be lying to?"

"Yourself. You're just lost without scent."

"Shut up." Dox turned away.

"Why don't you trust me anymore?" I urged.

"Leave it alone, Phoenix."

"Tell me!"

"Shut up Phoenix! I'm leaving and that's final."

"Yeah right," I scoffed, "You'd never leave the group, Ex and Vess can't lead just yet-"

"They're ready. They'll lead while I'm gone."

"You keep forgetting that you'd never want to leave her. You'd never leave Kareen all alone with your sons. You know that, it's an instinct now to never leave your family."

"Shut up, you don't know what I think," Dox growled.

"I do. I know that you're fighting yourself, and that you can't decide."

Dox growled fiercely and the chains snapped from the wall. He grabbed me, and pushed me outside, before he stormed off and I flew off after him.

"You're not helping yourself by running away."

"I'm not running, I'm walking."

"It's the same thing, Dox."

"If you stop now I won't pull it out."

"Yeah right," I scoffed, "you'd never hurt me, especially after you helped me to my feet when I was younger."

"You seem so sure," Dox pulled a gun from his pocket.

"I also know you'd never shoot me."

"You don't know that either," Dox pressed the trigger, and the bullet shot through me. I saw Dox run, not looking back. I struggled to my feet, and limped back to Rogue and Fangs.

"Phoenix are you alright?" I collapsed in the grass, and Rogue rushed over. She hurried off, and came back with the injections. The wound healing, I sat up feeling weak.

"He pulled a gun from his pocket. I thought he couldn't do it, but I guess I was wrong."

"Where is he?" Rogue growled.

"Don't Rogue, he's still dangerous. Where's Fangs?"

"He's doing patrol for you, why?" I bolted to my feet and Rogue's eyes went wide, and we rushed off to find him.

"Phoenix?" I grabbed Fangs pulling him away from the Wall.

"Go to the Willow, now." I pushed him off toward the tree, and he flew away. I joined Rogue and looked down at Dox.

"Don't do this!" I shouted and Dox looked up at Rogue and I.

"You know if I could fly I would've punched you already. I have something better though," Dox pulled the gun again, and Rogue pushed me out of the way, the bullet hit her wing and she fell. I dove to grab her, but her wing slipped past my hand. I dove faster and caught her by her shirt.

"Are you okay?" I asked as Rogue clutched me, breathing heavily.

"I'm fine," she replied catching her breath. Rogue looked at her right wing, red and bleeding. I set her down in the Willow.

"Rogue? What happened?" Fangs slipped down the ladder from the branches and handed me the injections.

"It's alright, she'll be okay." I wrapped Rogue's wing, and Fangs kept her company.

16

I flew high above the trees looking down on the ground. I ran into some hunters but I was flying too fast and too high for them to fire. Scouring the ground I still didn't find him. It was midnight and I heard Dox howl, far away from the Groves. I circled over him but Dox growled at something in the shadows. Something with emerald eyes and black and white fur.

"It can't be without the male it's helpless," I thought, eyes wide. The Alpha looked up staying totally still, staring angrily into my eyes. Suddenly it rose off the ground, wings outspread. It howled and chased after me, I zigzagged through the trees and I flew up toward the sky, and dove jumping on the Alpha's back. It struggled and I grabbed it by the scruff of its neck. I sank my fangs into its neck and it pushed me off slamming me into the trees. I fell on the ground, I couldn't move, the Alpha grabbed me up with its tail and slammed me on the ground. I felt dizzy and sick. Dox pulled a knife from his boot and stabbed its leg and it fell, howling in pain. Dox put my arm around his shoulder and helped me. We ran and made it to the barrier by dawn.

My head was throbbing, and I felt sick to my stomach.

"Are you okay?"

"Yeah, I just got thrown into trees by a vicious Alpha. Other than that I'm perfectly fine."

I pulled an injection out of my pocket and stabbed myself, and my wounds healed instantly.

~

"It's not my fault I pulled the trigger!" Dox growled.

"You pulled a gun from your pocket! You know I'm afraid of guns!"

"I kept it if I needed it!" Dox barked.

"So you needed a gun in case if I stressed you out?!" I lashed.

"No, but I didn't know what else I could do. You wouldn't leave me be!"

"Here's something you could've done, not pulled a gun from your pocket," I shot back. Dox and I stormed off in different directions back to our families. Even though we were both in a fight we both had the same idea. To steer our families away from each other. To remake the border between our two sides.

By noon our groups stood on different sides, holding the gaze of the other.

"You brought this on yourself, Dox," I growled.

"If you hadn't followed me, we wouldn't be here," Dox hissed back.

"Phoenix don't do this, don't start a war," Rogue pleaded.

"This is his fault, everyone knows what he did to me. He brought this on everyone." I glared at him.

"Blame yourself, Phoenix," Dox shot back holding my gaze.

"You two fight over the worst of things," Kareen groaned, standing next to Ex and Vess.

"You three stay out of this," Dox flared. "That's why I tried to keep you away from the humans all that time. They'll just put you in a circus. I should know, I got locked up in a zoo for six months 'cause I got caught by animal control."

"I don't even know what that is?!" I shot back.

"Exactly! You haven't stayed in the city long enough," Dox hissed.

"When I got out you started to charge me. Your family is a bunch of thieves. You and your brothers asked me for food and money. Then I was broke! You hurt me and my family! You stole everything from me! I gave you everything I had, then I lost it all when the Morse was burnt! Where were you then?!"

"I was helping you! My brothers and I did our best alright?"

"I was hoping to stay away from this, but you're getting on my nerves," I snatched him up, looking down on the two groups.

"Once you let me go, I swear I'll tear your wings to shreds."

"Alright." I shrugged and dropped him. He landed on his feet standing on the cliffside unharmed. I held his gaze landing on the cliffside.

"I win and you don't leave."

"I win and I cut your wings."

"Fair enough." I flamed up and Dox lunged for me, and I shut my eyes, dodging him.

"You know I bet I could do this with eyes closed it's so easy."

"Open your eyes you idiot," Dox growled and I opened my eyes and smiled slyly, dodging another one of his attacks. We punched and dodged each other's attacks, and by the end both of us were done, neither of us could keep going. Our bet was finished, neither of us won. Both us knew why neither of us ever won. We were as strong as the other, so both of us were down after every fight. We kept the border between our sides, and walked away, keeping our families separated.

17

Rogue and I sat with Fangs on the cliffside looking over the border between our two sides.

"Hey." I turned to a back wolf, and I changed into a phoenix, walking off with my friend.

"Hey, Dox."

We walked along the cliffside, the sun rising over the Groves.

"I think we should destroy the border." Dox turned around facing me.

"It does make sense. Our groups are together and they've never been happier. I think we could make it work."

"Make what work?"

"We should unite the groups for good."

"Remember what happened last time we tried that. We almost started a war."

"Since when do you care about starting a war between our people? We start wars almost always," I laughed.

"Yeah, Kareen doesn't want to start any wars. She wants peace… too bad," Dox shrugged, "I would love to see some chaos again," Dox chuckled.

"Alright, we get the group together at noon, tomorrow," Dox walked off to his family and I walked back to Rogue and Fangs.

"What's wrong?" Fangs seemed worried there was another fight.

"We're uniting the groups... tomorrow. You can see your friends whenever you want, and Rogue, you can see Kareen," Rogue smiled and screeched to Kareen, telling her the news, and Fangs joined in calling his friends. Kareen and the boys howled back.

Dox howled and I flew off to find him. He was on all fours as a black wolf growling at the Alpha. I landed next to him scales shadowed. I screeched at the Alpha and it roared back. I turned back into a human and put out my hand. Its breath was warm and I pet it softly.

"What are you doing?" Dox groaned.

"Taming a lonely soul." I smiled at the black wolf, eyes gold and shimmering.

“You’re stupid if you think it'll stop attacking us, if you tame it. You can't tame a wild beast."

“If it were wild it would've attacked you already. The girl's soul shows through now that the male is gone." I smiled softly at the wolf's emerald eyes.

Dox wasn’t so sure about putting the Alpha in the Groves, so we decided to let it roam free. We had no fights, Dox and I. The groups merged and we were happy. Every now and then we saw hunters, but they didn’t fire. They came in small groups, and every day I flew over them, watching. I started to follow them often, I didn’t trust these hunters they seemed…Dangerous. I met with Kalo in the Willow that afternoon.

“What’s your plan Leader?”

“I want to send a group with me. I’m following these hunters, I see them in groups ranging from three to eight. They’re growing, and I’m concerned about the safety of the group. Bring our people, I want no one from Dox’s group getting hurt.”

“I’ll get my best guards Leader.”

Kalo came back with other phoenixes, he seemed serious as always when it came to my tasks for him.

“You tense too much.”

“I follow my orders Leader. These are some of my best guards, and fiercest warriors. They’ll be ready to attack if you’re spotted.”

“Beyond my expectations as usual, just what I want,” Kalo nodded smiling, and flew off.

The group stayed close to the hunters watching their every move. They went around the Groves, weapons loaded. Suddenly they moved in closer, until they were only a few feet away from the Wall. I signaled the group to be ready to attack.

“Try and shoot it down.” A hunter pointed at the barrier. One of the phoenixes screeched getting their attention.

“Shoot, quickly! They're onto us, they know!” A man hissed. One of them stepped forward, ready to shoot. I screeched at them in full form, the man pointed his gun.

“Not yet, he’s not alone… listen. He has something behind that wall. Grab him.” Hunters moved toward me and I lashed my fangs, growling. They unhooked ropes from their belts and inched closer. The rope looped around my neck, and I pulled back signaling the group. Kalo’s warriors burst from the trees scaring off the hunters. I formed into a human and slipped the rope off.

"Their easy to scare," scoffed a girl, and a boy laughed.

"Yeah well imagine an army of them. A small group like that will run, an army of them will stay and fight no matter what," I hissed, climbing a tree.

"Can I ask what you're doing Leader?" a boy asked.

"You can ask, and I'm climbing a tree. They spot us from the air, so stay on the ground, don't use your wings." From the top of the tree I saw the forest from above and searched for any other hunters. Far away, near the Caverns was a group of hunters. I dropped to the ground, and looked around at the group waiting for their next command.

"They're close. There's a group of them near, the Caverns."

"Should we head back?"

"I think we should, we've done enough, let's head home."

Slipping through the barrier, Rogue stood in front of us, she wasn't too happy. I told the group to head back to the Willow Forest.

"Where were you?" Rogue snapped.

"Don't worry about it. Just a patrol," I shrugged.

"You would've taken Fangs with you if it was a patrol. And you never leave the Groves to do it. What did you do?"

"Relax Rogue, it's taken care of."

"Why are you keeping me and Fangs locked up? We're stuck here all day while you're doing who-knows-what?!"

"I want you safe, that's all."

"You never take it this far! What's going out there? Tell me Phoenix!"

"Alright, there's hunters. There's groups of them all around the woods."

"Please tell me you told Dox about this?" I didn't reply, and Rogue sighed shaking her head. "He's going to kill you."

"Unless if he doesn't find out."

"Oh please, I already know." I turned around to see Dox standing behind me. "You idiot! Why didn't you tell me!?" Dox barked.

"Because I didn't want you to worry!" I growled.

"No, that's something you tell your wife. That's never something you tell me. I'm supposed to know," Dox sighed, "Where are they?"

"Near the Caverns," I groaned.

"What?!" Dox growled.

"See this is what happens when I tell you things! I didn't want to take any of your people with me. I knew if they got hurt, it's my fault. Then you blame me!"

"They won't get hurt! We're half-blood too you know!"

"I know but it saves me the trouble," I shrugged.

"You just can't trust me, can you?"

"I can but I don't want to stress you about it, that's all."

"You have me stress more when I don't know what's going on. You're my best friend though, so I always know with you. But then I can't tell if you could trust me. If you could you would tell me."

"Of course I trust you, I just don't want you to hold all the weight of the problem."

"You boys are stupid. Share the weight of the problem Phoenix, it will help. You don't want everyone to worry, that's what I love about you, but you're stupid by trying to hold it all. You two are like adorable kittens fighting over a ball of yarn that's twice your size," Rogue sighed, smiling.

"I hate adorable animals," Dox lashed, "When I was five someone mistook me for a puppy, then I trashed their house. They found out I was a wolf once I attacked their other dog. I loved how scared he was of me," Dox nodded smiling, then he pulled himself out his daze and stared back at me angrily.

"Oh one more thing. Phoenix, don't move," Rogue smiled nodding.

"Why?-" Fangs slammed into me pushing me to the ground. "Why do I always fall for that?" Rogue laughed.

"Get off!" I barked. "And don't do that again!" I groaned.

"You kid is crazy. Why would he stay in a tunnel all day?"

"He has fun in there, doing whatever he wants."

"That reminds me I finished it." Fangs flew off and we followed him to the tunnel. Inside he handed us metal clips.

"It makes your howls and screeches louder. You call to each other from further away. I would cover your ears if I were you."

Dox howled and it roared against the tunnel walls, he stared at Fangs amazed.

"Well, I definitely heard it." I felt at my ears still vibrating.

"It's powerful, the sound can stretch about twice as far as

normally," I screeched and Dox howled.

"We could've broken out of prisons with this," Dox laughed.

"You bet. With this much power just by howling and screeching you could break down walls!" We laughed and stopped, staring at Fangs. He seemed suspicious.

"We should've just told them everything."

"What did you do?!" Fangs groaned.

18

"We broke out of prison once or twice," I shrugged

"More like we've broken out of every prison in each city," Dox added. I sighed glaring at my friend.

"What I can't keep a secret from your kid that's just madness!" he exclaimed.

"You broke out of prison!"

"See your kids are the wild ones, my kid is more civilized, that's why I don't tell him, Dox," I snapped.

"Answer me!" Fangs barked.

"Yes, I broke out of prison! Happy?!"

"There's more to it," Fangs nodded.

"What was I supposed to do, starve to death? He and his cousin left me broke. Ford stole from me, Dox took my food and my money! I had to steal some things, then I paid the price when my home was burnt down."

"What?! You have two homes?" Fangs gaped at me.

"Don't you dare ask me to take you. I will never take you!"

"Wasn't going to ask, not now," Fangs mumbled. I pushed Dox against the wall, I growled. Dox just looked innocently at me, like he'd done nothing wrong.

"See, he asks questions, he gets curious then I scare him when he sees my past! I didn't want to tell him!"

"Sorry but your kid creeps me out. Looks just like Rogue with that angered look, and I can't lie to her, she'd kill me, seriously! If you get hurt she takes it out on me, she knows how much trouble we get into together."

"Don't hurt him, Phoenix." Fangs put his hand on me and I couldn't resist.

"Just like your mother, only one that can stop me." I let of go of Dox, and he sprinted off.

"How do I stop you? How am I like Rogue?"

"Because Rogue is the one there to sooth me. To stop me from hurting anyone, which comes in handy especially with Dox. You stop me because I would never do anything bad around you, if I did it would be to protect you. If I scare you I'm sorry, I only want to protect the people I love."

"Do you love Dox?"

"We have a tough relationship. I wouldn't really call it love. His family is the kind that will help you to your feet and then take your money. Our family is the kind that helps and then won't let go. Or as Dox thinks we're the family that cares too much. He likes to do things on his own and so do I, but we get along."

"If you two get along then why is Dox taking a hunting group into the woods?" Rogue stood at the end of the tunnel. I groaned and flew over the woods. I swooped down spotting his group below.

"What are you doing?" I snapped.

"Taking matters into my hands, now go home." Dox formed into a human holding my gaze.

"Yeah I'm never going home, not without you and your group."

"You'll want to trust me, we'll be out here all night," Dox stood firmly.

"You're not nocturnal like your cousin, you'll fall asleep and someone will catch you," I growled.

"Don't you dare bring my little cousin into this? Why do you bring him up anyway?"

"Because like Rogue and Fangs, he's the only one that can stop you."

"Go back home Phoenix. We don't need any help," Dox growled.

"I wasn't going to, I just wanted to get you back to the Groves. We shouldn't-"

"Listen...They're here, it's an ambush! Run!" Dox howled and the wolves were surrounded by hunters. I switched forms and lashed my fangs.

"This is all your fault," Dox hissed.

"We wouldn't be here if you'd come back with me," I replied staring at the hunters surrounding us. The wolves growled, and the hunters took a step back. I screeched calling for the search group, and they swooped down lashing their fangs. Some of the hunters took a step back, frightened.

"Oh please, their dumb animals," a hunter scoffed stepping closer. The phoenixes flamed up, wings outstretched and the hunters dashed out of the woods.

"Demons!" they yelled running off, terrified.

"I told you to go home Phoenix!" Dox barked.

"I said I would take care of it myself!" I shot back.

"If you had told me in the first place we wouldn't be here!"

"I thought I could take care of it!"

"You can't and I'm here to help you if you need it! Just like we planned!"

"I didn't need it!"

"Go back home!"

"Duh. I'm never going home. Not without you!"

"Sorry, but I have to get you off my back," Dox shrugged. The wolves growled advancing toward me. I screeched and my group followed me back to the Groves.

"Are you alright Leader?" one of the warriors was anxious.

"I'm fine," I snapped.

Hunters stormed through the woods, everyday getting closer to the border. The wolves and the phoenixes stayed inside the Groves, never leaving. We did meetings with the entire council everyday discussing the hunters surrounding the Woods.

"There has to be something we can do. We're like sitting ducks, we have the border but with all these hunters it won't last long." Kalo looked at the border worriedly.

"I agree, over in the meadows a group of hunters was shooting at the Wall. They found its weakness and are striking hard. Once the Wall is down, we're unprotected," a wolf nodded.

"Humans would be done for. Half-bloods, would fight until they're gone, and we're not human," Dox snapped.

"I say we prepare for a fight if needed. If not we'll just send groups to check for hunters. No one gets in, and no one leaves," I pointed out on the map.

"These marks show where they've been spotted. I thought we could try and find their hideout. Wherever they are they always run off in that direction," a phoenix pointed at the arrows on the map that all lead to the same place.

"That's the Morse, but it's just a field of burnt trees now. What would they want from there?" I looked at the map remembering what I'd left behind when we found the Groves. "I didn't leave anything important back there-" I turned to the woods and put my head in my hands, shaking my head.

"This can't be possible," I gaped at the woods.

"What?" Dox stared into my eyes.

"When I left the Agency I took what was left of the chemical that made me fireproof. I left it in the Morse. If they find it, we can't fight them. With that, they'll be as strong as us. I buried it somewhere in there, we have to find it."

"You idiot! How could you forget it?" Dox barked.

"I buried it the day I found that place, I was there for years, that's long enough for me to forget about it!" I shot back.

"Come on, let's go get it." We grabbed our cloaks, and walked out into the woods. By nightfall we were standing behind the trees looking at the Morse. Cabins covered the sea of ashes, and black tree trunks. Blackened branches scatter over gray rotting grass.

"How will we get over there without being spotted?" Dox whispered, staring at the people rushing about.

"We'll have to get caught, then we can make a trade." I held up a full bag. "The potion for a bag of food, and money. Sure we stole it but they won't care." I shrugged, pulling the hood over my head. We passed by cabins, and people stared suspiciously.

"Keep walking, don't stop," Dox snapped and I turned away, looking forward. Someone stepped in front of us.

"Who are you?" A man asked suspiciously.

"We're looking for something." I held his gaze.

"Where did you two come from? The woods are dangerous for two boys to be walking around without an escort."

"We live a long way from here, and we're hoping to get home by morning. Our families will be worried," Dox lashed.

"Well you just passed the market, and you seem to know where you're going. What are you boys hiding?" The man glared at us.

"Okay, I'm done hiding. My friend and I want what we came for, we're heading deeper into the woods, we're only passing by." I pushed past the man and Dox seemed anxious.

"Why did you tell him?!" He snapped.

"Because if we're still in the woods by morning, these people might notice we're the same people and question us. They'll kill us, Dox."

"Fine." Dox walked ahead and I followed.

"Over here." I pointed at a spot.

"How can you tell where it is?"

"I've lived here for eleven years, I know what it looked like before it became…This." I dug into the dirt, and grabbed the vial. I slipped it into my cloak, and we slipped into the shadows. We raced through the woods back home. We luckily made it back to the Groves before dawn. I slipped up to the top of the Willow, and Rogue climbed up the ladder.

"Go back to sleep, everything's fine, honest." I looked through the leaves to see Fangs sleeping.

"Why do you leave us so much? Can't you just stay for a while?" Rogue lied her head on my shoulder, looking up at the stars.

"I will once this is over, once we're safe. I'll relax once we're not being threatened."

"How about we relax now?" Rogue took my hand and we landed on the cliffside, we sat silently watching the sun rise.

"See, this is beautiful. I would sit here with Fangs while you were gone…But it never felt the same. I miss you. Let me come with you, please. I want to spend more time with you."

"Alright, me and you tomorrow, we can take a walk through the woods. Both of our families, we can all go together, including the kids."

"That's sounds nice. Kareen is really lonely without Dox. The kids play on their own, and she sits there doing nothing. She needs him, and I need you." Rogue nuzzled her head into my shoulder and I was so happy to sit with her. Nothing on my mind at all, just sitting with Rogue made me happy. Made me feel calm and… Loved.

19

Our two families walked through the woods, while the kids rushed about chasing after each other. Dox and I were so happy to see our families together, no attacks, all of us having fun.

"Why can't we do this every day?" Rogue sighed looking up at the trees.

"Because we're at home. While the boys run off doing whatever stupid things pop into their heads," Kareen glared at Dox who shrugged innocently.

"Hey, it's not my fault we get attacked every other day," he retorted.

"I love this field trip!" Fangs smiled hovering in the sky before flying off to find the others. I shot up after him and Dox sprinted after me joining Ex and Vess.

By midnight Rogue and I were curled up in a tree Fangs sleeping in the branches.

"This was beautiful. Thank you Phoenix, I finally got to spend time with you. Kareen and her family are so happy, it's amazing."

"I want you happy. That shimmering in your eyes is all I could ask for. That smile on your face just makes me happy." I pulled her close and she kissed me on my cheek. We stared at the moon glowing above the woods, stars sprinkled across the sky. Rogue dazed at the sky, amazed.

"I couldn't really see the stars at home. I could but I never wanted to…Not without you. These moments are what I love the most." Rogue leaned on me slowly drifting to sleep. I watched the stars fade and the sun rise. I was awake when Fangs woke up.

"Have you been awake all night?" he asked sitting with me.

"I love watching the sky change from night to day," I smiled gazing at the sunrise.

"She kissed you didn't she," Fangs sighed. "Every time."

"I finally got to see Rogue happy for once. That's all I could I ask for."

"She's my mom and your wife. She's kissed you a billion times, how does another make it any different?" I turned to him pulled from my daze at the sky.

"Unlike you, I never felt love as a kid. I felt what most humans should feel as teenagers at that time. So now, when Rogue does kiss me I feel... like I finally get that feeling for once."

"But how do you deal with it? Trying to make her happy, how?" Fangs pressed.

"Rogue is beautiful, smart, caring and loving. It comes easy for me trying to make her happy. She only wants a loving family."

"No, I want a loving son, and a caring husband." Rogue pulled me close kissing me.

"How do you put up with that?" Fangs stared at us disgusted.

"Please, I could do it all day, and so could Dox." Fangs looked down below. Dox was licking Kareen's fur while she licked him back. "Their love is more… wild." Fangs flew off to play with his friends. Dox and I went nowhere staying with our wives, relaxed. Soon enough a day turned into a week. Our families were relieved for some time away from the groups. No attacks, no fighting, just peace. I met with Dox that afternoon and we strolled through the woods.

"This feels so good, Kareen is happy I'm home, and the kids are glad to be fooling around again."

"I mean they're kids they're supposed to fool around and have fun, same as us. We had a lot of fun, breaking out of prisons, stealing from the markets. Now we're top criminals, we put bandits to shame," we both laughed.

"I have to admit I would rather be in prison with you than a bandit. I was once, he beat me up after I told him he was worse of a stealer than ten year old."

"Why don't we bring back the past?" We smiled slyly and slipped into town.

I jumped over a fruit stand snatching a piece of fruit.

"HEY!" A woman shook her fist as I dashed off down the streets. I slipped into the police station, and bit into an apple.

"Hey so I understood there was this boy, that you guys were looking for and-"

"Grab him!" An officer yelled and I rushed outside and flew close to the ground. I slammed into Dox who was sprinting in the other direction.

"Police?" I huffed.

"Yeah," Dox panted. Police stood around us guns drawn.

"You can do better than that people," I scoffed.

"Put your hands in the air boys!" An officer barked.

"Okay," I put my hands in the air and flashed flames at the officers. The stumbled back and I grabbed Dox's wrist and flew off. I let go and Dox fell, sprinting off into the woods.

"Let's do that again!" I yelled flying above him.

"You bet!" Dox panted.

20

"You idiot! Phoenix why?"

"We had fun. Plus we didn't get caught," I shrugged biting into a piece of fruit.

"Where did you get it?" Rogue pointed at the plum in my other hand. I tossed it to her and she bit into it.

"Stole it why?" She spat it out and glared at me.

"Dox was involved I'm guessing?"

"Yeah," Rogue screeched and Dox bolted up the tree.

"What's wrong-?"

"What happened, Dox?"

"Oh," Dox stared at the ground innocently.

"Why?" Rogue pressed.

"We wanted to have some fun," I shrugged.

"You know how I feel about stealing. Ever since you brought me to that town I knew this would happen," Rogue groaned.

"Don't worry. So long as I get back safe, that's all you ask right?" I asked wrapping my arms around her.

"Yeah. It's just... I don't want either of you to get caught. Especially Dox, Kareen has been worried sick about you. I had to drag her out a cave, she wouldn't eat, drink. She needs him, and I need you Phoenix," Rogue hugged me back.

"Alright, alright. We won't leave...Without telling you," Dox added.

"Fine. But if you go behind my back again, I'll have you lose your sense of smell for good," Kareen snapped and Dox turned to her.

"I won't I promise."

"You better not, I starved because of you, and both of us were lonely without you." Dox kissed her and she held him close. Our families ate what Dox and I had stolen from town. We feasted on fruit, bread, vegetables, and cow.

"You didn't have to kill it," I stared at Dox and Kareen feasting on a dead cow.

"Hey it was free," Dox pointed out.

"You took it down after being chased by shepherd dogs."

"I say well earned," Dox nodded, looking over at his sons fighting over one of the legs. I nodded, fairly agreeing.

We sat around doing nothing. The kids slept in after staying up all night, fooling around. By noon we walked back to the Groves we had nothing to do but go home.

"Leader we've been attacked!" Kalo and a wolf ran up to us.

"How?"

"Hunters they broke the Wall. Twenty of our people, wolves and phoenixes. We can't heal them, the injections are gone. We can't save them all, but we can keep them alive."

"Keep them alive, I'll go find more of the syndrome-"

"I'm going too," Dox put his hand on my shoulder, "You'll need help, trust me." He turned to Kareen who hugged him and let him go. Rogue nodded, tears in her eyes. I kissed her and raced off behind Dox.

We slipped inside, everything dead silent. We slipped into the lab and searched for the syndrome. The capsules were open and the floors covered in water. Our footsteps echoed in the empty room, with every step. Dox loomed over one of the screens, a red light blinking. The screen appeared with a video.

"Who's Jamie?" A boy appeared on the screen.

"Stop fooling around, come home Jamie...Please," A man and a woman begged him.

"He listens to a different name now, actually," Ferdinand smiled slyly, "The side effects of the antidote finally kicked in, so now we'll tell you the truth. Your son was never sick at all, we needed him for an experiment. Though he wasn't sick, he has something special that no other child could ever have... Ultimate powers, half animal you could say. Well we call them half-bloods, the side effects are permanent, sadly."

"What did you do to him?" The woman asked, "What did you do to our son?" The man stopped her, begging the boy once again.

"Come home with us Jamie, you're just scared."

"Like I said, I don't know anyone named Jamie. I also know I'm not a foolish little kid," the boy snapped, "My name is 208, my subject number."

21

"That black souled, evil, murderer!" Dox roared.

"She wiped our memory. Dox those people are your...parents," I breathed.

"208 please move back to your chambers, I'd hate to tempt them," Ferdinand nodded, but Dox stayed still, staring at his parents. He looked as if he was fighting the urge not to leave.

"208, leave now," Ferdinand hissed, and Dox stayed by her side. She pulled a dog whistle and Dox rushed off….

"Get them out of my sight," Ferdinand ordered as guards pushed his parents away. "And wipe 208's memory, while you're at it."

I joined Dox at the computer. I tapped at it and a list of names came up.

"What are you doing?" Dox was puzzled.

"Finding Ferdinand's history. Someone in her family must've started it and Ferdinand would try to end it. Look."

A man and woman popped up on the screen.

"Lacey and Radley Blanch, future scientists created the first half bloods. Subjects 1204956, and 1204952, creation date unknown. (Now living in Xven). Their daughter Ferdinand Blanch, created the first GAP subjects…"

"What?!" the girls gaped at us stunned.

"It's true. Data, backgrounds, subject numbers, and title codes. All there. We found our human names." Dox nodded handing them the syndrome. "Kareen your real name is Irene, and my real name is Jamie."

"Gross, I'm sticking with my name," Kareen scoffed.

"Rogue your name is Irene, my name is Jack," I smiled.

"Yeah, I'm good." Rogue shook her head.

"Anyway we're going out into Xven." Kareen jumped on Dox nearly toppling him, not letting go.

"Don't leave me," she begged.
"It won't be for long, I promise," he promised.
"Fine," she grumbled.
"Please come back safely," Rogue sighed.
"I'll be fine, Rogue," I hugged her and we left the Groves.

22

A mass shadow of black cloaks stooped through town, people had their doors shut. We knocked on doors trying to find Xven.

"Hello?" I stood in front of a door.

"Get out of town you freak!" A voice barked from behind the door.

"I just want to know about a town called Xven?"

"You're standing in it, and no one wants you here!" The voice shot back.

"Well, I'm looking for Lacey and Radley Blanch." The door opened and I signaled the group.

"What do you want?" A woman stood at the door.

"Answers, please." I kicked down the door and she bolted back in shock. I flamed up and the guards pushed them against the wall.

"Who are you?" The man pleaded. My flames went out and I smiled slyly.

"I'm the one that killed your daughter, and your grandson," I hissed.

"Why?"

"She burned down my home, and almost killed my wife, and my son." I stared at them tears in my eyes.

"Your daughter, killed our parents, then wiped our memory of them. We finally found out today," Dox growled.

"We're sorry but what does this have to do with us?" The man begged.

"What did you do when you started GAP?" I stood firmly holding their gazes.

"We only used science, I don't how you have parents. We created a human life form then improved it, it's the truth really," the woman panted.

"Well your daughter, Ferdinand, took four regular children and formed us into these," I growled and flamed up, Dox formed into a wolf. We formed into humans and the couple gawped at us.

"We're sorry she did that to you. We weren't there to stop her, she ran away-" the woman cried.

"What do you mean? She worked and lived at the Agency." I stood puzzled.

"When she was sixteen. She planned to take over our researches, so she ran away into the city. She bought our old building and used it herself. She sent a messenger to-" the woman stopped staring at me. "You! It was you! She sent you with the message."

"I don't remember. We found footage, she wiped our memories, and trained us for combat," I signaled the guards, and they let the humans go. Instantly the man grabbed me, and me to the floor.

"You killed my daughter! I didn't know she even had a son! You killed her, and her son!" The man yelled and jumped on me, he turned to the woman, "Go get help!" The woman ran, and I kicked him off, bolting to my feet. A bunch of townspeople rushed in, the man stumbled back, and hands grabbed me. Dox was pinned and the guards screeched at me, worriedly.

"I'm fine! Get out here!" I yelled and a man pulled me to the floor. I beat my wings trying to break the man's grip.

"Behind the wings you idiot," the man snapped, and I yelped as the man positioned his hands in between my wings. Another man grabbed me, and I bit his arm, lashing my fangs. Something hit me in the head and I fell to the floor, Dox lied on the floor weakly, he struggled badly.

I bolted awake and felt the rope tied around my body. I turned, trying to bite the rope, I hit my head and Dox turned to me.

"We're tied together you idiot," Dox snapped, "Don't do anything stupid please, I already tried."

I groaned, "My guards are locked up too, aren't they?"

"Yeah. They wouldn't leave you, so they tried to help. They got electrocuted, and were out cold," Dox scoffed, "Your people don't listen at all. They won't even listen to you."

"Let's get out of here. How should we do this?" I smiled at Dox and he smiled back slyly.

"This is a cabin, which means all wood. I can slip out of that broken shaft in the wall. Quick question, are your guards fire proof?"

"Why wouldn't they be?" I smiled back, and pulled a dagger out of my pocket.

"Do your thing man," Dox nodded, as I passed him the dagger. We cut ourselves loose, and I set a flame on the wall. I screeched toward the guards, and they called back. Dox and I slipped out the shaft in the wall, and my guards stood outside. Dox formed and sprinted off, I flew off with him into the woods, the guards behind me.

Rogue hugged me, and I knew she was happy I was home. She stared up at me angrily, pushing me away.

"You said you'd be back by the end of the day," she lashed.

"We got captured but we're closer. We still need to find them."

"Why does it matter, Phoenix?! They wouldn't remember! They might be long gone! Then you'd be chasing after nothing!" Rogue cried.

"Because, I want to know why? Why would they give us up?!" I shot back, "You don't want to know, how we got here?!"

"If we never became what we are now! I wouldn't be here! I would've never met you!" I pulled her close and she cried into my shoulder.

"I'm sure I would've met you either way," I whispered.

23

"We need to go!" Dox begged.

"I'm not going to the Pride. He won't let it go!" I barked back.

"You're still mad at him, that's all," Dox shrugged.

"He gave me a position, I turned it down now every time I see him he blames me!" I growled.

"I don't care, I'm going." Dox started to walk off but I stopped him.

"Fine, I'll go, but I want nothing to do with this," I groused.

"Still playing with dogs, Phoenix?" The boy lashed.

"Still prancing with unicorns, Malley?" I shot back. Dox sighed standing between us.

"Look, this isn't a good time. My people are dying from the heat, and none of them plan on moving on."

"Malley we need your help to find someone," Dox growled.

"What! No! I'm not going to have my people, work with him!" I barked, and Dox smiled slyly. "You tricked me!"

"I had to man! You two have problems," Dox shrugged.

"Fine, let's settle this for good." I stared into Malley's eyes and he smiled slyly.

"What are you doing?!" Dox snapped.

"He annoys me, he frustrates me, and I'm done with him." I looked at Malley who stood innocently.

"Dude, he's going to kill you," he hissed.

"Not if I kill him first," I growled, holding Malley's gaze. I stood face to face with him, and Dox stepped back.

"Phoenix!"

"Rogue?" I turned to Rogue, and Dox grabbed her.

"Still thought you were alone? Instead you left for a girlfriend? You're weak," Malley scoffed, "Since she cares just back down, you won't win this one."

"I leave, then I come back and you're still prancing around with dumb flying horses? You make me sick," I shot back. He slammed me to the ground, and I kicked him in the gut. I grabbed his wing in my fangs, and I felt his wing break. Malley yelped, and punched me back. I formed, and pushed him to the ground. Malley flapped helplessly, unable to form. He formed and shoved me off, clamping his hooves on my wings.

"Stand down, and I won't finish you," he hissed.

"I'm still fighting, aren't I?" I choked him, and we both lost form. By the end, we were both on the ground, bleeding terribly. I stood on my feet, and stood face to face with Malley.

"Let's make a bargain, instead," Malley nodded.

"Fine by me." I held his gaze.

"We'll find whoever you're looking for."

"I can send supplies for your people." I flew off and Dox, and Rogue went after me.

"What did you do?" Rogue asked worriedly.

"I'm fine, and we won't be seeing Malley any time soon." I kept my gaze ahead.

"Who is he?"

"He gave me a position when I was with his group. I was ten and could've ruled his group, but I left. He blames me ever since, and now he has the position."

"Why didn't you tell me?" Rogue cut in front of me.

"Because he was going to fight me, and I didn't want you to get involved. He luckily, still thinks you're my girlfriend. But if he knew the truth, he would go after you, and Fangs."

"Tell me, next time. I can help you."

"Maybe, next time. Malley isn't safe to be around. Especially his group, they follow his every order, including to kill. They don't have an opinion, if I took the position, they'd be my slaves. I left him 'cause I would rather have my people an opinion, than to follow my orders blindly."

"You really do care," Rogue sighed happily.

24

I flew next to the Alpha, and it followed me toward the Pride. Malley stood on the ground, he nodded smiling. I helped pass out food, and water. I put a whistle in Malley's hand, and he smiled. I nodded, "If you need help, just call." I flew off and the Alpha followed. Days passed, and I assumed Malley and the Pride had moved on. Hunters disappeared from the woods, and I strolled through the woods with Dox.

"You helped him. Why?" Dox asked.

"He needed help, and I wouldn't fight him any longer. It's better to bargain than fight when you can't keep going," I shrugged. I heard Malley and looked off into the woods.

"You heard that too?" Dox looked at me worriedly.

"He's in trouble. Get the guards." Dox howled and I screeched. Kalo and a wolf stood with guards behind them. The wolf bowed to Dox, and Kalo bowed to me.

"What did we tell you two, about bowing to us?" Dox groaned.

"You don't have to." I smiled and Kalo nodded.

"Now listen up. There's a distress call from the Pride. We're going to check to it out. Our queens, are protected, right?" Dox stared into the wolf's eyes.

"First thing we ever do when called," the wolf shrugged.

"Find anyone who's alive and report back." We flew off and landed in the dry plains. I gaped at the Pride, lifeless, and dying.

"Leader! It's Malley!" one of the guards called and we rushed over. Malley lied on the ground, bleeding badly.

"How did this happen?" Dox looked at the plains, Malley's group, was dying quickly.

"Hunters. They stormed us, millions of them," Malley croaked.

"Spread out! Find any survivors!" Dox barked and the guards rushed off in all directions. Using the syndrome we healed Malley, and seven others. The rest of the Pride, was gone forever.

We helped them back to the Groves, and rested them in the marshes.

"How many did you find?" Malley asked, sipping some water.

"Only seven, but we're not sure that that's all of them. We'll look tomorrow," Dox nodded.

"We were supposed to hold up our end of the bargain. I'll pay double, for the next trade, how about that?"

"This one's on us." Malley smiled back at me, "It's the least we could do."

"Let's hope we find more of them tomorrow, you'd become a rare half blood." Dox stared off into the woods, toward the Pride.

"Tomorrow? Why wait, we can go now," I said and Dox sighed.

"I can't, Kareen won't let me leave the Groves overnight. I can't go behind her back, she'd kill me if I did."

"She worries about you too much. You'll be with me anyways, she'll be fine Dox. Since when do you care about going behind her back?" I scoffed.

"Ever since she did that." Dox pointed at a huge scar across his back. "That really hurt, I was bleeding for a week. Her claws went deep into my back, I swear she'll kill me. That or she'll break up with me, I can't lose her," he sighed.

"You'll be fine, she's never going to leave you. I never seen you fight her before," I shrugged, but Dox was serious.

"I fought with her just yesterday. She thinks I'm not being a good father since I'm gone all the time. She pushed my sons away from me, said that I would only leave them heartbroken in the end. That I'm so wild I could rip our family apart." Dox hung his head, and his muscles tensed. I knew he was fighting the urge to leave them.

"You just need to show her you still care."

"How? I've tried everything I could to please her."

"Just tell her. She can't stay mad at you for that long." Dox formed and sprinted off.

"I feel bad for him in some ways. I never fought with my family but it sounds harsh." Malley watched Dox leave. I nodded.

"He's just confused. Love was hard for him when we were younger. He just can't find himself. He's so used to being alone, this father thing is pretty tough on him."

Dox and I met at the edge of the Groves, each with six guards. We sat in the grass and spread out a map, circling any places where hunters were spotted.

"They attacked the Pride coming from the East and West. They're far away from the Morse, I've never seen them that separated from their hideout." I drew a red circle on the map, close to the Pride.

"Unless they have another hideout. There might be... More of them." The council members looked at each other and Dox scoffed.

"Sure there's more of them but who cares? We're two times as strong as any human," Dox shrugged.

"He does have a point." I nodded smiling.

"Let's check it out, but stay on guard," Kalo commanded and the guards nodded.

We walked through the Woods and reached the Pridelands by noon, scouring the grounds for any other survivors. We searched for days and by the end of the week we'd found another sixteen that we saved with the syndrome. Malley and his group came together and grazed on the sweet grass in the meadows. Dox and I strolled through the woods every evening with nothing to do. We talked and talked for hours on end, and by nightfall we stood face to face at the edge of the cliffside smiling at one another.

"Ready?" Dox asked.

"Why wouldn't I be?" I smiled back. Dox pushed me off the cliff and jumped after me. We fell and landed on our feet in the grass. We walked to edge of the Groves, and slipped outside. It was dawn and the both of us sat in a birch tree looking down over the cities. Our guards spread through the city in black cloaks, the humans' doors, closed and locked.

"They really are scared of us." Dox smiled slyly looking out over the city. When he wasn't looking I shoved him off the tree. Dox grabbed a branch and glared up at me, and I was laughing. A lightning bolt shot past me, and I looked down at Dox.

"When did you learn that?"

"I don't know I think I jumped on a powerline. Whatever happened now I can do this," Dox shrugged before shooting another bolt. I shot a flame and dodged his attack.

"When did you learn that?" Dox smiled.

"I don't know." I laughed before a fire ball whizzed past Dox's ear. Dox sent lighting through the branches and it shocked and burned me. I fell and Dox looked down the tree and I jumped on him from behind and tumbled down to the ground, laughing.

Dox smiled at me, before a blast of lighting rushed toward me, and I burst flames in its direction. The two forces clashed sending us both flying in different directions. Dox and I howled laughing so hard.

"What are you up to now?" Kareen and Rogue were up in the trees, out of view. I shot a blast of fire and Rogue poked her head out from the branches. We started laughing again, and the two of them joined in.

"Since when did you learn how to shoot fire with that much power?" Rogue smirked looking out over the Groves.

"I have no idea, but I love it," I smiled, I took her hand and laid a small flame in the palm of her hand. She coiled the flame around her finger and turned into a ring. She handed me another, a pair of wings carved into it.

"Now we can always be together," she whispered and I kissed her on the lips. We sat there in silence leaning on each other. Dox and Kareen joined us on the cliffside and soon the boys did too. All of us enjoyed the sunset, watching it fade. Fangs leaned against me fast asleep, and so was Rogue. I laid blankets over them and Dox and I went off on our own. We strolled through the woods quietly, and Dox stopped on the trail.

"Cover your ears." I nodded doing as he said. Dox howled and suddenly howls erupted from the Groves. I looked in his direction, a full moon and I soon remembered. Dox always howled at a full moon with his group, always wild. Suddenly shadows emerged from the darkness and we were swallowed and blinded. I hit something and landed on solid ground. I tried to light a flame but nothing happened. Dox stared at me worriedly. Suddenly Rogue's ring glowed, and Dox had a blue ring on his finger with a carved symbol, just like mine.

"They really take this seriously," Dox scoffed.

"We're fine, we just don't know where we are," I shrugged.

"Back home, where else?" My ears twitched noticing that familiar voice and it wasn't Dox. Lights blinded us again, and Saube stood with a group of hunters. I gaped at him and he smiled slyly.

"I killed you. I killed you!" I yelled tears in my eyes.

"These men saved me." Saube looked at the group of hunters.

"Where is she?!" I barked.

"She's here too." Saube nodded and Dox grabbed my shoulder.

"Don't Phoenix. He's not worth it." Dox stared at Saube oddly.

"So you're the one my mother was talking about. Interesting, she let you go but that was mistake," he shrugged, "When you thought to kill me the first time, I assumed you'd kill my mother too. That's where you messed up. You should've kept me alive and killed her. She would hand the business over to me when she was gone." Saube glared at me, "If you weren't such a pain, I might have saved you. But you drove me mad, so I planned on telling my mother. Of course she was dumb enough to leave you be. That was a mistake as well… and it won't happen again."

"You know, you're about as dumb as your mother. You side with hunters, that's enough to make you a total idiot," Dox shot back. "I don't care if I didn't kill her, I'll end it this time."

"Are you sure about that?" Saube shrugged, and Dox shot a bolt.

"Impressive, new powers, I'll have to put that in." Saube nodded at the hunters. "Find them." The hunters walked away and Saube turned to us.

"I'm not your enemy, Phoenix." Saube held out his hand.

"I would rather side with the people I can trust," I hissed.

"How's the family then?" I stopped cold, and Saube laughed. "You really think I don't know?!" he scoffed, "Why else would I bring you here? They'll come for you, and you and your friend's little games are over."

"I hate games," Dox lashed, "and our rein isn't over. You can't kill us and end it that way. You need the group's support, and they'll never bow down to you." Dox glanced at me and I nodded-

"Behind you," Saube pointed out and guards grabbed us. I lashed my fangs the man yelped, blood dripping from his hand.

"It's just a little blood," Saube shrugged clasping his hands over my mouth.

"Yeah, and that wasn't my plan." I sank my fangs into his wrist and he wrenched back,

"You bit me!" he gawped at me in surprise, "You don't bite me we're friends."

"Sure believe that, if I could've revealed my secret at MJD, I would've done that days ago," I hissed.

"I thought you were human at first? Guess I was wrong." Chains pushed me to the ground, and men chained my wings.

25

I pulled at the chains on the wall.

"Well this is fun," Dox mumbled.

"When I get out here, I will rid him from my life for good," I growled, and glanced at Dox. He started whistling a soft tune. "What are you doing?" I lashed.

"Whistling," he shrugged.

"Really now?" Dox shrugged and kept whistling. A scratching noise came from the vent above us. Dox whistled louder, and a girl jumped from the vent.

"I thought you'd never call darling," she sighed.

"Enough flattering, get us out of here," Dox barked.

"Oh but darling, you're really not of interest to me anymore," she shrugged.

"Oh enough Snake. I don't care if you're interested or not," Dox hissed.

"Who's this cutie?" she hissed at me, I shook my head disgustingly.

"He's got a family, now get us out," Dox growled, "We don't have time, unless you want to become a snakeskin robe," The girl gasped. "Yeah, I said it, now hurry up. If you don't help I might just do it myself." Dox growled again.

"Fine, but you know what you owe me," she mumbled. Dox sighed, as she cut us loose. We made it outside and rushed into the woods. "You can stay with me for the night, it's a long way back."

"You better not pull any tricks, Snake."

"Oh darling, I never do," she hissed, I stopped dead cold.

"She's a snake?!" I gawped at Dox, and shook my head, "I hate snakes, they're cruel and cold blooded. How can you trust her?!" I snapped.

"I don't but I guess I owe her the company, after she's repeatedly begged for love." We walked ahead and came to a den overlooking a meadow. Snake coiled up and hissed at us, and we sat with her.

"Has the position been filled darling?" Snake hissed.

"Years ago, and she's not leaving Snake," Dox growled back.

"Well you two really get along," I mumbled.

"Snake here expects Kareen to give up her position as queen. She has nobody to love her, and she really wants me. I hate her more than life." Dox glared at her.

"I don't see why you're so pushy darling," she smiled. "I'm not holding grudges," she shrugged.

"I don't care if you are or not. I will never let you around her," he growled, "I'm not even going to deal with you. Come on Phoenix, let's go home." He turned and walked away, and I joined him. We formed and disappeared into the shadows leaving Snake coiled up in her den all alone.

"He'll come back. He always does…" she hissed.

"He's alive?! That's impossible!" Rogue paced at the edge of the cliffside.

"Will you stop pacing, you're going to hurt yourself," I groaned sitting on a rock.

"I need to it helps me think-" Rogue tripped and I grabbed her wrist before she fell off.

"Now will you listen to me?" I growled.

"Fine," she moaned, sitting with me.

"I don't want to worry you." I put my hands on her shoulders and she hugged me tight.

"Just stop! You tell me the same thing, then you end up killing yourself for nothing! This time you're starting a war?! We won't have a place to go when the Groves is destroyed, you know that!"

"We're uniting every group. You won't lose me this time, I promise…" I stopped and Rogue looked at me worriedly.

"What is it? Phoenix, what's wrong?"

"Traveling. I'll be gone for a while, I don't want Fangs to know. I need you to keep him distracted while I leave."

"You promised me! You promised me you wouldn't leave!"

"I never said that!" I shot back.

"You're going to fight in a war and have me not know. Go ahead you idiot! Get yourself killed, for all I care!"

"Rogue please…" I put my hand on her shoulder and with a blast of flames she shoved me off the cliff. I quickly grabbed the edge and pulled myself up.

"GO! GET AWAY FROM ME!" She roared. I flew off back to

the Willow. Dox leaned against the trunk, smiling.

"Ready to go?"

"More than ever."

"Never thought I'd hear you say that," he shrugged.

"She's mad at me, and Fangs will be when I come home. My family turned on me, but so what. It'll be me and you for days, just like old times," I smiled.

"You never told her we weren't bringing guards on this mission did you?" He scoffed.

"She'll find out sooner or later." I walked with him to the edge of the Groves and we passed through the border, and I didn't look back.

26

We strolled through the woods. I took Rogue's ring and turned it into a flaming snake. It coiled and wrapped around my wrist, setting it aflame.

"I thought you hated snakes?" Dox glanced at the flaming creature.

"No, I hate that girl that's half snake. Plus I possessed Rogue's ring, now it can form into anything I need. Just concentrate." Dox stopped and concentrated, his ring turned to electricity, and into a horse. I turned my ring into horse and we rode out of the woods. Days had past and we were now in the Snowy Mountains. I formed my ring into an owl and it stared at me waiting.

"Find her, bring her here, no matter what it takes." I hissed and the owl flew off. It came back hours later, landing on my shoulder.

"Took you long enough," I snapped.

"Takes me awhile to get here, considering I visited Snake long before you," a voice moaned, and a brown lynx stepped from the shadows.

"Stop with the excuses, and round up your troops," Dox barked.

"I don't have any," the lynx purred, stretching her back.

"Where are they?" I growled.

"They're at the top of Mount Aven. Long way from here boys, better leave it to me." The lynx turned her back to us.

"We're going to find them. You'll just retreat to your den and we'll still be here," I barked, storming ahead. I turned my ring solid and pressed ahead. We were close to the top of the mountain by nightfall, Dox and I sat in the snow, starving.

"Just let me hunt. I can get enough meat to last us three days," Dox lashed.

"I don't like to be smothered in blood like you," I shook my head.

"Just once Phoenix, you'll starve," Dox pressed.

"I would rather die," I shot back, "I don't need food, I need to get this over with and go home," I growled, pulling the hood of my cloak over my head. I gripped at my stomach in pain.

"You're hungry just admit it," Dox scoffed.

"I'm starving," I groaned. Dox and I feasted on a white rabbit and I ate slowly, disgustedly too.

We kept moving, and made it to the other side of the mountain by dawn. I shook my head, staring at a frozen and my body flamed up.

"Just calm down until we get across," Dox shrugged, and I shook my head again.

"I can't, my body will overheat, and we'll fall through."

"What do you mean you can't control it?" He snapped.

"I'm thinking about warm things, I'm not meant for this weather."

"Just think about something else." I nodded and we inched forward across the icy pond.

"Think of something… different. Something… different," I thought, "Think of her, and think of Rogue. She's beautiful, smart, and she loves me, even though…"

My eyes darted to the ice below my feet. I breathed a sigh of relief and kept moving

"Are you okay?" Dox glanced back at me, "Don't think about it-" Without even thinking about it my body flamed up and the ice below my feet cracked.

"Run! It's melting!" Dox hurried to the other side of the pond I tried hovering but my wings were frozen and covered in ice. I bolted for the edge of the pond and tumbled into a snowbank. I brushed snow off my freezing skin, and glared at him.

"Let's get this over with," I growled. We trudged through deep snow and by nightfall we were close to Mount Aven.

"One flame that's all you have to do," Dox snapped. "It's never hurt you before."

"I'm sorry okay? I'm not used to this weather, I hate winters like this." I lit a small flame in my hand, its glow was dim and slowly fading.

"We're going to die looking for these troops," Dox mumbled.

"No, we'll die long before we even get to Mount Aven," I scoffed.

"I'm sure we'll get caught in an avalanche." We sat in silence, we were sure we'd be long gone before we made it to the troops. Dox fell asleep, I formed and laid my wing over him.

We woke up the next morning and walked across fields covered in layers of snow. I melted my frozen wings and Dox climbed on my back, and we flew closer to Mount Aven. I flew upward toward the peak of the mountain.

“Phoenix what are you doing?" Dox asked worriedly.

“Get ready, but no worries, I'm sure you'll survive,” I shrugged before throwing Dox off my back and he went flying over the peak. I raced off behind him, and he fell onto my back and we landed on the other side of the mountain. We saw no one around, just another mountain dead ahead. We gaped at each other, both thinking the same thing.

“There are no troops…Are there?” Dox breathed and glanced at me. I screeched angrily and Dox wrapped his hands around my mouth.

“Shhhh! Be careful!” He hissed, “Even the slightest noise could bury us in snow far over our heads.”

I sighed, “What do we do now? It’s almost nightfall, we’ll never make it back home now-”

“Turn around so we can see you!” A voice shook worriedly.

“You don’t think there are police in the Snowy Mountains, right?” I ask turning toward a man and woman.

Dox shrugged, “They don’t look like it.”

“Easy now George, they’re just boys,” the woman coaxed. I screeched stepping back, looking at the weapon in his hand. I slammed into Dox who was frightened too.

“Boys that can scream like girls,” the man shrugged, putting down the weapon.

“Come with us, we can get you sheltered,” the woman smiled. I looked at Dox who gaped at the woman.

“I don’t know what to do,” he hissed. “Run or form?”

“I’m thinking scare them off then run,” I snapped.

“No need to worry, we don’t get a lot of company out here. You must be a long way from home,” the woman smiled.

“Of course they are Lucy, they’re not boys they’re demons. Why else would two teenage boys be up here in the mountains,” the man stood his ground.

“Let’s take them back, they’re not dangerous at all.”

“I think we should take it, we’ll escape.” Dox glanced at me, and I nodded. They led us to a wooden cabin, at the edge of a cliff. They gave us a room, with a bunk bed and a view of the mountains.

"I hope it's enough for you two," the woman smiled kindly.

"Thank you, it's just enough," I replied staring out the window.

"Sorry about the weapon this evening, we were out hunting. George should have never pulled a weapon on you two. After all you've been through a lot, you must be exhausted, I'll leave you be so you can get some rest." The woman shut the door and disappeared. We sat in silence and Dox glanced at me worriedly, I looked in his direction and we both looked away. He looked at me again.

"What?!" I lashed.

"You're not flamed up, something's wrong," Dox shrugged.

"I'm fine."

"You're overheated," he snapped.

"I had to help you last night, you'd die." I pulled up my sleeve, my arm was bright red.

"Ice it," Dox handed me chunk of frozen ice from his pocket. I wrapped the ice with a cloth and it began to heal. I fell asleep leaning against the window.

"Why do you have ice in your pocket?" I looked at him again.

"Don't ask me how my brain works," he snapped, "Even I don't know."

27

We woke up the next morning and the humans were still there, fast asleep.

"Thought they'd be gone by now. We can't get out the windows there's an alarm on the wall. They might catch us if we try," Dox glanced at a padlock on the wall.

"I don't want to hang around with humans," I scoffed, and Dox nodded.

"We can tell them I guess. It'll be tough though, humans are social creatures," Dox lashed.

"I wouldn't call us creatures, we don't have tails, wings, or fur. We're beings." Dox and I looked up at the top bunk. A girl looked down at us, she had long brown hair and emerald eyes.

"I hate kids even more," I groaned.

"Then why do you have one," Dox spat, glaring at the girl.

"Actually you two are still kids, but older. I'm Dixie." She held out her hand to Dox.

"Put it back or lose it," Dox growled, and Dixie climbed off the bunk bed.

"You're funny," the girl laughed.

"Won't be so funny when you lose your wrist," Dox spat.

"Who are you? First time my parents ever brought two teenage boys home for me."

"We're not your friends, kid. We're not worth getting to know," I shot back.

"At least tell me your names...And if you're in love," she giggled.

"My name is Dox, this is my friend Phoenix." Dox glanced at Dixie.

"Who do you like?"

"Not happening," I snapped again, I didn't dare tell her anything.

Oh, one more," Dixie smiled, and Dox and I put our heads in our hands, both sick of questions. "Why don't you take off your blankets? Are you cold?"

"I am not taking off my cloak, don't even think about," Dox snapped. Someone knocked on the door and the woman poked her head inside.

"Get out of there Dixie, give these two some space. Sorry if she's bothering you," the woman smiled.

"No she's not bothering us, she's annoying us. We're used to it though." I glared at Dixie who ran off down the hallway. The woman smiled once more and closed the door behind her. Dox and I glared at each other, in silence. We stood face to face until we couldn't bare it any longer.

"This is all your fault!" I lashed, "They're already trying to find us out!"

"How is this my fault?!" Dox barked, "I would've let Lynx go find her own troops in the first place!"

"We would've waited forever! Saved us the trouble!" I growled.

"Now we'll never get home! We're further away than before!" He shot back.

"Who's to blame for talking to the kid?! Because I didn't want to talk to her at all!" I lashed.

"If you don't answer the questions, they keep asking until you can't bare it any longer!" Dox exclaimed.

"That one's on you! Said we'd be home by nightfall, and look at where we are now!" I roared back.

"You're the one that trusted Lynx! I know not trust to cats, they're nothing but bad luck!"

"Then why didn't you tell me?!"

"Because I thought you knew! Never trust cats and snakes, they're the real demons!"

"Then why are you friends with one!?"

"She's not my friend! She was in love with me when I was six! No one should be in love at that age, it's stupid!"

"We need to get home! You're the one that got us into this, how do we get out?!"

"I don't know, I didn't think we'd take it this far!"

"We always take things further than they should! Why else are our lives so tough?!"

"Our lives are already tough with Rogue and Kareen after us! Plus, we're about to dive head first into war!"

"So you're going to blame that on me?!"

"You're the one that started this thing with Ferdinand's son in the first place!-"

Dixie knocked on the door. "My parents made breakfast, want some?" she asked. Neither of us payed any attention to Dixie who stood outside the door waiting for a response.

28

"I'm going to kill you," he growled.

"I'd like to see you try," I shot back. Dixie hurried into the room and outspread her arms. She looked between us, and turned to shout out into the hallway, "Mom the boys are trying to kill each other!"

"Get out of the way kid," Dox shoved Dixie aside and glared at me, "This'll be an easy fight."

"Have you forgotten that neither of us have won a fight?" I shot back.

"I will hurl you into that mountain, see how you like it being stuck in an avalanche," he growled.

"I will toss you over the cliff-" The man pushed between us, and glared at us both.

"Have you two lost your minds!?" The man barked, "Get a grip! You two better get this under control or you'll burn the house down!"

"If you want it just say so." I shrugged, a small flame in my hand.

"Don't even think about," the man glared at me furiously, and the flame disappeared.

"So nobody wants breakfast I guess?" The woman stood in the doorway with Dixie, smiling as always.

"I would rather starve," I growled at Dox.

"Over my dead body," he shot back, and I noticed a blue spark in the palm of his hand. I burned another flame, holding his gaze.

"Mom, they're magicians." Dixie pointed at the glowing spheres in our hands.

"Yeah let's go with that." Dox shrugged before hurling a spark at my head. I tossed a fireball and he ducked just in time, and the flames crashed through the window. I shot a blast of flames at the flying sparks and like fireworks they popped and faded away. The family ran down the hall and disappeared into the bedroom, locking the door. Dox shot sparks at me, I ducked and turned back to him smiling. He nodded and we jumped out the window. I formed and Dox jumped on my back, as we flew off over Mount Aven.

"You lied to us!" Dox barked at Lynx, pinning her to the ground.

"I had to, they'd kill me!" Lynx croaked.

"Who?!" Dox growled.

"He's working with the....Hunters. They're coming...They'll destroy you."

"Who is he?!" Dox pressed.

"Saube, he's rallied the hunters." Dox glanced at me worriedly. "We'll be fine, we're just going to go extinct!" I growled, "Tie her up, we're taking her hostage." Lynx's eyes went wide, and I snatched her up and we brought her back to the Groves. Rogue was happy to see me, and I explained everything.

"I don't care about that, I'm just glad you're home."

"You're not mad at me?"

"Of course not, I just don't want to see anyone from Ferdinand's family ever again."

"You might have to, but I will be sure you don't get involved. I would hate for you to get hurt." I hugged Rogue and she lied her head on my shoulder. "Does he know?" I asked.

"He knows now. You were gone so long he just knew." I flew off to Fangs' cave but he wasn't there. I checked the meadows, the Willow, but there was still no sign of him. I went back to find Rogue, but she was gone too. Dox ran up to me, as confused as I was.

"Either we're not good at hide and seek, or they just left us." Dox was worried, and so was I.

"We're both thinking the same thing, right?"

"Yeah, that if the group finds out that they're gone...They'll look to us. If we don't know what to do, we're going to be torn apart."

"Should we tell the Council?"

"I think we should send a search group." I nodded at Dox and we called for the warriors, who as always were ready. Kalo gaped at me when I told him the news, and I nodded.

"Where would they go?"

"Hunters I bet, I want you to check the lab."

"We'll try our best," a wolf nodded.

"Yeah, you can't do your best this time, this is important. Bring them back and we might just reward you, how about that?" The warriors looked between each other and nodded. They disappeared through the meadows and Dox and I joined at the Willow.

"How could I let this happen!?" I growled, "How are you not freaking out?!" I looked at Dox who seemed fine about his family missing.

"Please, I am going to have a meltdown if they don't find those three. Until then I have slight hope that they'll find them. You have a sense to care so much that family is like your heart, lose it and you die." I took a deep breath, and lit flame in my hand.

"What are you doing?"

"Playing with it, it keeps me calm, and from killing you." I shrugged and Dox stepped back shaking his head.

"Why do you want to kill me?!"

"Because I have no one to blame except you," I shot back.

"What?!"

"You're the one that dragged me into the Arctic in the first place. I hate anything about the Arctic, I would burn those snowy plains until they were nothing but rock."

"And you blame me for that?!"

"I thought Lynx had troops! You know her more than I do."

"I thought you'd come because you wouldn't let me go by myself!" I looked down at the flame, it was brighter than before. My ring softened and formed into a phoenix, twice my size. Dox gaped at me.

"You should know by now that I don't have the slightest bit of patience." The phoenix wrestled with me as I held it still. "Find them, you're my only hope."

29

The search party never returned and neither did my ring. Dox and I were worried sick, and our tribes were lost. The phoenixes kept looking for Rogue, saying they needed her help. I couldn't wait to tell her how much they needed her. Kalo came to me the next day, he looked suspicious but he wouldn't say.

"What do you want?" Dox snapped at him. Kalo looked at us both worriedly, "I know we came back empty handed, we tried honestly. Give us another chance, please-" A dagger stabbed the tree, right above Kalo's head, another at his side. Dox was flipping another dagger in his right hand.

"I would happily stab at you again," he hissed, "and if you were in my tribe, I'd kill you."

"I was planning on it," I shrugged. Kalo began to run, and I grabbed him. He fell out of the Willow dragging me with him. Somehow, he ended up on my back when we hit the ground. Kalo ran off deeper into the Groves.

We had met with the Council, since they were smart enough to keep calm with the Royals gone. Or at least they faked it with the tribes, dealing with their questions. Now they were grouped around Dox and I all worried. They were all asking questions at once, and it was hard to understand. Dox was puzzled and leaned against the cliff side, some of them asking him too.

"One at a time! I don't understand!" Dox growled. I had my head in my hands, with the members of the Council surrounding me.

"ENOUGH!" We roared and the Council stepped back, dead quiet. They were stunned, we'd never been mad at them before. "We'll find them ourselves," I sighed.

Dox and I were on our knees in the vents above one of the hallways in the lab. Dox sighed with an angry look on his face.

"I'm going to pretend that whatever happens after this, never happened," Dox growled.

"I thought you didn't pretend?" I shot back.

"We need to get one of those uniforms. If you even leash me, I'll kill you on the spot," he glared at me.

"I won't, I'm not that stupid," I mumbled. When there was no one in sight Dox kicked the hatch open and we jumped down to the floor. We slipped inside a guard chamber and broke into one of the closets. We used try on the guard uniforms a long time ago, hoping to escape. Now when we put on the uniforms they fit perfectly. "Finely fit," Dox looked at me and for the first time in a week we were smiling. I handed Dox a dagger, and he passed me a gun to clip at my side. "Grab them and get out, I'll take care of the guards. I'll be right behind you, I promise," Dox explained the plan, and I nodded. I slipped outside and down the hall. I knew exactly where I was going, but I still had the dagger in my hand. I found the chamber and quickly checked behind me.

I began to work at the lock, when a voice came from the other side.

"Phoenix! You came?!" I couldn't have been happier to hear Fangs' voice.

"Get back," I replied, ignoring the fact that he doubted me.

"Phoenix?!" Rogue spoke from the other side. I checked down the hall one more time, and picked the lock, before slipping inside. Rogue, Kareen and the others all looked up at me as I went to the window.

"Are you going to get us out of here or what?" Vess lashed.

"I will, if you give me a second!" I barked, slipping the dagger in my pocket and pulling out the gun. "I'd like to get out of here for good." I fired a couple of shots at the window and the glass shattered. I broke away the glass and scraped the pieces out the window, grabbed the boys. Fangs looked at me worriedly.

"Something's wrong with you. You've never been this way before," Fangs whispered.

"Of course something's wrong with me. There always is," I shot back, as he stepped onto the edge and looked down. "Look forward, and keep that mouth of yours shut." I shoved him off the ledge and Fangs fell forward but flew off, taking Ex and Vess with him. I looked back at Rogue.

"You're next," I nodded, but Rogue shook her head.

"Don't even think about it," Rogue snapped at me Kareen took Rogue's hand and they both went out the window next. Then I slipped outside and down the hallway, as a guard started down the other way.

"Maybe you didn't hear the order, but you're supposed to be in the chamber hall. From the looks of it, you're going the wrong way." The guard looked me over and I groaned.

"Do I really need a nametag or something? You should know who I am Laurence." I flung a dagger that pierced his shoulder. He buckled to his knees and I kicked him against the wall. I ran down the hallway and slammed into Dox. He was panicked and looked back at a mob of guards storming down the hall behind him. I pulled his gun out of his pocket, and began firing shots, and with a running start we both went for the large window at the other end of the hall. I spread my wings and Dox positioned himself on my back. I changed course and went up for the ceiling and we shot through the roof. Guards burst out and pointed their weapons. I coiled my tail around him, trying to keep him protected, but he slipped from my grasps as I burst through the roof above me, he fell to the ground. I pulled the gun from my pocket, when I stood on the ground in front of Dox who had blacked out.

"Put the gun down Phoenix, save yourself the trouble," a guard laughed.

"I'm going to fire as many shots as I need to! Just because you moved your lab doesn't mean I'll stop! I'll tear this building brick by brick to pieces!" I shouted at the guards, and I closed my eyes. For the first time ever, I stopped thinking. I was the last one standing when I opened my eyes, with every guard around me dead. I fell to the ground and pain washed over me. I then noticed I got a couple hits to the chest, arms and legs. I felt Dox put his hand on my shoulder.

"Nice job killer," Dox smiled.

30

"I am not going to tell my tribe I'm a murderer." I shook my head, trying to stop the panic that was rushing through my brain.

"I know a place we can go," Dox shrugged, "We need a break."

Dox led me to the Trader Tunnels, and I shook my head.

"Dox, are you crazy? They'll kick us out."

"Of course I'm crazy, I'm the dumbstruck one in the family," he shrugged. He disappeared inside and was flung out the second he got in. He was scratched up, and growling.

"How did it go, idiot?!" I barked.

"Never mind then! I know another place we can go." I sighed when he led me to an old shed. It was worn down and abandoned.

"Your brothers own this shed?"

"Actually, I do. I usually came here to get away from them. It's the only thing they haven't taken from me," he grumbled. I climbed up after him and we sat up on the roof looking at the sunset. I couldn't remember the last time I'd looked at the sun. I felt calmer but still a little worried. It should've been normal for me to be that way, to be a criminal and all. I knew that I'd get used to it like Dox, but changes somehow took longer to get to me. I never seemed to understand why these things were so hard for me, I grew up stealing, robbing, and breaking out of prison. I grew up that way. I grew up with all kinds of dangerous people, Dox being one of them. He was a criminal against the state, and a killer like me. I'd learned to take what I got.

We returned home and the Council was relieved to see the Royals again. I was up all night thinking about what Dox had told me that afternoon. I was officially a killer, and a criminal against the state, wanted in every city, just like him. I had to admit it kind of felt good, now I could stay away from the city as long as I wanted. I never really wanted to go back anyways, the guards were after me as always, and Ferdinand would kill me. Rogue came and sat next to me, she kissed me and smiled at me worriedly.

"Are you okay?" She asked.

"I'm fine, there's just a lot on my mind," I shrugged. Rogue kissed me again and leaned her head on my shoulder. I kissed her and we looked down over the Groves in silence.

"What were you doing with Dox? After you saved us we thought you two were behind us. Where did you go?"

"We needed a break, the Council was all over us for the past two days. Dox has some kind of special hide-out. Said he would hide from his brothers for days on end," Rogue shrugged, and smiled.

"Sounds like you too," she laughed.

"I don't hide from you." I didn't seem to understand the joke.

"I'm joking silly. But it is true, you boys will disappear for days and then come back saying nothing happened. Just like today, I got a little worried that you were captured." Rogue's eyes sparkled, as she stared into mine. I smiled, now noticing that being a criminal, I can appreciate.

"I'll never get captured, because now Dox and I are criminals of the state." I pull a crumpled piece of paper from my pocket. "It was a wanted sign I found in the Woods, we're wanted dead or alive. We're heading into the Woods for the day tomorrow."

"Please don't do anything stupid," she smiled.

Dox and I ran through the Woods, pulling wanted signs from the trees. The old shed became our hideout, we gather a bunch of signs in the shed and one by one tore them to pieces. We gathered up the pieces and I set them on fire. And after a few minutes the papers had burned to ashes. We had some fun too. Dox decided to call up the whole family, thinking it was a good idea. They shook their heads like we were crazy. Dagger practice, was what we called a good time, at least Dox and I.

"Fangs, stand against the tree. Trust me." Fangs stood against the tree, eyes wide.

"You stab him and I'll claw your eyes out," Rogue snapped.

"Don't worry, we've got good aim." Dox shrugged and flung a round of daggers at Fangs. Fangs flinched trying to stay still.

"Why are you flinching? You can trust us," I said flipping a dagger in my hand, "I've got to work on aim."

"Bet you can't hit the tree a hundred feet away," Dox laughed.

"Watch me." I stood a hundred feet away like he said. I flung the dagger with all my force. It was a little too much because the dagger had caught fire and went hurtling toward the tree. Fangs bolted back from the tree, when the flaming dagger shot through the tree and fell to the ground. Dox and I switched places and Dox's dagger went right through the hole and stabbed into the tree behind it.

Our families left and went back home after some time. We were stabbing at the trees all day, then we checked for more signs. We snatched a couple more, and went home. We gathered the tribes and showered the wolves and phoenixes with the papers. We threw a party, having them tear those papers to shreds. We ran through town taping the strips of burnt paper all over town.

31

Standing in dead silence, Dox and I glared at Ford and Evian.

"What did you call us here for?" Dox asked holding Ford's gaze.

"I don't know, maybe to ask you why we found this on our door." He held up one of our signs.

"We did it to everyone," I shrugged.

"What did we do to you now?!" Evian groaned.

"The whole city wants us dead or alive. Mostly dead, and our bodies are worth a million dollars!" Dox laughed.

"Then what do you need us for?" Ford grumbled.

"To hide us. I don't want to put my family in danger because of me. We can't hide in the Woods...It can't protect us anymore." It was hard to stay away from the home you grew up in. Dox looked at me and I could tell he was worried. "Once we get the signal we'll leave," I promised. I nodded toward him, and Dox seemed a little reassured. We turned to Ford and Evian. Ford nodded at Evian and she sighed.

"Alright, you can stay. Just don't leave the house." Dox and I were relieved, we'd be sheltered for some time, which felt good.

We did what they wanted and stayed inside. I sat at the window and Dox lay on the floor, neither of us spoke. Ford came and stood in the doorway. He seemed a little worried.

"Are you two okay?" He asked. Dox looked at him, and I shook my head. "I get it, you're homesick."

"Home-what?" I'd never heard of this emotion before.

"Homesick. When your sad being away from home. I leave home a lot, so it doesn't affect me," Ford explained.

"I'm not...Whatever that is. We leave home more than you could ever imagine. We just miss the others, trying to protect people is hard when you care so much. You want to protect them from everything."

"I just worry that I scare her," I shrugged, not taking my eyes off the window.

"Scare her? How?" Ford seemed interested, so I looked to Dox, because I didn't want to talk anymore.

"They worry about us when we leave for a long time. Kareen and Rogue are really sweet and all but they worry too much. He's just worried he's scaring her," Dox explained.

"So you're just depressed?" Ford asked.

"I guess so," I sighed. I wondered if I was scaring Rogue. I didn't want to, I just wanted to keep her safe.

Part 3

Prologue

Dox and I stayed with Ford and Evian for more than a month. We watched the news, checking for any new attacks, but nothing happened. We decided to head home, until a news report came up on the TV. A reporter was interviewing two of our own. It was the lead patrol guards, Kalo and Jillian.

"So what can you tell us about your leaders?" The reporter asked.

"Nothing," Kalo shrugged.

"I don't need much honestly," the woman begged. "Is there anything I can do to get you two to talk at all?"

"You can leave us alone, how about that?" Jillian snapped.

"I'm afraid I can't do that until you give me some information," the reporter shot back.

"What do you need to know?" Kalo asked.

"Where are they?" The reporter shoved the mic into Kalo's face.

"I think they're in Canada. Wherever…Canada is," he shrugged…

1

"You're okay!" Rogue grabbed me. She started to speak again but I pulled her in and kissed her. I never wanted to let go, I was so happy to see her.

"You should've seen it. Kalo and Jillian were interviewed, and told the reporters that we're in Canada!" Rogue and I laughed.

"They seriously fell for that?!" Rogue laughed. I felt so happy to be home, and so was Dox. We stayed in the Groves for an entire week and everyone was happy. Dox and I promoted Kalo and Jillian. They were now our messengers. We were safe, happy and nothing could've been better. Dox and I decided to take the family for a night in the city. We sat together on the roof of the house where Ford and Evian lived. We watched the moon fall below the horizon, and the sun rise, as if the moon and sun switched places. We played with security guards doing their shifts that night too.

Dox and I hid on the side of the building, I shot a flame their way and we ran before they could catch us, laughing. We jumped from building to building chasing each other once the others had gone home. From then on we spent our nights out in the cities, playing games and having fun.

By dawn we started back to the Groves. "Bet you can't outrun me on foot!" Dox called before run off, and I chased him through the trees. I was right on his tail when suddenly something caught me and grabbed me by the ankle, and I was upside down hanging from a tree. Dox had kept running and then noticed I wasn't behind him. He found me up in the tree and laughed.

"I thought you were behind me," he smiled.

"I was," I groaned trying to fish the knife out of my pocket. It almost slipped from my hand but I caught it just in time. I cut the rope and landed on my feet on the ground. I held a piece of the rope in my hand and tossed it to Dox.

"What kind of rope is it?" I asked. Dox was good with building, and he could tell where a piece of rope was from and what type it was. Dox sniffed at the rope and inspected it carefully. His eyes went wide and he looked to me.

"It's Saube. He set traps," he sniffed at the rope and closed his eyes. "He has others set around the woods. They're around the Groves and all over the woods." He looked at me, as if he wasn't sure what we should do. I thought for a moment, and flew to the top of the tree. I checked a couple of trees for traps, and went back to Dox with no luck.

"There aren't too many in the trees. We should warn the Council about this, right?" I stared down at Dox from the tree, and it was his turn to answer.

"I guess we should."

"...Traps? Why should we worry about traps? We can fly," a phoenix scoffed.

"Not all of us can fly, idiot," Jillian snapped.

"Well, what are we going to do? And, I hate to be picky but can we not seal ourselves inside the Groves this time?" Kalo added. The Council members seemed to agree, but Dox and I were taking it seriously.

"Alright! That was a bad decision I get it!" I barked, "But we need to do something!"

"I agree. We can't just wait around to get attacked again," Dox nodded, and the council members began discussing the situation. We stepped out of earshot so Dox and I could talk without worrying the others.

"What's the plan?" Dox sighed, "We need to come up with something. I can't fight with these people anymore."

"I think I have an idea?" I guessed. I really didn't have an idea, I was too busy wondering why Saube would set traps. Dox noticed what I was thinking and grabbed me by the shoulders.

"Phoenix, focus!" Dox snapped looking toward the council, "We can worry about Saube later."

"I know, I know. But why would he set traps? He watched Ferdinand do whatever she did, we're smarter than that!" I scoffed.

"Or we could actually believe that there is a problem to take care of right now. And if we don't figure this out the group is going to fall into absolute panic." Dox shook me by the shoulders trying to snap me into reality.

"Okay, but why do you think he's doing it using traps?-" I pressed.

"Pay attention Phoenix!" Dox barked. I stopped to think and I came up with something.

"I got it!" I smiled at him wide-eyed.

"Great," Dox nodded.

2

Dox and I sat in the Willow with Kalo and Jillian.

"…Let me get this straight? You want us to rally the troops and storm them?" Jillian seemed confused.

Dox groaned, "It's not that hard to process, Jillian. You and your troops are a diversion, while Phoenix and I kill the leader of the operation."

"But we're the messengers?" Kalo seemed confused.

"You are, but you're also lead guards still," I explained. Kalo and Jillian nodded.

Dox and I were hiding by the side of the building. Dox nodded, and cupped his hands to give me a boost. I pushed off and used my wings to reach the roof. I pulled the security cameras from the walls and gave Dox the signal. He formed and backed up a couple feet. Then with a running start he bolted up the side of the building and reached for the ledge of the roof. I grabbed him by the wrist and helped to pull him up. Dox pulled his dagger from his pocket and reflected the sun's glare onto the ground in front of Kalo's feet. Kalo looked up at him and he nodded. Jillian and Kalo wore those guard uniforms, and grabbed two of the troops by the wrists. They pulled them inside and Dox nodded toward me. I used the heel of my boot and kicked the lock on the door. I wished they didn't need locks on the doors but I guessed that was the reason why. We hurried inside and I almost couldn't believe it. A group of guards had their gear on and weapons drawn.

"The back door? I thought you guys were better than that?" Laurence stood in the front row, smiling under his helmet.

"We are better than that," I shrugged, and pulled out a gun. I remembered I'd stolen it from the Agency, and I was surprised I'd remembered that at that certain time.

"Go ahead then, shoot us if you can," the officer scoffed. I handed Dox my gun and he began shooting at the officers. While he began to fire I formed and jumped to the ceiling above. I climbed through the maze of pipes, crossing and overlapping one another. I kept weaving through the pipes while dodging bullets as the officers starting shooting at me too. I quickly climbed to the grate of the vent, and started to ply it open with the dagger. I pulled away at the cover and dropped it on the floor. Dox hurled the gun in my direction and I caught it, starting to shoot from where I was. Dox started up through the vent and I chased after him as I shot my last bullet. We raced through the vents on all fours and after crisscrossing through the vents, we found the lab. Scientists were doing something inside, working over an operation table. I noticed the capsules were empty and the floors were clean, which was a sign, since the floors were always wet in the lab. The scientists cleared away from the table and I was surprised they weren't working on anymore combinations this time. Instead they were working on...Weapons? On the far wall in front of the table was a rack full of guns, blades, and swords. The table was covered with tools, and behind it was two more rows of tables. Scientists were moving around grabbing tools, building things and taking the racks of weapons out of the lab.

"Psst. Phoenix, look at this," Dox whispered, looking out of another gap in the vents. I crawled over and looked down at one of the old training rooms. Guards were lined up, each with a weapon. They went down the line shooting at targets on the far wall. One of the guards was using a gun, but instead of a bullet it was a rushing comet that hit the target but nothing happened.

"Dox, they're not working on more combinations, they're building weapons to come after us," I whispered, realizing we'd just sent the others into a trap. Dox didn't answer, he was under one of the tables in the lab. I gaped at him but he put his finger to his lips, telling me to stay quiet. The scientists suddenly grouped together and left the room, so I joined Dox in the lab. He was scanning the rack looking at the guns. I looked at another rack full of blades. I noticed the blades were glowing, like the one Ferdinand had used on me, and I almost screamed. I grabbed Dox by the wrist and dragged him to the open grate on the ceiling.

"Dox, we need to get the others, they're in danger. It's a trap, the whole thing is a trap!" I climbed up into the vent, and Dox started up after me. The door opened and scientists came in, and I quickly grabbed Dox by the wrist. We hurried through the vents and found Kalo and Jillian in one of the rooms.

"Go find the others, I'll get them here," I called to Dox as I silently opened the grate and Dox kept going through the vents. Kalo and Jillian looked up at me, wide-eyed. I tossed Kalo the blade and he passed it to Jillian once he was loose. I went around the room and ripped out the cameras, which I always did. They put security cameras in every room so it became a habit to rip them out. I climbed up into the vents after them and stopped.

"What is it?" Jillian asked.

"Dox, they have him, I'm going after him. Take the others back to the Groves," I commanded, and the two of them nodded and disappeared. I went back to the lab and grabbed two of those guns before I started off through the winding hallways to find Dox. Running through the hallways I could hear him howling at me, and I knew I was getting closer. I pressed my ear to one of the doors and I heard him howling louder, then I stopped.

"Will you please be quiet, you're going to give me a headache with all this howling," a voice groaned.

"You can't expect to bait him with me. He's smarter than that," Dox paused, "He's already here." I slid the gun under the door and climbed into the vent. I looked down over my friend, and Saube standing in the control room. Dox stood with the gun pointed at him. He howled one more time and I dropped down beside him.

"Look, I'm going to make a deal with you two. We need to run some tests, and we need you two for it. If you leave your tribes will be experiencing absolute pain, including the two of you," Saube smiled slyly, a hard decision to decide was hard for us to do. I thought for a moment and looked up at him.

"If we stay, what happens then?" I asked.

"What are you doing Phoenix?" Dox whispered.

"That's what he wants, he wants to run tests on the both of us," I nodded turning back to Saube.

"Although if you stay, we can give you what you need. Upgrades," Saube smiled. This was a good deal, we hadn't received upgrades in almost a year. Upgrades were exactly what we needed. I looked to Dox for an answer and he was thinking the same thing.

"We'll stay," Dox nodded.

"I guess I've taught you two quite well," Saube smiled.

"Don't push it Saube, we're just here for the upgrades," I growled, walking out of the room. Dox and I walked down the hallways toward the chambers. We decided to share one together since we weren't sure what to do.

"I guess we wait now," Dox shrugged.

"I think this was the right thing to do. Plus, upgrades are exactly what we need," I added, staring up at the ceiling. "Our last upgrade was like six months ago."

"That's true. What kind of tests do you think they're planning to do?" Dox wondered.

"No idea. All I know is that we should still be alert. Saube is tricky, and we don't know what he's planning to do with us. But, why does he need us for it?" I wasn't sure about that. Maybe I wasn't thinking then and was too busy thinking about upgrades. Then again, the tribes would be safe, and the troops would go back unharmed.

3

I stood in one of the training rooms, waiting. Saube wanted us to follow his orders, and if we did we'd be sent home. I hated to follow orders but I had to if I wanted to get home with Dox. I grabbed a handful of daggers and started hurling them at the targets. One of our latest upgrades was stronger hand-eye coordination, so it was bullseyes each time. I kept throwing daggers until I ran out. Then I was bored again.

"Good job, looks like that upgrade worked," one of the scientists smiled. She flicked a couple switches and the daggers raced back to their places on the table.

"Stand in front of the targets, and I want you to try stop the dagger before it reaches you," the woman explained. Before I could entirely understand the test a dagger came whizzing at me and I set my arm aflame slowing the dagger to a halt. The next one I split the blade slicing it open with a shot of flames. Before I could react to the next, it zipped past me, cutting my shoulder. I grabbed the next one that was heading right for me. I set it aflame and dodged the blades cutting them from the handles to the edges of the blades.

The test was actually easier than I had thought.

When it was over I sealed the wound on my shoulder, as the scientists clapped, astounded.

"Not even a scratch! Absolutely extraordinary! A wonderful work of art!" one the scientists smiled, looking me over.

"What are you talking about?" I growled at the man.

"Obviously, you're one of the rare models. Your friend is too. Rare models contain those interesting specialties. You two are much stronger, faster, and far more powerful," the man explained.

"Rare model? Specialties?" I didn't seem to understand what he meant, so man kept explaining.

"Look, we're running some tests to see if the upgrades improve the survival status of the combinations we've created," the man further explained.

"Then why do you need us?" I scoffed.

"Because we've only given upgrades to the both of you. If we improve your mental and physical survival status you can give that to your people. Then all combinations will receive the improved status."

"We're not combinations, were improved human beings," I pointed out.

"Exactly, you're a genetic prototype." Saube walked into the room smiling, "You two have succeeded at one of many tests the others failed at."

"Let's just get to the next test, I want to get out of here." I hurled the dagger at the closing doors, and it kept the doors separated.

"Hand-eye coordination is excellent, I'm going to note that," the scientist nodded and left the room. Saube stood still, smiling.

"Now what do you want?" I snapped.

"To give you an upgrade. Unlike my mother, I do set traps, but I don't lie to my clients," Saube pulled a little device from his pocket and handed it to me. It fit comfortably behind my ear and I couldn't feel a thing. "You'll have to use this device until the upgrade clicks in. If you focus enough you can hear some pretty interesting things. Plus...Tell me what's behind that wall." Saube pointed at the wall, and I focused in on it. Suddenly I could see the lab on the other side of the wall. I focused out and I could see normally again. I felt a little dizzy switching visions.

"Don't use that upgrade too much for the next couple hours. It can be a little blinding to the eyes when switching visions. Dox has the same upgrades," Saube added walking out of the room. I focused and I could hear Dox six rooms down. He was practicing with the same upgrade. I could hear his ears flicking, his heart pounding, he seemed out of breath. I loved these new upgrades.

"Can you hear me Dox?" I asked.

"Phoenix? You got the upgrade I'm guessing?" Dox laughed.

"Yeah, and I love it. We can hear thing that are far away, see through things. This is amazing," I smiled. Then I began to focus in on something else, home. I focused in on the sounds of the woods. The trees were swaying, and I heard...footsteps. I listened in closer and it was Rogue. She was sitting with Fangs, Ex, Vess, and Kareen.

"Do you think they're okay?" Rogue asked.

"You worry too much, I found out they can handle themselves," Kareen replied.

"They're fine Rogue, Phoenix and Dox are the toughest people I know out of the whole group. I bet you they're fine…," Fangs sighed…

4

The scientists did six more tests, and Saube kept his promise like he said. They let us go, and we were able to head home. Dox and I were home by sundown, and the others were happy we were back. We had a quick meeting with the Council to explain the deal, and Rogue and Kareen sat in too.

"What do you think they were planning?" A wolf asked worriedly.

"Don't know yet, but we'll figure it out," Dox assured him. I wasn't really paying attention to the conversation, I was too busy using that hearing upgrade to find out what the Agency was going to do.

I could hear Saube instructing something to the guards explaining the new upgrades.

"We gave them a vision upgrade, so be sure you have don't have any extra bullets or spare weapons in the uniform pockets. They can find that easily, and prepare yourselves. They'll be twice as strong with the new upgrades. But those upgrades do and can backfire eventually," Saube explained.

I focused out and turned back to the Council. They were all giving me worried looks, except for Dox who was listening in for more. He opened his eyes and looked at me.

"I don't want to worry anyone but all I can tell you is you should start worrying," Dox stared at the ground, he looked stunned.

"What did you hear?" I whispered.

"I can't say." Dox kept his eyes gluing the ground. He seemed terribly stunned, and I was dying to know, we all were.

"Dox, what did they say?" I asked again.

"They said that…Once this is over...That the ground will be soaked with our blood," he whispered.

"I'm done. I'm done! I can't do this anymore." I stood up shaking my head, "Just shoot me and get it over with!"

"Relax, we'll figure something out," Rogue placed her hand on my shoulder.

"Did you not hear that? It's like another war, and for a change, we're not ready," Dox snapped, "What do we do then?"

It caught everyone, everyone knew he was right. We weren't

ready, and we were finally giving up.

"We can't afford to lose anyone. And those weapons can kill us all-" a phoenix sighed, and worried looks were passed around.

"We have to go," I interrupted.

"What?" Rogue looked at me worriedly.

"We have to go," Dox repeated, "Don't worry about it." We both got up, and left without explanation.

5

Dox and I sat on the roof of one of the skyscrapers, overlooking the city. It felt really good being away from the chaos for a night. I had to admit I was trying my best not to give in, but I couldn't resist long.

"...You want some?" Dox handed me a strange silver can. Apparently, it was what Humans called, "getting drunk". I'd heard it from Ford, he said it was dangerous if you kept up with it, that you could go to jail. It didn't seem to bother me though, apparently the alcohol didn't affect us. Dox and I used to drink it all the time when we were kids, which worried some people but we were fine. I took the can and Dox started on another. We stole a whole pack of the strange-tasting drink and drank the whole thing in one night. The alcohol didn't affect us too much I guess. It only cleared our minds of any possible thoughts. It felt like a strange sort of head-clearing magic.

Later on that night Kareen and Rogue came over that night, and we went with our families. I gave Rogue a can and she smiled. She took a sip, her eyes half closed. I thought alcohol didn't affect us, but I guess it could in some ways. All I knew was it took our minds off of the chaos. We were relaxed, and maybe too relaxed. The girls fought to stay awake and decided it wouldn't be safe to fall asleep in plain sight so they went home. Dox and I stayed up drinking and silently enjoying the view. I started to fall asleep and so did Dox. He would shake me awake every now and then, trying to keep me awake. But soon enough, neither one of us was alerting the other that we were in plain sight. We both fell asleep.

I woke up tired and dazed. Saube stood over me and I was terribly confused.

"I thought she taught you better than to get addicted to alcohol," he groaned.

"We finished the tests what are we doing back here?" I asked, still half asleep.

"If you get caught by security the blame will come back to us. We'll get sued, and the both of you will be in solitary confinement! If we get sued, we'll be shut down. And if we're shut down we won't have any way to help the both of you," Saube explained, "This stuff corrupts minds. We can't help you if it gets to you too."

"Help us?" I growled, I didn't want his help.

"If we get shut down," he continued, "they'll find a way to destroy you. If that happens, you'll die. Ferdinand's lifelong work and thriving succession...Gone."

"And this all will probably happen if we get caught drinking? Cool, but stupid." I pulled another can from my pocket and he slapped it out of my hands.

"What happened to the both of you? Ferdinand told me you were supposed to work on building a sustainable society someday. Where these kind of things would never happen. You're not building a society...You're destroying it." Saube seemed pretty disappointed but I shrugged.

"Look, I don't care if you're disappointed in me or the rest of us. Ferdinand tortured us in order to succeed, she took random kids and turned us into what we are now. You shouldn't expect anything from us except this. She created us for the building of a society, and guess what? I didn't work that way. Instead she got us. A bunch of normal people that are stronger and faster than the average," I lashed, "I'm sorry if that's not good enough for you, but I can't fix that." I chucked the can at his head and Saube ducked just in time.

Dox was standing in the hallway sharpening a blade when I got outside.

"You stole it, I'm guessing?" I asked walking down the hallway with him and out the door.

"Duh, of course I stole it. Do you know me?" Dox scoffed.

"Of course I do, and I also know you stole that box of liquor last night," I added.

"I can't believe they can get shut down because of us," Dox looked back at the lab.

"Who cares? We want to shut them down, but we don't want to die doing it," I shrugged, "I feel like I don't want to go home for some reason. How about you?" I asked

"That's why you're my best friend," Dox nodded smiling.

6

We flew around the city before heading home.

"...I guess people would rather get a job and own a house. All those things that we don't have and that we don't need," I explained, as we walked through the Woods, on our way home.

"Yeah, I guess. Why do think people want a house? Then you close off social contact...What is social contact? I overheard some scientists saying that they should move us to a disconnected state." I looked at the ground. Dox stopped next to me.

"Disconnected Social Contact, DSC. They wanted to put me on some sort of medication for DSC when I was a kid. DSC medication is where they turn off your emotions, your need for social contact, they'd be disconnecting our memories," I said softly.

"Then, we wouldn't remember our families, our wives, our children. We wouldn't know each other anymore-" Something crackled in the bushes ahead of us and we both turned. There was a glow coming from the bushes in front of us. When we got a little closer, I couldn't believe it.

7

Fire crackled against the barrier of thorns and stones. The wolves were scaling the walls and jumping from the cliffside. The phoenixes were flying off in all directions. I focused in to see Rogue holding on to Kareen and flying off from the meadows. Fangs, Ex and Vess were standing a little bit away from the fire waving to the girls.

"They're safe!" I pointed to Rogue, and Dox took off toward the Groves.

"Come on! We can stop it!" He yelled and I dashed after him. Half the Groves was in flames. I stood on the ground below and Dox stood on the cliffside. We built a barrier to close off the Willow Forest where the trees were.

Two planes were hovering over the Woods, and I looked to Dox. I flew up to the cliffside as the fire began to rise upward. I grabbed him by the wrist and gave him a push. He jumped, but couldn't reach the plane. I flew up to grab him when a grappling hook grabbed him by his shirt. I fell on the cliffside and felt my wings break. I jumped trying to fly off after him but I could barely get off the ground. I ran to one side of the cliffside and the other, coughing from the smoke. I backed up and with a running start I jumped, and flapped my wings trying to reach higher. I started to fall and suddenly a grappling hook grabbed my wings. I yelped in pain and it jerked me backwards. Suddenly it jerked me back and I hit the floor of the plane. I felt people grab me and pull me away from the edge. Some man was talking to me, but with all the commotion it was hard to understand. I felt the smoke clogging my lungs and I starting coughing again. I felt dazed and light-headed. The plane started moving and I stood on one knee looking out the window. There was a plane in front of us and I focused in on it. It was Dox, he was looking down over the Woods, and I knew he was okay.

I looked down over the woods then, looking for Rogue and Fangs. I saw them down below, sixty feet away from the flames. I suddenly heard Dox's voice, I saw him look toward me, but I didn't hear what he said. We were both thinking the same thing.

"I'm going to get them," I growled.

"Phoenix, you're going to kill yourself!" Dox looked at me worriedly.

"I'll be fine just get ready to pull us up-" I went to the edge of the landing dock, and went to jump when two men grabbed me. I kicked them away and jumped.

"Phoenix, wait! You can't fly!" Dox called after me, but it was too late. I flamed up and dashed toward them.

"Phoenix!" Fangs rushed over to me, wheezing from the smoke in his lungs, the others followed close behind him. "There's too much smoke…For me to fly…Rogue broke her wing," he tried to explain between coughing.

"Are you insane?! There's no way to get up there!" Kareen shouted to be heard over the raging fire.

"It'll be fine!" I waved up to Dox and he lowered the hook, but it was too short.

"Come on!" Fangs grabbed Ex and Vess and they grabbed the hook. Dox pulled them up and looked down at me.

"Take her up with you!" I looked to Rogue, and she grabbed Kareen by the wrist.

"What about you?!" She looked back at me worriedly.

"I'll be right behind you!" I shoved them off and ran for the cliffside of the Groves. The flames had grown and were close to the cliffside. I looked up to see Rogue and Kareen getting pulled to the planes, but the hook got stuck. Dox and Fangs kicked at the lever but it wouldn't budge. "Phoenix, it's stuck!" Dox called. Rogue screamed for me, and I knew I had to hurry. I formed and flew up toward them and snatched them from the hook. I flung them up into the plane, before I lost form and started to fall. My wings were burning in pain, and I couldn't move them. "Phoenix!" Dox suddenly jumped after me, and grabbed me. He grabbed hold of the hook, and I held on.

"You are so stupid," Dox glared at me.

"I can see that now," I panted.

8

When I woke up we were off the plane and in a hospital. I woke up in bed, and I felt slightly dazed which was common for me. I was still in my regular clothes which were burned and smelled of smoke. A woman was sitting near me, typing on a computer. I looked around the room, with its blue colored walls, and beige tile floors.

"Where's my family?" I asked, sitting up in the bed. The woman turned to me, and smiled.

"Finally awake I see. You've been out for a couple hours," she smiled.

"Where's my family?" I repeated the question assuming she hadn't heard me.

"They're okay Phoenix, and so are you. You broke your wings so you'll-" she said looking at a clipboard.

"How do you know my name?" I interrupted.

"You are just full of questions aren't you? All your questions will be answered soon enough," the woman continued what she was saying before. "Your wings are broken so you won't be flying for about two weeks or so. Just rest for now okay? We're going to run a couple tests on you to see if there was any other damage."

The doctors ran a couple blood tests and they all left. They told me to stay in the room, but while they were gone I slipped into the hallway. I looked at the clipboards on each door giving a background of each patient. I looked down the hall before I cracked the door open and saw Rogue asleep in one of the beds. I slipped inside quietly trying not to get the attention of the doctor in the corner. I snuck up behind him and dragged him into the closet. I locked the door and stood next to Rogue. She slowly opened her eyes and sat up. I sat on the edge of the bed as she leaned against me, quietly. She looked over at where the doctor had been and back at me oddly.

"I locked him in the closet," I looked over to where I could hear the man banging against the door.

"I love it when you reject orders to do stupid things. It's cute," she sighed.

"Coming to see you wasn't stupid. I had to see for myself," I shrugged.

"Yeah, and you did it by shoving a doctor in the closet," Rogue explained.

"That's true. What else was I supposed to do?" I smiled.

"That's easy, don't hurt people," Rogue laughed.

"That's instinct though," I pointed out.

"I guess you're right. You and Dox rely on instinct more than thought most of the time." I looked toward the door and Rogue looked up at me.

"What is it?" She asked.

"I have to go, someone's coming," I kissed her for a second and left. I ran back to my room, before the doctors returned. They came back and asked me some questions, and I answered what I could. I was bored with all the questions but I guess I could trust them.

"What were you doing the night before?" One of them asked.

"I don't remember," I replied keeping my tone straight so it didn't sound like I was lying. Humans always assumed that I was lying and that they couldn't trust me so I always kept a straight tone.

"Do you have any family? Any parents, or guardians?" Another asked.

"None of us have parents. They're gone." I looked up at the blue ceiling, there were no windows so the ceiling was all I had to look at. The questions continued for another couple minutes.

"Do you have any close family members that aren't in the hospital with you?" the woman asked.

"My friend, has a cousin who lives in the city, and he has a sister..," I replied lying back. I felt my heart racing, my head pounding, and suddenly I felt my heart stop. The nurse was shaking me and stopped, she believed I was dead. My heart really didn't stop, I was just really tired and wanted the doctors to leave the room. While I was faking it, I was exhausted from the questions and fell asleep. I assumed faking it would make them go away, but this pushed it too far.

9

I opened my eyes and Dox looked at me wide-eyed. He was stunned, he looked down for a second then back at me.

"God, Phoenix," he sighed, "I actually thought you were dead man. What did you do that for?"

"They were asking me so many questions it was hard for me to process. I needed a break." I began breathing normally, and glanced up at the ceiling.

"If you want them to go away just say so. If you didn't wake up by tomorrow they were going to put you down. Faking your death is dangerous." Dox put his hand on my shoulder.

"How long have I been out?" I asked looking around the room, as if I expected it to change.

"Three days. Four days is the max of how long they keep a patient that's actually passed on," he groaned, "Don't do that again Phoenix. You just put your family at risk, and we made a pact to help out, remember?"

"I remember, geez. I'm okay. I thought that if it looked like I was in a worse state they'd leave me alone." I pulled away the cover and stood up.

"Come on. I want out of here." Dox went out into the hall and I followed. Dox went to get his family and I went to get mine. I went to Rogue's room and Fangs was there too, so it saved me the trouble of trying to find him.

"You are so stupid," Rogue sighed, climbing out of bed.

"I can see that now," I said walking out of the room.

"You scared us, Phoenix," Fangs lashed.

"I know. I don't understand why you're surprised, I've scared you before," I shrugged.

"Faking your death. You're a bigger idiot than I thought," Dox growled walking up beside me.

"You were stupid enough to jump and get me. That's called wasting your life, stupid," I shot back.

"Let's just settle this," Ex put his arm around our shoulders. "You're both stupid idiots, and that's a fact."

"I couldn't agree more," Vess sighed.

"Look who's talking," Dox scoffed.

"Hey, when it comes to you two being total idiots, I have to give input," Vess sighed.

"What's with you and those words, I don't understand you," Kareen snapped.

"What's your problem?" Dox asked.

"Maybe that you shouldn't be trying to save the day, now look at where it's going," she shot back.

"You guys are out playing superheroes and then coming home six days later. Say you'll be back at sundown. No, you'll be back at sundown a week later," Rogue shook her head.

"I don't even know what a superhero is," I shrugged.

"Some kind of superhuman that saves people's lives. Normal people," Fangs explained.

"Saving the lives of humans?" Dox scoffed, "When I'm dead."

"I wouldn't save a human over my dead body," I laughed. I wouldn't save a human, or in fact, any human. After everything they'd done, I'd never help humans.

10

I checked the woods for traps with Dox. We counted at least twelve or more. We started checking every day and more started showing up.

"How many traps do they need?" Dox wondered, testing a trap with a struggling mouse.

"Do you really need to test it with a live animal?" I asked.

"If it survives I'll kill it and give to Kareen. If it dies, I'm still going to give it to her," he shrugged.

"She doesn't have a birthday though, does she? None of us have one." I really didn't understand why my friend would give his wife a dead mouse. We had really different opinions on presents for our wives, I thought flowers.

"I'll give her a little surprise sometimes just to straighten things out," he explained and I nodded.

Luckily when we tested the trap, the mouse survived and disappeared before Dox could catch it. We set up the trap and went back to the shed behind the Tunnels. We had placed a huge piece of paper over the walls, marked with certain spots in the woods. Dox tossed me a marker, and we plotted each trap we'd found on the map. We had marked certain places too: the Trader's Tunnels, the Morse, the Groves, the Agency, the Caverns, and Ford and Evian's house near the border between us.

I drew in red marker wherever we'd found a trap. Every trap Dox and I had tested was reset so I drew a checkmark in green next to the marks for traps.

We stepped back and looked over the map. There were red marks surrounding the Traders' Tunnels, and the Groves. The only place untouched was the city, and they hadn't placed any traps around the Agency.

"Why are we worrying about traps again? Shouldn't we be worrying about who set that fire?" I asked, marking another couple traps we forgot to mark the day before.

"I was thinking the traps had something to do with it. Maybe it set it off," Dox suggested.

"It may have been the Humans, they're all metal traps, they would've melted with that big of a fire," I added, and Dox nodded in agreement.

"We can take it to the leader of the Humans, they'll find out who it was," Dox nodded, and we went to the Tunnels for more info on their leader. I was surprised Dox would go to his brothers for this advice, but they did know all the Richies in town.

"...Their leader huh?" Mori thought about this.

"Mori, straight answer," Dox lashed.

"Okay, okay. Well, he lives right here," Mori spread out a map and pinpointed the location.

"You sure about this? That's deep Richie territory Phoenix," Dox looked to me unsurely.

"Who cares, last time I'm dealing with Richies, that's for sure," I scoffed.

"You say that now, until you have to pay to talk," Mori grumbled.

"You forget that I'm broke right?" Dox snapped.

"Because you lost some of it to hunters, and the rest of it to our cousin. At this rate, you have a zero percent chance at getting what you're looking for. Also you have a one-hundred percent chance at going broke and living on the streets," Mori pointed out, grabbing something off the shelf. He handed us some glowing bottle and we were terribly confused. "Pour this on your cloaks when you leave for town, whenever you need it you can be invisible. It only works when you're in real danger."

"We won't need this," Dox hurled the bottle over Mori's head and it smashed against the wall. Mori growled at his brother, but Dox was already walking out the door.

"You'll thank me Mori! I just got you broke!" Dox barked. I placed a gun on the table and Mori nodded slyly. Mori and his friends gave stuff away for a price, and weapons were worth a fortune in the Woods. I walked off after my friend and he groaned.

"You did not just hand him that gun," Dox groaned.

"No, I just saved you from the streets," I smiled, handing him the money. He threw it in his satchel, and glared at me.

"I already live on the streets, remember?" He growled, and handed me my cloak and we slipped them on over our clothes. We never wore clothes weather-wise. Just some ripped up jeans and a black T-shirt. Cloaks, we always wore when going into town, it became a habit and something we always did.

11

We sat in the man's office, looking at all the expensive wood and leather. We had our hoods up over our heads, and waited in silence. He said he was going to meet with us, and that he'd be right back in a couple minutes. The man finally came, wearing a black and white tux. He sat down and looked between the both of us.

"Humans have no concept of time," I sighed, and we both pulled off our hoods in unison.

"Let's get down to the point. We need to talk about the fire in the woods," Dox explained, and I jumped up on the desk.

"Sit down please so we can discuss this," the man snapped. I growled at him and flipped off the desk, to stand behind him with my dagger to his neck.

"Yeah, you never tell me what to do," I hissed, "I would gladly claw your eyes out if you'd like that."

"So what would you like to discuss then?" The man looked back to Dox.

"You know, I really hate Richie territory, what about you Phoenix?" Dox asked me, and I screeched at the man.

"So tell me, human. Who started the fire in the Woods? I'm sure you've heard about what happened?" Dox asked.

"There was a fire? I didn't know?" The man rasped as I pressed the knife harder, getting angrier with the man the more he spoke. He surely knew about the fire, and I would track down whoever it was. I would make sure they saw what they'd done. Dox noticed my muscles were tensed, and stared me down. I let go and jumped over the desk to stand with him. The man felt at his neck and cleared his throat.

"Ah, yes. I remember there being a meeting to discuss the stealing you two have been doing. One of the men suggested to burn the Woods, but I had disapproved. He may have spoken to the other members of our meeting afterward," the man shook with fear, his voice shaky.

"Can you contact this member for us?" I asked, and he nodded. He called them up and when the man entered the office he almost fell back in shock. I sat him down, and the man looked at the both of us worriedly.

"Who did you contact?" I growled.

"What?" The man seemed confused.

"To burn the woods, who did you contact?!" Dox barked.

"I contacted an agency up north that specializes with genetically improved humans. His name was Saube Blanch, he said he was looking to find you two," the man stopped and smiled slyly, standing up. "I believe he mentioned, a great deal of money for the both of you." A guard grabbed Dox and I by the wrist, and I spread my wings. I tried to hover and it slowly loosened the guard's grip. I flapped harder and faster, and grabbed Dox's arm. He climbed up and held on tight. I dashed forward and changed states, forming. I swerved between buildings trying to keep Dox on my back. I grabbed him with my tail and tossed him into the air. I flew up skimming over a building, and caught him in my claws.

"You better not drop me," Dox glared up at me and I shrugged, before tossing him again. Dox screamed, and I rushed forward to grab him. It was more fun for me to throw him then have him on my back. He jumped, running to the edge of a building, before jumping onto my back again. I changed course and flew upward. Dox read my mind and shook his head.

"Phoenix, we need to get to the Agency," Dox snapped.

"It's a shortcut, Dox," I nodded and stopped flapping. We fell quickly. Dox screamed again and held on tighter. I spread my wings five feet off the ground, and formed back into a human. Dox jumped off my back and sprinted ahead, while I went up over another building. I took a sharp turn and grabbed Dox's hands. I dropped him down on the roof of the Agency and landed on my feet.

12

There were no guards when we dropped in, the security cameras were off, and the door was open. It was almost nightfall when we arrived and the whole town started to fall silent. I sat on the ledge and leaned over the side of the building to get a closer look. I used my vision upgrade and I could see the offices, empty and dark. I focused in deeper, and all the lights were out. I searched every hallway before my eyes got tired, and I felt a little dizzy, having the blood rush to my head. I sat upright, and thought for a second.

"All the lights are out," I said, thinking still.

"Did you check the lab? They're usually people there by now," Dox suggested.

I shook my head, "I already checked, I can tell because now I have a headache," I sighed.

"Let's go inside, I have a feeling it's an ambush, or that they're expecting us." I nodded and we checked the doors, but they were locked.

"Definitely an ambush," Dox started down the stairs and I followed him.

We found ourselves in a long dark hallway, and Dox's ears started twitching.

"Something doesn't feel right," Dox stared down the hallway, pitch black. Instinctively, my ears started twitching too, back and forth, something wasn't right at all. There was an odd buzzing noise coming from the walls.

"It might just be the pipes, considering what they've been doing the system must be backed up," Dox and I shrugged, thinking nothing was wrong. We were probably paranoid anyways. But the buzzing came again, and suddenly something hit me from behind, shoving me to the ground. I was shocked, and confused, that odd buzzing noise now ringing in my ears. As if the volume became ten times louder, and I couldn't hear. The noise disappeared, and through the darkness a streak of light came rushing at me. I put my hands out in front of me, hurling a blast of fire. Only the flames were consumed by the comet, and it hit me in the chest. I buckled to my knees, the pain struck me all over. I tried to call for Dox but I was suddenly hoarse, and couldn't find my voice. The volume increased and all I could hear was my racing heartbeat, and feel shocks of pain everywhere. I felt my voice return and I was ready to call for him but all I could yelp and cry in pain. The pain surged all over my body, like a river of electricity. The pain stole my energy from my body and I felt numb.

I was strangled almost instantly, and gagged. The lights suddenly flickered on, and guards were wrestling Dox and I down different ends of the hallways. I yelled toward him and he looked up, before wrestling against the guards, in their black uniforms. Their silver logos glistened under the bright lights, and I was shocked to see…The police? My eyes went wide with shock and I knew where they were taking us. A policeman grabbed my wrists and handcuffed me. I couldn't do anything and neither could Dox. He stopped fighting, losing his energy and the numbness weakened him even more. The policemen dragged me away, and I didn't resist.

They shoved me into a truck and drove off. I lied on the floor, helplessly, knowing there was nothing I could do to escape. I was in one of those moving vans, probably owned by the police department. It seemed easy to break out, but I was still too weak. I set a flame in my hand, but it was dim, and close to fading. I fell asleep, having no way to conserve the last drop of energy I had left.

I woke up in the police department, in a jail cell. I looked up and in the cell, sitting across from me was a man, glaring at me oddly. Two other men were chatting and glancing at me every couple seconds.

"Looks like they finally caught the boy!" One man snickered.

"Wonder how long his sentence will be?" Another man stared me in the face. I clicked in my attention, finally waking up. I backed up against the wall now noticing where I was.

"Where is he?" I asked, standing up and pulling against the iron bars. I stopped and looked down the hallway at all the other cells and prisoners.

"Who are you looking for? I bet you he's here now if they've finally caught every criminal in town. You and that dog boy, were the last ones. The police have been trying to track you down for years. I should know, my sentence has lasted long enough for me to see," one explained. I stopped, and turned back to them wide-eyed.

"Where am I?" I asked.

"One of the highest prisons in the Seven Cities. Your friend is at the highest, he's caused more crimes than you. At this rate you two might be sentenced to death or a life in prison," the third added, and one nudged him in the side.

"No need to scare him before his actual trial," he said.

"Dox!" I screamed, pounding against the bars, though it was no use. "Let me out of here! You don't understand!"

"Understand what?" One of them asked, but I didn't answer, trying to melt the bars. I started screeching at the top of my lungs, and the men covered their ears. I formed and the men backed up into a corner, frightened. I grabbed the bars with my claws and started flapping my wings. The three men called for help, and soon guards came over, opening the cell. I changed states, and ran down the hallway.

"FREEZE WHERE YOU ARE!" The guards shouted, surrounding me with their hands on their weapons. I put my hands in the air, and hung my head.

"You have to understand. He can take any other charges, just please don't kill him!" I pleaded.

"I'm afraid that's not your decision, kid," one of the guards sighed. I stopped to think for a second.

"Actually, my friend doesn't have a lawyer," I explained, "He's not human, and every criminal needs one."

The guards nodded in agreement, and put me in car that drove me to see Dox.

13

Dox wasn't too happy to see me, but I understood. It was almost dawn when I got there, and I had fallen asleep in the car. Dox on the other hand, looked like he hadn't slept all night. I sat next to him and saw that he was asleep. So I sat there in silence with him, and eventually he woke up.

"What did they do to you?" I asked worriedly.

"Nothing but interviews. Just a bunch of people asking a bunch of stupid questions. 'Where are you from?' 'How old are you?' 'Do you have any spouses or people we can contact?'" Dox groaned.

"Did you get to any trials yet?" I pressed, even though I knew he was tired.

"No. They did two interviews, and then they put me here to wait while they discussed something. Probably charges, and what my sentence is. I told them you were with me. That way we're not separated," he explained.

"So they were going to bring to me here?" I groaned.

"You tricked them into thinking you could be my lawyer, didn't you?" Dox groaned, reading my mind.

"Every word. But also I'm supposed to be here, so I can't defend you. Then who will?" I wondered, now realizing my plan was useless.

"My messed-up cousin, actually. He'll do what he can, but he doesn't have the money to bail us out," Dox scoffed.

"Hold on, what about your brothers? They could've given him the money. Or your brothers could've given it to the people themselves," I suggested, and Dox laughed at little.

"My brothers wouldn't bail me over their dead bodies. They hate me, and want nothing to do with me. Plus, they're charged with selling dangerous weapons and drugs. They were let off the hook, but they paid the price not being allowed to bail anyone from our family. Ford is broke, so the only thing he can do is keep us from dying," Dox explained, " You're too busy worrying about me, when you're going to get charged for almost the same things as me."

I had totally forgotten about all the things I'd be charged for. Thievery, murder, abduction...And so many others considering all the things I'd done in my lifetime.

We talked for a long while and then fell asleep, tired and bored of sitting around. I rested my head on Dox's shoulder as he leaned against me.

Someone started shaking me and soon I woke up. Ford was sitting on the floor with a bunch of papers and folders, and packets.

Dox woke up and joined us on the floor, looking at everything.

"What is all this?" Dox asked.

"Everything I possibly own that can help save you two. I rummaged through some files in the police department and the lab and found everything I possibly need. I found your files, which didn't have too much information. So I put in some stuff that I collected."

I took my file and went through it. Papers with my charges, and my identification papers. "Where did you find this?" I asked.

"Mostly from Rogue and Kareen, they left the papers with Mori and Edgar so they'd be saved for things like this. We're not the closest group of people, but I told them about what happened-" Dox pressed him against the wall, and I put my head in my hands.

"You're not supposed to tell them. It worries them, that's why we told you," Dox snapped.

"Okay, okay. One more thing though...They're coming here...For the trial," Ford added, and Dox sighed.

"Fine. Let's just get out of here." Dox let his cousin go and we reviewed everything we had. Ford tried to explain what to do in a trial since we were clueless. It took a while, but I thought I understood what he meant.

14

"...You two are charged for the murder of two innocent human beings, is that correct?" The judge asked, peered over the podium where he sat.

"Objection!" I put my hand in the air, and the judge sighed.

"Objection sustained," the judge nodded.

"Innocent is wrong," I pointed out.

"Well, either way, both of you are charged for the murder of the same person. Can you explain?" The judge asked again.

"She brought herself back to life using some kind of syndrome," Dox explained.

"Another one of your greater charges was thievery-," the judge added.

"Objection!" Dox raised his hand, and again, the judge sighed.

"Objection sustained," he groaned.

"Thievery is wrong. Whatever the people leave at sundown belongs to us. We steal from the markets, and considering how much they leave out, it's not stealing," Dox corrected him, and technically, he was right.

"Either way, we would like to speak to the defendant." The judge leaned over the podium, and Dox and I stared at Ford. He stood from his chair where he sat behind us.

"I believe you live in the city, considering your family member is telling the truth," the judge glanced at Dox.

"Absolute truth," Ford nodded.

"Then have you seen your friends committing these crimes?" The judge continued.

"Yes, but may I object?" Ford asked, and the judge nodded. "My friends are broke, almost our entire family is broke. Considering where they live, what they get from the city is all they have."

"Do you have any proof that this is true?" The judge asked.

"Duh, why else did I come here?" Ford scoffed, pulling one of our capes from a bag. "The materials were stolen from the town. Left out overnight," Ford explained as he placed it up on the podium and the judge inspected it for a bit. He nodded, and turned back to us.

"This is your crest, I believe?" The judge pointed at the shimmering gold clip, and we all looked from one another as if unsure whether to tell the truth or lie.

"Yeah, that's ours," I replied. The judge and other trial members left the room and soon returned. It was hard to tell what they were thinking, they all had straight faces.

"We've discussed, and you are innocent." the judge explained, and Dox and I were relieved. "Considering, that with the capes your friend place a certain file with it." I looked back at Ford, and he nodded smiling.

"What did you do?"

"I asked Dox's brothers for some past information, which led me to a government video. Mori and Edgar said I could borrow it but need it back though. It was an idea for an advertisement of turning children into soldiers, I took it and gave it to the judge with your capes. I already knew they would discuss it with the evidence being reviewed," Ford explained.

"That's why I brought you here. I knew you'd have something. Plus you're the only person that would defend us," Dox shrugged.

"I never wanted to defend you. I called to see if you were okay and you pleaded with me and forced me to do this," Ford snapped.

"Either way you saved my life, and kept my best friend out of prison. So my plan worked out anyways." Dox ignored him, only seeing that he wouldn't go to prison.

"Can I go home now?" Ford groaned.

"Yeah sure," Dox shrugged and Ford left without another word.

15

Ford had left and Dox and I went to see Kareen and Rogue, but they had already walked out of the room and were gone. Both of us were confused, and feeling the same thing. Were they avoiding us?

We rushed out after them but they were ahead of us, and we ran to catch up. I ran down the hallway shoving the door open, and cut in front of Rogue. She was upset, but I could understand why.

"I don't want to talk, Phoenix," Rogue sighed.

"We don't have to talk, I know," I shrugged.

"Just stop, okay?" Rogue looked away from me and know I was confused all over again.

"Stop what?" I asked.

"I know you don't want me to worry, but you worry me when you keep secrets from me." Rogue wouldn't look at me. I had never thought about that. I was too busy trying to protect her from everything else, I didn't think she'd worry about secrets. I guess I underestimated her too.

"Okay, no secrets," I nodded, making personal notes on how to keep her happy.

"Then tell me what happened. And I want to know everything," Rogue met my eyes and I knew I couldn't keep anything from her anymore.

"We went to find out about the fire. We went to the leader of the city, which led to the lab. But when we got there, everything was dark. The last thing I remember I was hit with some kind of weapon, it paralyzed me and then I got put in prison. Then I was able to trick the guards into getting me over here. So I waited with Dox until Ford came with almost every criminal record we ever had. And, I mean everything. So after that, it led to the trial which leads us to where we are now," I explained. I wasn't too good at thinking but I was really good at explaining. I could take a span of three days and explain it easily. I guess it was out of habit though, since I had to be serious with Rogue. She wanted the truth and I could understand that.

So we went home and I was able to clear things up with her. I told her everything, and she was happy, just like I wanted.

I sat up in the Willow, overlooking the Groves. I was bored and everyone was still asleep. I really hated leaving the group by themselves, but if they were going to be safe, I had to leave them. But right then, I was happy to be home. I went over everything that had happened in the past few days, and a lot had happened.

The lab, the police, the trial, the judge, all that had happened in only two days.

"What are you doing up here?" Dox came and sat next to me.

"How did you get up here?" I asked, and looked down the side of the tree. Claw marks, I wasn't surprised.

"What do you want to do?" He asked this time.

"I don't know, I'm bored. That's the whole reason I came up here," I shrugged.

"I found a new spot, come on. This one is fun," he suggested. I nodded, seeming interested.

We smiled at each other, and looked up into the trees. The trees were covered with vines, and far up, was an old treehouse. There were swaying wooden bridges held with vines, and it looked like a playground to me. The bridges went to other trees and other treehouses too. We climbed to the top, and I was amazed. This was definitely not Dox's place to be. It was his brothers'. The moment I realized this I looked down and climbed to the ledge.

"Are you sure we should be up here? I love heights, but doesn't this belong to your brothers. They'd kill you if they found out you were up here." I was worried about Dox but I was also worried about what they'd do to me.

"Again, you should be worried about yourself. They'll care that we're up here, but they'll never find out," Dox shrugged. That's what I loved about my best friend, he just didn't care. So I went along with it and looked around the place. It was full of piled up books and maps tacked to the walls. They had different colored circles all over the large sheets of paper. Dox was looking over a map, and stopped, pointing at where the Groves were on the map. I looked over his shoulder, and there was no circle there, but a big huge "X" in red.

"They really don't like us." I stared at the X and I was a little worried.

"It's probably because of us. Who cares though, we can do whatever we want." Dox shrugged it off again, and grabbed one of the books up off the floor. He looked it over, skimming through the pages.

"They need manuals to help keep their business going?" Dox scoffed, "Pathetic." He took the book in both hands and ripped the book in half. I was laughing at this, but I stopped.

"Did you just rip that?" I asked.

"Yeah, so what? They don't need it," Dox snickered.

"You got any money?" I snapped. Dox stopped laughing, and threw the book behind him. Mori caught the book, standing behind him.

"I'm going to kill you," Mori growled, standing in the doorway.

"Dox, run," I snapped. He grabbed my wrist and jumped off the ledge pulling me with him. I grabbed his shoulders and spread my wings, looking back behind me. Mori wasn't happy at all.

"Don't worry about them, let's go," Dox said, I let go of his shoulders. He hit the ground running and I looked back behind me. Mori couldn't possibly reach us now, I thought to myself.

"Phoenix look out!" Dox barked, but it was too late. It came flying at me, and wrapped around my wings, and I fell to the ground.

16

I would've been fine hitting the ground like that, but falling from a height like that and slamming into a rock, wasn't the same. I felt my wing snap, and I yelped in pain. I tried flapping my wings, which was a stupid idea at the time since the rope ends were magnet. They were stuck together and hard to reach, so it was no use. Dox was still ahead of me, his black wolf was barking but I couldn't get to him. Dox's legs were tied, and now both of us were stuck.

Edgar grabbed me, and Mori grabbed Dox. I flamed up and Edgar let go of me in shock. So I lied on the ground, my body in flames, until I felt the rope snap. I broke away from Edgar, and formed, snatching Dox from Mori, getting him in my claws..

I took off, and heard Mori's voice behind me, "Leave it be, he can't get too far, not with a broken wing."

I ignored him anyways, but I noticed he was right. My right wing was sore, and hurt badly.

"Phoenix?" Dox looked at me worriedly, freed from the ropes.

"I'm fine," I said, looking ahead at the Groves. We got pretty close, when the pain got worse than before. Dox climbed onto my back, and looked at me worriedly again.

"Something's wrong with you, my instincts tell me everything," Dox said. I grabbed Dox in my claws, I couldn't fly anymore. I hit the ground again, harder than before, but by now I was used to the pain. I switched states automatically, and Dox and I were lying side by side, our faces smudged with dirt, neither of us moved. I was so tired, I didn't feel like getting up, but we were only a few feet from the Groves' barrier. Dox kneeled over me, and put his hand on my shoulder. He helped me, and we sat there together, out of breath.

It was almost sundown and we still hadn't moved from our spot, we just sat there quietly, talking.

"...Why didn't you tell me?" Dox asked.

"I thought I was fine, I guess. I've broken my wings before so breaking them isn't that bad," I shrugged, "It should be fine by tomorrow."

"Well, what now?" Dox sighed, looking up at the sky, smiling.

"We could watch the others get food in town. We're never around to see it. Plus we get something ourselves." So we stood up and walked into town, and all of them were there. Running through the streets, and hurling food into bags. Dox and I climbed up an apartment building to watch from above. I noticed that all the doors were locked, and the only noises were from our people. I liked looking over these kind of things, seeing what was happening. We sat on the ledge with our legs dangling over the side, just like before. I never noticed how beautiful those towering buildings looked in the setting sun. The sky was a mixture of colors and made the glass buildings shine. I looked over at the Agency, and again all the lights were out. I remembered what Saube had said about getting shut down. Dox was now looking at this too, we were both worried suddenly.

"Do you think…?" Dox wondered quietly to himself, but he couldn't finish the sentence.

"I don't know. I thought that was just them warning us but I didn't think they meant it." I couldn't take my eyes off it. The Agency wasn't too far from our borders, and it was easy to see considering it was another towering building in the city. Most apartments had windows with shades, or were entirely made of glass, but the Agency had few windows with shades, or made of glass, or anything. From the outside it looked normal, but from the inside...Well we knew.

"Should we check it out?" I suggested.

"Remember what happened last time we went to 'check it out'," Dox snapped.

"You have a point, but it would be nice to know that they're shut down. Don't you think?" I really wanted to go but if I knew my best friend, I knew he wouldn't let me go by myself. Dox thought about this, and nodded.

"Fine, but we're not going inside. And if we get captured, it's all on you," Dox sighed, and stood up, and started for the door. But I just sat there.

"Are you coming?" Dox looked at me oddly.

"Since when do you want to take the long way?" I scoffed, and slid off the ledge. Dox lunged to grab me but he was too late. He looked down over ledge, and fell back in shock to see me flying again.

"You said tomorrow," Dox groaned, getting up.

"I forgot that it heals faster once it's been broken before," I shrugged. I switched states and Dox jumped from the ledge and climbed on my back. We got to the roof of the Agency and looked around, all the cameras were out with the screens still cracked, and lights were still out. There was a soft noise coming from inside. Dox said he didn't want to go in but at this he pressed his ear to the door.

"What is it?" I asked.

"It's our sons, and I'm not surprised. The Agency will do anything to get us over here," Dox groaned.

"We should probably get them, right?" I suggested.

"Way ahead Phoenix, keep up," Dox tossed me a gun, and I felt at the knife in my pocket. These kind of things happened in my life more than they should've but by then I'd gotten really good at saving people with my best friend.

17

We got inside and I looked to Dox to find them. If he could search out anything it was our sons. Dox switched states and sniffed them out before stopping five feet from a door.

"Dox! Phoenix!" The boys called out, but we said nothing.

"I'll let you call to them all you want, but it won't change anything," Saube's smooth voice sighed.

"They'll come for us, they wouldn't leave us," Ex barked.

"Are you sure about that? How do you know?" Vess asked.

"They're coming, and they'll do anything to get to us," Fangs reassured him.

"You are right, but you're forgetting what will happen after. I've grown up with them, I've seen what they can do. You're lucky to have them, and it would be tragic to lose them," Saube shrugged. This angered Dox and I kicked at the door, and we pulled out our guns. Saube took a step backward with his hands in the air.

"Look who it is, right on time as always. You know, you may live in the woods but you have a really good concept of time," Saube nodded.

"Might have to thank your mother on that one. Actually give her our thanks when you see her!" Dox barked and the trigger clicked in his palm. I burned the binds around their wrists, and they stood behind us.

"Get out of here, we'll be right behind you!" I looked to the three of them but they didn't move.

"Just get them out of here. It'll be my fault in the end," Dox glanced at me before looking back at Saube.

"You really think I'm leaving my best friend? I'm not as dumb as I seem," I grabbed a pair of handcuffs off the rack on the wall and clipped them around Saube's wrists.

"I'd be surprised if you could get out these. You can tell me how it feels to be cuffed afterwards," I growled, shoving him with us out the door, and Dox kept the gun on him.

"You'd really shoot me?" Saube asked.

"You hurt my sons, and you're as good as gone," Dox growled.

"You know, for a bunch of criminals you two are really interesting, doing anything for your sons," Saube smiled.

"I'd do anything for my family. Including shooting you in the head," I snapped.

"You wouldn't mind if I did a few more tests right? I really want to research you two," Saube asked.

"Over my dead body. What are you going to do this time, wipe our memories? Won't work, I'm telling you. We'll never forget." Dox and I looked at each other again for a long moment.

Dox and Saube were on my back, and Ex and Vess were with Fangs.

We went home, overlooking the group as they rushed back through the woods, all going to the same place. For that evening our only plan was to go home, and home was all I wanted.

Dox and I met early that morning with Rogue and Kareen.

"Ladies," Saube nodded politely.

"Don't even think about it," I barked.

"So what are we doing with him again?" Rogue asked.

"Whatever you want, so long as we get something from him," Dox shrugged.

"Fair enough," Kareen nodded, "How about this, if he doesn't want to talk we can get a good deal at the Traders' Tunnels." We all nodded in agreement at the idea, and that was the plan.

"What do you want us for?" I asked first.

"Research, honestly," Saube nodded truthfully.

"That's what Ferdinand said, and we all know how that ended," Dox groaned.

"Come on, it's the truth, I just want to know what happened, how you got here. If you talked with every scientist at the Agency, they'd give you the same answer. I just want to finish it, a complete lab of your actions and thought process. That was all she ever wanted," Saube explained, "I watched her write it out in her log, every detail, and exact number. If you let me finish it…" Saube stopped short, trying to think of a good bargain, and we waited patiently. "How about this. If you let me log a few more tests in the record book, you can have it."

"Why would we want a book full of testing scores?" Rogue scoffed.

"No, no, that's not it at all. It has everything. Your ages, your thoughts throughout the simulation tests, your actions, all of that. How would you not want to know?" Saube was out of breath, trying to convince us.

"I'd take it if I were desperate to find out my own log times," I shrugged, "But, I don't want them. That's old news that none of us care about." We all looked at each other and nodded, nothing convincing, no reason to keep him any longer.

"I've got a better plan," Dox smiled, "We could sell him at an auction. Getting a deal is good, but at an auction, you get more than you asked for. My brothers pay big money for the good stuff. It sounds weird, but trust me. I killed a duck and got twenty bucks out of it. They'll pay money for almost anything. For a threat of the entire Woods, they'd pay a fortune to hold him hostage."

I found this a little odd to be giving away a living being at an auction, but it sounded like a good idea. We could use the money. Dox grabbed Saube by the wrists and I walked with him to the Tunnels.

18

Dox shoved Saube onto the platform in front of the Traders. The wolves were seated at tables talking and enjoying themselves, but they fell silent when they saw our offer.

"How much do want him for?" A wolf asked.

"As high as we can get. He's got to be worth something," Dox shrugged.

"Hold on. Is that, Ferdinand's kid?" One of the wolves stood and walked to the front of the room. He gaped at Saube in silence.

"They're not lying, it's him alright!" The wolf went back to his seat, cheers rose from the crowd and Saube went pale. The wolves held rolls of money, ready to pay a hefty price for him.

"Wait! Please, you can't sell me! That's a charge of child abuse!" Saube protested.

"Charges don't apply here," Edgar stood over Saube smiling. Saube went ghost white and looked at Edgar in shock.

"Good job guys. Mori and I will take him for seventy." At this the wolves stopped short. No one paid a bigger price than Dox's brothers that's for sure. No one could top their payments at any auction, those two were rich beyond compare.

"We'll take it," Dox nodded.

"Please, I'll do anything. Don't give me to him! He'll kill me!" Saube begged.

"What's wrong with us kid? You got a problem with us?" Edgar snarled.

"You're wolves. Dangerous, vicious, man-eating wolves," Saube was horrified, and quivering.

"Looks like this one takes from his mother. I've got a bone to pick with her, she owes me big time. In fact she owes these two also. Ferdinand's got a lot of debts to pay on the Woods," Mori joined at Edgar's side, towering over Saube. He spoke softly gesturing toward us. "You owe my brother and his friend big time kid," Mori smiled at us trustingly, "Surely you could pay it forward."

"I might have to join you on that. Ferdinand owes me big time because I still have that scar across my chest," I grabbed Saube's wrists, dragging him away from the others.

"Phoenix, what are you doing?" Dox snapped.

"Getting more out of the deal, I forgot about those debts. I'll do whatever it takes to get more out of this," I whispered.

"You got guts, Phoenix. No one's turned us down in years," Edgar nodded impressed with my decision.

"I'll split a hundred with you for the offer, but the traitor's mine," I growled. The wolves had no hesitation and handed Dox the money.

"How did you do that? What did you that for? Just let them kill me and get it over with, since that's what everyone wants," Saube snapped, as we shoved him forward along the path home.

"I was going to keep you so I get my revenge." I shoved him to the ground, and he looked at me worriedly. I'd never seen someone look at me that way, Saube's heart was racing and pounding in his chest, and I could see that he was frightened. "You owe me for this." I showed him the scar across my chest, and looked at Dox.

"Your mother owes me for experimenting. That's the last time she ever messes up her calculations," Dox growled.

"Look, I'm sorry she did that to you, but just a bit more testing, please. I need it. If I can complete this, the Agency will be known as the first lab to have successfully completed a genetics human test. It'll be the start of another world!" Saube explained.

We turned away from him to think about this.

"Should we? It'll only be a few more tests and we're done," I shrugged.

"We're not dumb anymore, we're putting in limitations," Dox nodded.

"Nothing can be done without our permission," I nodded, as we turned back to him with our decision.

"So, is this a yes?" Saube asked hopefully.

"I guess so," we shrugged, "But first we have to tell our families," I added.

Rogue and Kareen let us go after we explained everything. We said we would visit, but we both knew we were lying. They didn't notice the lie and we left.

19

"We need to do a few simulations if you don't mind," Saube said, flipping a few switches behind the glass wall. I remembered the last time I had broken it, and the other time when Rogue and I had shattered it, but through all that it was replaced with another wall of glass.

"By all means, as long as there are no secrets," Dox shrugged, and we strapped ourselves in. I felt a quick shock from the connectors, and fell into the simulation. Dox was standing in front of me, I knew it was fake because he showed no expression or feelings.

"Dox?" I asked.

"Who's Dox?" Dox looked at me oddly.

"Sorry, Jamie." I turned to see a boy smiling at Dox. It was me, but that's when I noticed it was younger versions of ourselves. I was confused until Dox had passed right through me. Suddenly I was in a dark room, and saw Dox sitting in the corner of the room his eyes glowing a bright gold color.

The second I saw him, I knew. I had seen my fears before but these were someone else's. These were, Dox's fears. I went to go to him, but I couldn't move. Suddenly I was dragged under by a wave. They were mixtures of our fears, not just our own. I fell on the ground, choking and coughing up water. Dox loomed over me, a dagger in his hands.

"Dox please!" I screamed, as he wield the dagger at me, and everything faded…

I pulled the connectors from my skin, and fell to the floor.

"Phoenix, are you alright?" Dox shook me worriedly. I might not have been thinking then because I punched Dox in the face. That's when I realized I was still half asleep.

"What was that for?!" Dox barked, covering his bloody mouth.

"You...You scared me!" I screamed.

"I didn't mean it! You think it's easy for me? Have you ever wondered why I don't sleep at night? I haven't slept in what? Years!" Dox wiped the blood from his face, and inched away from me.

"I've been in a simulation, but...I have to admit it. I'm horrified, I'm really scared and I don't want to see that again." I put my face in my hands, and waited for my breathing to go back to normal.

"I scared you? I swear, I feel like I'm going to throw up. You have no idea how many times I took a shot in the head in the simulator back there. I felt like I had died ten times and couldn't keep myself from dying. I have to say it, I'm scared. I don't want to go back there either." Dox hung his head. Saube wasn't in the control room anymore, he had disappeared. We hadn't noticed, too busy admitting our fears. But he came back to explain what had happened.

"You did good, and surprisingly, each of you had the same last fear. Being killed by the other. See, this is why I wanted to test you again. You should receive your first upgrade by the next test," Saube explained, kind of proving his point.

"Whatever, can we just move on?" Dox shrugged.

"Of course, but that last test I'm afraid is the one we'll be practicing in the exercise." Saube held a clipboard in his hand and starting scribbling on, walking out of the room. We stood, and followed him into a training room.

"The hard part is you will be fighting each other, and this will be real," Saube explained, "Each of you can take a weapon and we'll get that started." Saube disappeared, and reappeared on the balcony up above. Dox and I looked at each other, after the first test neither of us could do it. Saube leaned against the balcony and waited for us. He must've thought that we were confused, so he explained it a bit further.

"It shouldn't be too hard, all you have to do knock them down. That's all," Saube shrugged, speaking into a microphone.

"I'm not fighting him, that's madness," Dox protested.

"It's going to be fine, believe me," Saube nodded.

"We're not doing this, you can convince us to come here. But we're not fighting, not each other," I added.

"There are limitations, I understand. Alright, let's take a break then," Saube nodded, smiling slightly through his frustration.

The guards moved us into a cell together, and we sat there bored.

"I don't know if this was right," I sighed.

"Saube just wants us to do as he says with no questions asked. Whether we like it or not," Dox nodded.

"He doesn't want to finish the log, he wants to get famous. He'll do whatever it takes, no matter how many tests he does. He's not trying to finish the log, he's trying to be world known," I scoffed.

"I think we need to tell them," Dox shrugged.

"We should've seen it coming in the first place. I think we just wanted them off our backs," I nodded, and we stood to find him. Saube was shocked at this, and we tried to make him understand as calmly as possible.

"We need to leave," Dox said.

"What?" Saube gaped at us.

"No need for an explanation. We're going home, and that's final," I snapped. We grabbed our cloaks and walked off.

"You might want to rethink that boys," a voice said. We turned, and weren't surprised to see the guards.

"I'm not surprised," I groaned.

"Don't got any weapons this time, so it's either you come back, or we'll open fire on both of you," a guard explained. Dox felt his pockets.

"Shoot. My dagger's gone," he whispered.

"So is mine," I added.

"Seems like a simple choice to me," the guard shrugged, "life or death." Dox looked to me for a plan, and surprisingly, I felt the upgrade click. Usually I'm asleep so I never feel it but that was good.

"Well?" Dox snapped.

"Start running, I'll be right behind," I nodded reassuringly and Dox got a head start. The guards opened fire and I spread my wings to block my body. I suddenly felt nothing, but heard the bullets snake a clinking noise against my wings. I started after my friend and he looked at me in shock.

"What upgrade did you get?" Dox smiled.

"Bulletproof wings, that's going to come in handy."

"Great. Keep going, I'll hold them off." So I hurried up the stairs and onto the roof, and climbed to the ledge. I crouched on the edge and waited for him, when I noticed the security cameras were up again. I pulled them out, and Dox got out to the roof.

"Well, what is it?" I asked.

"Some kind of mind trick," Dox shrugged, and jumped on my back. I switched states and we took off for home.

20

"You're back already?" Rogue asked.

"It didn't work out the way we had planned," I shrugged.

"Who cares, if Saube kept you any longer we would've stormed them looking for you two." Rogue leaned against me, her head on my shoulder.

"I don't care what they do to me. So long as I have my family, I'll be fine." I kissed her on the forehead, and she smiled.

"I like it when you say those things, it's cute," she laughed.

"I'm not trying to be cute." I was confused at this.

"Yeah I know. You're just naturally caring and cute, I like that. I also like how you're clueless at romantic stuff, that's something cute," she laughed silently. I again, felt happy to be home. I guess I was only happy coming home because I got into a fight every other day. So being home felt pretty good. Like before, we watched the sunset, and talked quietly kissing each other every now and then. It felt good that is, until my hearing clicked in, and I heard something far off.

"What is it?" Rogue asked.

"Aw you have got to be kidding me," I groaned.

"What?" She snapped.

"Troops. Get the tribes together, and get out as quick as you can," I explained.

"What about you?" Kareen asked, standing with Dox on the cliffside.

"We'll be fine." Dox and I raced outside to barrier, to see an army of troops.

"Shoot," Dox groaned.

"What now?" I asked.

"We don't have any weapons except our powers. And they have those new weapons," Dox snapped, then it was my turn.

"Shoot!" I moaned.

"'Shoot' is right, we're done. Did you see what those guns did to us?" Dox put his hands on his head, in panic. This was bad, really bad.

"By the way, what were you thinking!?" Dox shouted at me as we both began to realize we had no plan, and that we had sent our army off to hide.

"I don't know! I thought it would save us the trouble of losing more members!" I shrugged.

"Yeah, and also get us killed! We can't take on an entire army!" Dox barked.

We were too busy fighting to see the army now fifty yards away from our borders. Dox put his hands out and focused, staring at the army.

As they began to run for the barrier, they were shoved back by an invisible force. With a wave of his hand the ground beneath the feet was pulled up into the air and showered down on the troops. They all ran.

My ears started flicking again, and I focused on the sound. Footsteps, lots of them.

"It's not over yet," I whispered.

"What? How many?" Dox asked.

"Thousands or at least that's as much as I can hear." I looked at Dox and he looked at me, we had no plan for this, but jumped in anyways. I thought for a second, having no idea what to do though.

"I need you to do something." I knelt on the ground, and Dox knelt beside me. "I'm going to heat the ground below us, I need you to spread the heat around the Groves."

"Oh I get it, so it's like a big shield," Dox nodded.

"Exactly. When it happens I want you to get to high ground, that way it can't touch you. Find the group and lead them off, I'll be right behind you." I put my hands in the dirt and set them on fire, which made my hands glow like candlelight. I felt the ground begin to warm up and get hotter and hotter.

"It's getting too hot, I'm going up, will you be okay?" Dox looked back at me one last time.

"I'm a phoenix, fire is my thing," I shrugged, and Dox left without another. I could handle it, I thought. I felt he ground grow warmer and warmer, burning. The army ahead had stopped dead in their tracks, the ground unbearably hot. I flamed up and advanced toward them, my left arm outstretched. Dox barked toward me and I saw him with the group.

"What is he doing?" Kareen asked.

"Fire wall," Dox smiled. Just like he had said I raised the fames from the ground creating a line around the Groves. I was at least five feet from the army, and the troops pulled out their weapons as if they had no other choice. I spread my arms, making the wall rise, and spread my wings. I shot upward and lit a flame in my hand, and molded it into a ball of fire. I made multiple fire balls, hurling them at the troops, and they retreated bit by bit. Until one was left, Saube.

"Give your respects to Ferdinand when you see her!" Saube shouted.

"NO! Phoenix!" Rogue screamed. Saube shot one of those comet guns, and for a moment I let it come toward me.

"Phoenix move!" Dox yelled, only I dove toward it. I flamed up and went toward the comet at full speed, as I flew toward it. It got closer and closer, until I lit a growing flame in the palm of my hands. I stopped, hovering and with my arm outstretched, grabbed the glowing orb. It fought against me, and I grabbed it with two hands, and watched as the flame surrounded the orb and the comet turned to fire. I held it my hand again, looking at it closely. This was odd, because last time the comet had stopped my flames instantly, but that time it didn't. For a moment I could control it,, and just as I went to redirect it back at Saube I was hit in the back by another comet.

21

I woke up and had almost forgotten what happened before, but everything came back when I couldn't feel my body. I again felt paralyzed and couldn't move at all. So I lied on the floor, and realized I was back at the Agency all over again. I lied on the floor for a while until my body returned, and I sat up in a room that I for once didn't realize.

"Finally awake?" I looked up in alarm to find my best friend, and felt a little safer with him there. I relaxed a bit and looked at him a little closer. Dox was cut and bruised and bound on the other side of the room.

"What happened to you?" I asked.

"What does it look like? I came to save a stupid boy that would die if I didn't. But apparently it's not going to work that way," Dox growled.

"Yeah, I see that now. But how did you get cut? You're bruised and cut all over, how?-" I wondered.

"Get off my case Phoenix!" Dox barked, and I stopped asking instantly. "I don't want to talk about this, I'm not in a good mood. Look, we have to get out of here. The troops are going back to the Groves. I saw them. We need to get out now. I overheard Saube talking with some scientists-," he stopped, and hung his head trying to keep calm.

"What did they say?" I didn't like how he stopped mid-sentence..

"Not going to say, but if we don't get out here soon you'll see," Dox glared at me angrily.

"Alright, let's get out of here." I lit a flame in my hands and set it under the binds, but I hadn't noticed the titanium ropes. I sighed angrily, and looked around the chamber but there was nothing we could use to escape.

"Now what?" I asked.

"I don't know, wait until the titanium kicks in I guess," Dox shrugged, and glanced the binds around his arms. We sat there in silence for a long while, when our attention snapped to the ceiling. The lights started to turn off one by one, until the lights above went out, and someone was outside unlocking the door. There was a soft glow under the crack of the door, a candle. I started to struggle against the binds but it was hard to because by now the titanium had weakened my arms. I lit a small flame behind my back one more time, but I was so weakened it shook and disappeared. The swung open and it was Saube with two guards at his sides. He must've seen my temptation at the flame because he waved it in front of my face,

"Go on, take it. You need a little energy I understand." Saube gave me one of those sly looks, and I grabbed at it but missed and he pulled it away from me. He turned to Dox waved it in his face, doing the same thing he did to me.

"It's not your element I know, but it affects you just as much as everyone else." Dox turned his head away from the flames, and Saube moved the candle closer instead of away. I craned my wrist to face my palm toward the candle, and the flames were pulled from the candle just like I wanted. Saube glared at me angrily, as the flames flickered and moved toward until they were in my hand. I made my hand into a fist and the flames disappeared.

"Give that back. Come on," Saube said blindly. Without the candle it was pitch dark in the closed room, and I could see why he needed it, but I only shook my head. I grabbed onto the ropes and felt them start to snap. I was almost there when a guard kicked me in the gut, I immediately lost the flames, and hung my head weakly. I couldn't breathe, and felt sick to my stomach, the pain was so strong it was as if I had forgotten how to breathe. I watched as they pulled some device and it switched our elements. Dox's ropes started to set aflame and he screamed in pain. The guards grabbed me and back me up against the wall, and Saube stood in front of me.

"I thought you'd like to watch, to see destruction with your own eyes. If don't cooperate tonight, his family we'll be in the same state as he is right now," Saube whispered and stunningly grabbed me by the neck. "It's nice to see what destruction you can cause isn't it. To see how much it hurts." He held me there for a moment and I didn't fight back as I felt my breath slip away, my body weakened to a breaking point, and he let go. I bowed my head weakly, looking at my friend screaming in pain.

"STOP! DON'T HURT HIM!" I roared with my last bit of energy and Saube stopped. The flames on the ropes when out, and Dox didn't move. Saube threw a knife at my feet, and the guards untied me.

"I'll give you some time, but Phoenix...You're next." Saube left without another word, and I snatched the knife, and ran to Dox.

"I'm so sorry," I whispered, as I cut him loose. I shook him rapidly trying to get him awake, but he only kept his eyes closed. I stayed knelt on the ground, and put my face in my hands.

"What am I going to do?" I whispered to myself, in the darkened chamber. Saube was right, all I could do was cause destruction. All I could do was hurt people, even the people I loved. I knelt on the ground in silence, before placing my hands on his chest. My eyes and hands glowed, and faded but nothing happened. It felt like an eternity that I sat there.

"What have I done?" I felt tears roll down my face, it was over. I hung my head again, when Dox starting coughing. I looked up to see my friend, he was alright. I hugged him tightly, and he hugged me back, and we sat there for a while.

"How? I thought you were dead?" I asked.

"No, I passed out. I would've gotten up earlier but I couldn't move, it's kind of like being paralyzed," Dox explained. We heard the door unlock for a second time, and the guards grabbed us and dragged us away in different directions. They threw me into another chamber, where there were four posts at each corner of the room. "Hope you enjoy this one, it's very...Shocking," a guard laughed, before flipping a switch on the wall and leaving the room.

The posts started buzzing and soon there was a circuit of electricity, connecting all four. For some reason I got close to it and went to touch it but it zapped my hand and I pulled it away. I was too busy trying to get out that a shock wave came and hit me in the chest. I clutched my chest in pain, when another hit my leg, until more of those shock waves came one after the other hitting my body. I was doubled over on my knees, still clutching my chest weakly. Another shock hit me in the stomach and I fell to the floor. My body shook in pain, my ear drums had shattered, and I felt my body weaken and I could no longer move but the shocks kept coming.

The buzzing noise stopped, and all I could here was the voice of my best friend, trying to help me from my daze.

"Phoenix, Phoenix can you hear me?" He asked, but I said nothing, I was still in pain and had to wait for my body to loosen up. Dox kept repeating the same question as I was still waiting.

“Phoenix can you hear me?!” Dox asked worriedly, shaking me a bit. I took his hand and we stared into each other's eyes for a moment. He helped me to my knees, and I lied my head on his shoulder.

“Yeah, I can hear you,” I rasped. ‘Please...Don’t leave...Me….”

“I won’t, I promise,” Dox whispered. We sat there in silence again, and I thought it felt good to know that my best friend would never leave me. That he’d always be right there, and never leave. I felt comfortable with my head on his shoulder, as he supported me, like he had for so many years.

22

"…Now, are you going to cooperate?" Saube asked,

"Alright, we'll do it," I nodded, finally back to my full strength.

"Good, because I couldn't let your families watch you suffer, it'd be torture," Saube smiled, and my heart sank. Dox and I lunged for the boy but the guards held us back.

"Where are they?!" Dox barked.

"Oh no worries, we're taking you to them, that is, if you'll cooperate like you said," Saube explained. I wrestled from their grips and moved forward with Dox to follow Saube. He led us down the winding hallways to another chamber. Rogue and Fangs ran to me and I grabbed them held them close.

"We thought you were dead," Rogue whispered, tears rolling down her cheeks.

"No, I'm okay. It's okay." I promised her and leaned her head against my shoulder.

"Phoenix, can we go home?" Fangs asked, and I looked into his sparkling blue eyes, but I couldn't lie to him. I said nothing for a moment,

"I have to stay, but I'll get you two home no matter what. I think the only reason they attacked us was because we ran off. If we leave again, it'll be putting you in danger too." I couldn't look at my son, not that way, not to disappoint him. I knew what he meant but he kept going.

"I don't want to go home, not without you. We've been going home without you for so long, it's as if you're not there. I want to go home with you for a change," Fangs pressed.

"I would say yes, but I have to say no," I sighed.

"He has a point, we made deal, and we never break them," Dox added.

"Really because you broke that deal about lying to your family. And this is the what? Something hundredth time you've broken it," Rogue growled.

"We're serious about this one," I nodded.

"Wow, so what's this now? You'll protect me but you won't tell me the truth!" Rogue shouted.

"So now you're going to push it?! I've been going through a lot trying to protect you and this is it?! You're upset with me now?!" I yelled back.

"Maybe if told me I wouldn't be!" Rogue screamed.

"I'm doing what I can to keep you safe! I'm trying to make things better!" I felt the anger begin let loose, but I couldn't control it.

"What happened to no secrets?!"

"If you haven't noticed, I don't have time to tell you everything!"

"Well you could at least try!"

"Trust me, I have tried!"

"Really?! Because it doesn't seem like that now!"

"Okay, I admit it, I wasn't thinking about it then, but it's not like I forget about you all together!"

"Well sometimes I wish I could forget! You think I like this? You having to come save me all the time?! Well guess what?! I hate being captured, and I hated being saved! I can save myself, okay?! Without you!"

This made my rage flare, and my eyes suddenly glowed an orangish-red. My body lit up, and I tried to stop it but I could. My muscles tensed and the flames grew. Rogue stood face to face with me, her eyes the same way. The light from our eyes collided push against the other. The light grew, the flames sweltered, Fangs made a shield to protect everyone as the blast flooded the room and suddenly Rogue and I were thrown against the walls on opposite sides of the room. The force of the blast threw me against the wall and I blacked out, unconscious.

23

I woke up, at home? I was at home, in the Willow, and I almost thought it was a dream. But I woke up, with a black wolf asleep under my arm. I stroked his fur, and smiled, he kept his promise like I wanted, and I would do the same. Dox woke calmly and licked my face. I laughed and shooed him away, and looked back at my friend in human form. I smiled still, but it vanished when I remembered last night. My fight with Rogue, my rage gone wild, the screaming and fire, flashed back into my memory, and now I was lost.

"Is she still mad at me?" I asked.

"She seems fine now," Dox shrugged.

"But how do I know?" I wondered, trying to make the right decision to win her back. I wasn't sure if she'd fight with me again, or if she'd forgive me or not.

"Just do what I do, get her a present. I would suggest rodents, girls love them," Dox suggested.

"I am not give my wife a dead rat. She's a phoenix, not a wolf," I looked at him terribly confused.

"Just get her something pretty then," Dox said picking another suggestion. So I left the Groves for a bit trying to find something pretty. Which was hard since there was nothing but trees and leaves. I had to make it up to her at any costs, which included going into another land. I went for the Pridelands, where it was nothing but green grass, hills and the occasional trees. But the good part was that these trees bore fruit and flowers, the perfect thing I could give to Rogue. The Pride was down below but I didn't think they'd care that I was there, so long I stayed out of their way. I found a tree with colorful roses and fruit, so I grabbed hold of a branch with one hand and picked the flowers with the others. I carefully pulled each flowers getting the stems with it.

"Is that a..." I glanced at the ground to see some Pridelanders but I just kept picking the flowers. I didn't need each one from the tree, but I had to be careful to not burn them with my hands. I decided to pull a piece of fruit that was a bit higher up that I couldn't reach. I went for it anyways but it slipped from my grasp and hit the ground near a boy's feet. The boy looked up and it was Malley.

"...Never mind the search, I can deal with it myself," Malley groaned, and climbed the tree. I quickly used my flames to encase the flowers in fire, and the flowers didn't burn.

Malley glared at me angrily, and I just gave him an innocent look.

"What are you doing in our territory?" Malley growled.

"I need these, never mind the reason," I glared back at him, holding his gaze.

"You're breaking the rules, step out of here with those flowers and I'll march over there myself." Malley gave me a nasty look and I laughed.

"Yeah right. You know nothing about nature, Malley. Flowers grow back, no matter what the season," I scoffed.

"Fine. They'll grow back. Take them, but I'm warning you, Phoenix, if I see you again, you know what's coming." Malley swung from the branches to the ground, landed on his feet, and walked away. I shrugged again and switched states before flying back to the Groves.

Rogue sat in the oak tree in the meadow, with her legs dangling through the branches. I nudged her shoulder, and she smiled at me.

"I got you a present." I handed her the bouquet of flowers and sat next to her. I saw that her wrist was bandaged, and I almost thought to leave.

"I'm okay, its fine, " she laughed a little and placed her hand in mine. "I broke my wrist in the blast."

"I never want to see that again." I looked away from her remembering my rage.

"See what?" she asked.

"Myself. I couldn't see myself then, but I could tell I scared everyone, I never want to see myself like that. Where I couldn't control it, and I tried," I whispered softly.

"Hey, it's okay. I should've never started fighting with you. It got out of hand, so that's my fault. Fangs isn't scared of you, you should talk to him," Rogue explained. So I stood and went to the cave where Fangs was and I stopped. What if he didn't want to see me? What if he was still angry with me? What if…? I started doubting myself but didn't move any further.

"Go away, I don't want to talk," Fangs growled from inside the cave.

"At least come out so I can see you," I sighed. Fangs stood at the edge of the cave, shadowed by the darkness. His piercing blue eyes glowed in the darkness.

"What are we talking about this time?" He groaned.

"Rogue wanted me to talk to you again," I shrugged. Fangs said nothing but stared at the ground for a moment.

"I've never seen you so upset with Rogue," Fangs whispered.

"I know, and I'm sorry, I couldn't control it anymore." I looked away from him for a moment.

"No, it's just...You looked like you were splitting up For a second I thought it was true," Fangs explained and neither of us could meet each other's eyes. We stood there for a long moment in silence.

"Why couldn't we just be human for a change? Humans don't deal with these things every day. They get hurt easily but not as often. Why couldn't we just be normal for once?" Fangs sighed.

"Normal? Human? Fangs, there's no such thing as normal, no one's normal. People made up normal, normal doesn't exist in our world. If you were human you'd fall victim to these lies and believe that there is a way to be perfect. Humans don't see the truth, and meant to think that they're the only ones, that they're the reason the world is so perfect. Humans live in what's called seclusion, where they're cut off from the real world. Why would you want to be like them?" I explained.

"I guess you're right, we don't bleed as easily, we're stronger, and faster than them. So I guess there's a good side of it too," Fangs shrugged.

"Exactly, just see the good side of it," I suggested and Fangs nodded, agreeing with my advice.

Dox wanted to talk with me next, but apparently it was a secret to keep away from the family. We walked outside the barrier toward the city, and I stopped.

"We're going into the city?" I asked.

"We need to talk to Ford, he'd know what to do," Dox nodded handing me my cloak, "I thought you'd need it." We went to Ford's house in the middle of the day. We never went into the city during the day, I never liked the noise, the distractions. I went anyways, and sat down at the kitchen table with Dox and Ford.

"So what did you want to tell me again?" I asked.

"My sons want to be human. Is this happening with your kid too?" Dox gave me a panicked look and I buried my head in my cloak. "What does that mean?" He asked.

"Yes," I sighed. I looked up and both Dox and I were looking to Ford for advice.

"What's happening?" We asked together, hoping for some help.

"I can see why," Ford snickered, and continued. "You don't see it do you? Your kids don't want to have to be dragged around by the Agency, or steal food from town. They want to be normal." There was that word, "normal", again

"My son is turning human and he's supposed to take over for me," I groaned.

"Come on guys, this is good, they'll be making your families a bit more human friendly," Ford smiled.

"Just get it over with, and shove them into the city already. Then we can leave them there overnight and they'll be out of our lives forever. On the bright side then we'll really be carefree," Dox moaned.

"What!? No! I can't leave him, he's like...The pride and joy of my life. Getting rid of him is like cutting my heart in half," I sobbed.

"You guys are so stupid," Evian sighed, leaning on Ford's chair.

"How would you know, you blood-sucking little leach. You want to know something about yourself. When you get to be an adult you're programed to destroy and consume. That's all you'll ever do. You're like all the other Riches in this town, now my son is going to be one of them," I growled, almost losing my temper again.

"Cool it Phoenix," Dox snapped.

"How would you know what to do? You're freaking out too. I'm surprised you're not panicking about this. Dox, we're standing on Richie territory, and in a short amount of time, our sons will be here too....Permanently. Either we get a plan or we'll never be able to see our sons again." I felt my anger coming back and stood, grasping the table even harder.

"We'll get a plan, but if you keep being paranoid we never will. So calm down and let's think of one," Dox growled.

"Actually you mean Ford's going to think of the plan," I corrected.

"You know what I meant," Dox nodded, and we both sat back down looking to Ford again for a plan.

"Well, you can show it's a dangerous place. It's like one of those 'I was right, you were wrong' kind of moments in the end, and it scares people out of their skin. All you have to do is close them into the city for the day, and you can go and get them at sundown. Trust me they'll be so scared they'll never want to be human again. Hold on, do they take up the same things as you guys?" he asked.

"I don't know, I've never really exposed him to the city during the day, but yeah I think so," I shrugged, and then both of us looked at each other and nodded.

24

So we let them loose into the city, which was hard for both Dox and I to do. Neither of us liked the city because we didn't trust Humans, we only trusted Ford because he was Dox's cousin, and he was one of us, even if he lived in the city. But Ford had promised he would keep an eye on them and that they would return safely.

"If you're doing this to prove your point, you've done it already," Fangs shook his head as I tried to shove him through the barrier. It was barely even mid-morning but there were already cars, I hadn't planned that part for him.

"You haven't even tried yet." I stopped pushing.

"You're trying to prove your point, and it worked, I'm not dumb. I'll stop asking just don't put me in there. I like the silence, I like the caves, our people. Compare this to home. Our people are really nice and them…They're just nasty. They assume that everyone's bad, and our cloaks won't protect us." Fangs shook his head, and I pulled the cloak over his head anyways.

"You'll be fine, you've got your friends, and I'll be back by sundown for the stealing," I smiled and shoved him through. Ex and Vess grabbed his arms and pulled him away from the border.

"Let me through! Don't leave me!" Fangs yelled.

"Don't worry, I still love you!" I called, waving as the border closed. I started to regret it when I thought about. But I remembered Ford said he'd take care of it and I trusted him because he was a part of Dox's family. And I trusted anyone who had a connection with my best friend.

"That was the most reassuring thing you could possibly tell him? 'I still love you', he already knows that. Why not 'watch out for cars' or 'take shelter in a bar' or something like that," Dox suggested.

"They are not going to a bar, that's chaos. You can't bring your kid to a bar," I scoffed, and Dox gave me one of those regretting looks.

"What did you tell them?" I asked.

"I told them to take shelter in a bar," Dox sighed.

"Are you dumbstruck, or an idiot?! What's wrong with you?!" I growled.

"I don't know. I just thought they'd be safe there. They'd fit right in with the cloaks. Every time we went people had their hoods so it makes sense," Dox shrugged.

So now I was even more worried for Fangs but I knew he was smart so hopefully he would stay away.

The sun finally set and surprisingly Dox and I hadn't moved from our spots, still standing there and arguing.

"So you don't trust my family anymore?!" Dox shouted.

"No that's not it at all! I just don't trust Ford with my son! He can't watch them all day!" I yelled back.

"Fine then. If you don't trust me just go and get him yourself!" Dox growled.

"I'm surprised you're not worried about your kids. Since they grew up with Traders I guess they'll be fine!" I spat and Dox shoved me to the ground.

"You got a problem with Traders?! I'd be surprised if you did considering you chose to be with one your entire life. My sons have never met my brothers and that's how it's going to stay!-" Mori and Edgar towered over us, and Dox sighed. Mori and Edgar were serious stalkers when it came to Dox's life, much less anyone else's . I wasn't surprised that they'd find it about Ex and Vess.

"Oh, we knew. We found just a few hours ago when we were in the city ourselves. I was a little shocked to see your people in the city, especially youngsters like them. We noticed because we were stalking them too. You seemed worried so we brought them for you instead," Mori explained. The border opened and there was one of the Traders on the other side he nudged our kids back into the woods and the border closed. Fangs ran to me and didn't let go.

"What happened?" I asked.

"They got drunk. I swear I ordered one, but I didn't drink it. Then Vess took and told me it my loss and drank it. Just watching them made me sick to my stomach," Fangs explained.

"You're lucky we there. We decided to...Be nice, I guess, and bring them to you." Mori explained, but he stopped short at 'being nice', as if it was hard to say.

"I didn't know you had brothers? How big is our family?" Vess looked between Mori, Edgar and Dox with a surprised look.

"My question is what happened to you? You guys used to stay out of people's business, until now everything's your concern," I growled.

"That's not our fault. If it's family business it's our business," Edgar nodded.

"Yeah, you never talk about them, why?" Ex asked, and Dox groaned.

"You're not serious!?" Mori looked at Dox mockingly, and both Mori and Edgar broke out laughing.

"He doesn't talk about us because he doesn't want to get caught talking simultaneously-" Both Mori and Dox spoke at the same time. Even though their sentences started off differently, they matched at the end.

"I could've explained myself you know," they glared at each other for a moment as it happened again.

"Look, I want you gone, alright. I don't want you talking to them, I don't want you to ever talk to her either. I especially don't want you two talking about my past life, that's my life, not yours. Now I want you out of here, got it?!" Dox growled, and his brothers shrugged.

"Fine, that's what you want let's go right now," Mori changed into a massive wolf, with the same black fur as Dox.

"I want you out of my life," Dox lunged for Mori and shoved him into a tree, and the fights started up. I knew this wouldn't be good, so I had to do something. I changed my form and looked at our sons.

"Get on my back," I said hurriedly. They climbed on and I went for the Groves.

"Wait, why aren't we getting Dox then?" Fangs asked.

"If know him at all, he wouldn't want you there. He's fighting with Mori so Edgar could close in on you. Believe me, not the nicest of people. I should know, I grew up with him. Your group was in the Caves for a reason. Your group united with mine for a reason," I explained.

"What reason?" Ex scoffed.

"Duh, me. He's my best friend, we've been friends for almost our entire lives. Plus if he joined with me, he could get away from them. Same thing will happen to the three of you. You'll still be friends, no matter what happens." I wasn't too sure if I should've been explaining all of it to them, but might as well saved Dox all the questions. I heard him focusing in for me, so I listened in for his voice.

"You okay?" I asked.

"You have come get me," Dox rasped, he seemed out of breath.

"Where are you?" I wondered hoping I could get to him in time.

"By the outpost," Dox replied, "Hurry."

"I'm on my way." I changed course and I could tell that the boys were confused.

"What's happening? Who were you talking to?" Fangs asked.

I used my X-ray vision to sort through the trees, when I found my friend. Dox looked pretty beat up, and he was leaning against a tree, with little time. The Traders were closing in.

"Start back home, and whatever you do...Don't look back," I instructed. Fangs jumped off my back and changed into his purple phoenix. Ex and Vess jumped onto his back and they flew off. I went down and formed into a human, before setting my body on fire. The wolves started to get closer and closer, so I stepped in front of Dox, and covered him with my wings. He was bruised and bleeding like always after any fight.

"I'm here. Hold on alright?" I turned back to the wolves, and they seemed a little different. More dangerous, more wild than before.

"You really think you can protect him? Against all of us?" A wolf snickered.

"Why does it matter to you, dog? You hate me as much as you hate you," I spat.

"We spared you. We made him a criminal, he has our blood. But he won't anymore," a wolf growled, and they all stepped in closer. A wolf lunged for me and pinned me to the ground. I kicked him off and ran to Dox as the wolves came at him. I changed back to my phoenix and let my flames grow around us. The wolves tried to jump on me but as my flames grew it was no use.

"Can't hide forever," a wolf snickered, and I felt a pair of claws grab me by my back and pull me to the ground. They clawed and scratched, at my body, until one grabbed me up and threw me against a tree. I went to get up when another jumped on me, and started throwing me around. I felt my body weaken more and more, until one threw me again and I slammed my head against another tree. I fell back and everything went black.

25

I opened my eyes wearily, my head was throbbing and my body ached. The events of last night flooded back into my memory, I and pulled myself to my knees, feeling a heavy weight around my neck. I remembered I had blacked out, the wolves had chained me to the tree, where I had woken up. Chains were around my neck, my wrists, and my wings, and they were short too, so I couldn't get very far. I felt my energy levels rise, but fall as quickly as they came, I lit a flame in my hand, and tried to burn the chains from the tree.

"It's titanium, Fire Boy." I looked up to see a Trader, leaned against a tree. I felt the flame disappear instantly.

"Where is he?!" I barked.

"Geez, take it easy. You're going to tire yourself out," the wolf explained. That's what I hated about Traders, they never gave you an answer.

"I really hate you guys," I groaned.

"I know right? Being hated and feared is all you really need, honestly. That's our job, make money get rich and be hated or feared by everyone," the wolf shrugged. I lit a flame and hurled it at the wolf, but he ducked just in time. I thought about this for a bit. They'd catch us listening for each other, any bit of contact was cut off. I screeched at the top of lungs, and the boy shoved me against the tree. His ears started twitching, as there was a long silence. There was a loud screech in return, two phoenixes tackled the wolf, and pinned him to the ground. Kalo looked up at me and burned the chains around me. I stared the boy in the face, and he was now full of panic.

"Where is he?!" I growled. I saw the panic drain from the boy's face, replaced with a slick look.

"Check the bottom of river," the Trader hissed, and my heart sank.

"Leave him! Take out the other Traders, leave the leaders to me!" I ordered.

The phoenixes, went into the Tunnels, but I flew over it, a little ways away from the Tunnels, was the river. Two wolves were closing in on my friend, moving him toward the river. Mori jumped on Dox, and he fell to the ground. I saw his clothes were ripped and torn, and he struggled to get up. I changed my form and swooped down to grab him. I went down to Dox with my claws outstretched, when Mori came and jumped on me from behind. The second I hit the ground, Edgar was on top of me clawing my face and tearing my clothes. I got up, but he only hit me again, backing me toward the water, when he hit me so hard I fell in. The water rushed down my throat, and I immediately couldn't breathe. Being in the water healed my aching my body, but I was still sore and exhausted. I pulled myself to the surface, but the rushing water swallowed me back under.

I suddenly felt hands grab me, and pull me out of the water. I opened my eyes, as Dox helped me up out of the water. I stood and shook the water from my wings.

"We need to go, now!" Dox looked panicked, and we started to run, when a voice made us stop cold.

"Take one more step, and you're out!" Edgar roared.

"What do you want? Money?" Dox asked.

"We want what's rightfully ours. You," Mori explained.

"Why do you need me? I thought I was worthless. You wasted your time on me," Dox was confused and I was shocked.

"You need to choose. Family, or friends. You're a Trader and you know that," Edgar growled.

"Again, you wasted your time. I'm staying with my tribe, with my family. You don't love me, not like they do. You treat me like a slave, Phoenix, Rogue, they've put aside me being dangerous. They trust me. They love me like a family, not a slave," Dox looked his brothers in the eyes, and he was serious. Mori hung his head, and the rage bottled up inside of him.

"Mori, don't be like that. If you wanted me to stay you shouldn't have been such a control freak. You wasted part of my life that I could've used to do what I wanted. You can change, but you don't want to. You want me to do it for you. You're afraid...And you're not my family, I never was to you," Dox walked away, and I was dumbstruck, not sure what to do.

"Phoenix," I looked back to Mori and Edgar, who handed me a package. "We need you to give this to him. He'd understand it coming from you," I nodded, and walked away without a word.

I had caught up with Dox, but I didn't say anything. We were finally back in our territory, when he stopped.

"You understand it better than I do...Do you think I did the right thing?" He whispered.

"I was supposed to give this to you, but I'm not good at finding 'the right time'," I shrugged, and handed him the package. He opened it, and was speechless. I looked over his shoulder, and was pretty surprised myself. It was a picture, of him and his brothers. All of them wore matching, ripped up suits, smiling, and they were happy. His hands shook, and suddenly, he broke the picture frame in a snap. He dropped it instantly, and I could see tears welling in his eyes. He howled, but it was hard to tell. He seemed angry, sad, and kind of happy all in one. He lowered his head and his ears twitched, as there was a howl in the distance.

"What did he say?" I wondered.

"He said he forgave me...That he was sorry...That he loved me."

We stood there in silence before walking home. After what had happened I had to ask about Dox's brothers. I knew he didn't like to talk about, so I thought it over in my head, until I just spoke straight out without thinking at all.

"Why don't you go back?" I wondered.

"Because, if I went back they wouldn't treat me like family like you do. They'd put me back on overnight shifts, and running their errands in town," Dox explained.

"You still-You still love your brothers, right?" It was hard to say, but when it came out I immediately wanted his answer.

"I-I-I can't tell you. Let's just get home." Dox formed and ran off, so I spread my wings and flew after him.

When we got home Dox walked off, and I didn't follow hm. If I knew my best friend, I knew I had pushed him, and that he'd think it over. He must've been upset, and didn't need me.

"What happened?" Rogue asked, wrapping her hands around my chest. I felt a little tense, but relaxed when I felt her hands on my skin.

"I asked the wrong question, and I don't think I'll be getting the answer anytime soon," I sighed.

"Well, don't be here, go fix it." Rogue nudged me on the shoulder but I shook my head.

"We're far over talking it out Rogue. That was years ago, this is different," I added. Kareen ran up to us in a hurry.

"Where is he?" Kareen asked.

"Don't. Kareen believe me, this'll only make it worse." Rogue shook her by the shoulders and she took a deep breath. Then she looked back at me angrily

"What did you ask?" She wondered.

"If he still loved his brothers after he turned them down," I groaned.

"Are you insane?! He's about as dumb as you! He's going to think it over and make the wrong decision. His family is going to fade to only me and the boys, because of you!" Kareen barked and stormed off.

"Fade?" I was shocked.

"If he loses his brothers, Kareen and the boys are all he has left," Rogue explained.

"I'm doomed," I moaned, and flew off to the meadows as far away from Dox as possible. He came a while later and leaned at the base of the tree where I was sitting up above.

26

"We're good?" I asked.

"Yeah. But don't bring up my brothers ever again," Dox nodded.

"I won't," I smiled.

"Do you think our sons are going to be human anymore?" Dox wondered.

"Well, considering Fangs hates the city now, and yours got drunk. I don't think so," I shrugged.

"I actually told them what they did, and they thought they were brainwashed," Dox snickered, and we both started laughing.

"I think we're good for now," I smiled down at my friend and he climbed up to sit next to me.

"I like the views up here, it's pretty," Dox sighed.

"I haven't been up here in a while," I realized. We sat there talking, and I had my best friend back. His ears started twitching and perked up suddenly.

"I'm hearing something," Dox said randomly.

"Well, obviously, but what?" I wondered.

"The whistle." Dox stood and jumped from the edge of the tree to the cliffside and his ears started twitching again.

"Whose is it?" I now heard this too, which was odd, I should've heard it sooner.

"It's different. It sounds kind of like the one I gave to Ford. It sounds different though," Dox explained. I formed and he climbed on my back and we rushed off.

We dropped down on the roof of the Agency and just like last time the door was open. We sped down the steps and into the simulator room. The lights were on but no one was around.

"They're cowards," Dox scoffed.

"But they play really good tricks," I knelt on the floor to look at a trail of blood.

"I've seen some pretty bad things but this is like a scientific lab and a haunted house all rolled into one. Remember that crazy holiday the Humans had when we were kids?" Dox shook his head disgustedly, remembering the event.

"We're never going to a party like that ever again. More likely because I put that teenager in a coma," I added. When we were about nine or so, we went to a party during Halloween in the city. Let's just say that after that, parties weren't our thing.

The trail of blood seemed odd. It led toward the wall, on the far corner. Dox followed the trail and tapped at the wall. The metal suddenly faded to the brick wall behind it. The bricks suddenly shifted and opened to a doorway and a winding staircase.

"I knew it," Dox mumbled to himself.

"What?" I asked.

"When I was younger, I swear I heard screaming coming from the other side of this wall. They told me I was just being paranoid, but it's here," Dox explained and peeled back a panel on the wall. There was a brick wall behind that, and when he pulled out a brick in the center the other bricks began to rearrange themselves. A staircase appeared ,and both of us were amazed by the discovery, but nothing felt right about it. We pulled our weapons from our pockets, and started slowly down the stairs.

Suddenly there was a soft whistling comings from further down. Then two voices fighting back and forth.

"Do you think they'll come?" A man spoke.

"I hate to doubt Saube, but I don't think so. If they really do come like he said, they're dumber than I thought," the other scoffed. There was a third voice now, but we both knew who it was.

"Enough talk, keep sounding that whistle," Saube ordered, and the whistle was blown again. There it was again, that same sound Dox had heard on the cliffside.

"He already knows, that's not me," Ford's voice added. We both looked at each other in amazement, and I nodded. We were ready to attack when Saube came back with another order.

"Go to the door up top, they should be here by now," he explained. I jumped up to the ceiling and pointed my gun at the floor, and Dox formed. He started barking as the guards rushed up the stairs. I fired two shots and the guards fell beneath me. Dox rushed ahead and through the doorway, as I dropped on the ground and followed. We found ourselves in another chamber, walls full of vials and test tubes on racks. "Don't move." Saube smiled slyly like he always did, and I knew we were caught. He had his gun pointed at Ford as they stood in the middle of the room. I dropped my weapon on the ground, but Dox kept his in his hands.

"Drop it!" Saube shouted.

"Give him to me first," Dox growled. Saube pushed Ford away, and Dox shoved him behind his back.

"Drop the gun, dog," Saube ordered again.

"Whatever," Dox shrugged and dropped the gun. It hit the floor and the trigger was hit as the gun fired a bullet and knocked Saube's weapon out of his hands. Dox and I picked up our weapons again, when a mob of guards rushed in from the back door to cover Saube.

"Get down," I stepped in front the two of them, and my eyes changed from violet to orange, as my body flamed up. I balled my hand into a fist and punched at the floor, and my flames spread from my body and blasted the guards. My eyes went back to their normal color and I looked at the guards, surrounding us.

"You-They're gone," Ford was shocked.

"It's a good thing too," Dox helped him to his feet. "You need to get out of here." They turned to the door, and Dox looked back at me.

"Are you coming or what?" Dox snapped, "We need to go." I said nothing, but my ears started twitching again.

'Phoenix, are you okay?" Dox repeated.

"Someone else is here. One of them isn't dead," I replied, not looking at my friend. We looked around but there was no one around.

"GUYS, BEHIND YOU!" Ford shouted. It was one of those comets, and I spread my wings and set aflame. It slammed into me and I fell to the floor. Dox grabbed me, and fired a few shots, and the figure in the shadows fell. My energy was fading fast, and I couldn't warn my friends. With fire being a dangerous element they couldn't get it to me, I'd lose my energy completely.

"Phoenix!" Dox shouted.

"What do we do?" Ford asked.

"We need to get him out of here…" My energy drained and I closed my eyes. I only knew I was safe, because Dox would bring me home.

But when I woke up, I was in Ford's house.

"...It was closer anyways," Ford shrugged.

"We can't be here. More importantly he can't be here. If he's hurt we're vulnerable," Dox replied angrily.

"What's happening now?" I rasped. Dox and Ford looked back at me and both breathed sighs of relief.

"You're fine, you just got hit with one of those power surges," Dox explained.

"What's a power surge?" I asked.

"I don't know. Ford said it's something that can confuse the senses or something like that," he added.

"That wasn't what I said. Were you even listening to me?" Ford snapped.

"You lost me at power surges," Dox shrugged and ignored him.

I sat up on the floor and leaned against the sofa.

"Do you guys remember anything?" Ford asked, handing us a loaf of bread.

"Not really," I shook my head.

"Wait, how did I get it?" Dox wondered.

"When you touched Phoenix it had spread through you. That obviously proves that neither of you remember anything," Ford realized. "You might want to go the hospital, memory loss is really effective."

"I think they got rid of our doctors," I added, as Dox handed me a piece of bread.

"Go, or it might get worse," Ford snapped.

"How long was I out?" I realized.

"It's one in the afternoon, so hours, and I mean many hours. So I'm going to remind you again that you should go to the hospital," Ford explained.

"We'll stay at your place for the night and leave in the morning," Dox decided grabbing his cloak.

"Where are you going?" Evian wondered, leaning against the sofa.

"Never mind that, but I can't live off of bread, Ford. I'm starving," Dox flipped his hood onto his head and started for the door.

"Dox," Dox looked back at Ford. Ford tossed him a bag of coins. "Save us the trouble and buy it will you." He walked out the door, and I couldn't help but laugh.

"What?" Evian snapped.

"You know what he's going to do with that money, right?" I snickered.

"What?" Ford asked.

"He's either going to give it to Mori for weapons, or keep it to himself," I laughed.

"DOX!" Ford shouted, grabbed his coat and rushed out the door.

Dox and Ford came back later, while Ford shouted at his cousin and Dox ignored him anyways. He tossed me an apple and I bit into it feeling a bit better to eat. Dox dropped the bag of food on the ground and pulled a box of sardines from it, and started eating.

"I bought you food, but you never ate it!" Ford groaned.

"That's breaking Trader code, Ford. If it's not bought, it's better," Dox scoffed and shoved a sardine in his mouth.

"I have to agree with them on this one. They can't get this stuff in the Woods. I mean, when was the last time you guys ate real food?" Evian shrugged.

"I ate a dead mouse last week," Dox nodded.

"Last time I ate was right now. I don't eat rodents like he does," I added.

"I actually got one on my way over there," Dox pulled a small, squirming mouse from his pocket and Evian screamed.

"Throw it out, idiot!" Evian screamed.

"Alright, alright, geez." Dox opened the window and chucked the creature outside.

We tore through the bag and ate everything. I felt much better, with my energy returning, and my power being restored. We spent the night at Ford's house, sleeping on the rug in the living room. We never really cared for beds anyways.

We got up early the next morning and left for the Woods. I formed and Dox climbed on my back and we flew home.

"Who was that person who hit you, Phoenix?" Dox asked, riding on my back.

"How should I know, you were the one that was still awake when it happened," I shrugged.

"I was?" Dox wondered. I turned off course, thinking we needed a break from all the events. I was going to tell Dox my plan, but I noticed he had fallen asleep on my back. So I went to the shed by the Tunnels and rested there myself.

27

Dox nudged me awake. I opened my eyes sleepily, looked up at him and closed my eyes again.

"No, get up we overslept." Dox nudged me again and I got to my feet. I stretched my wings and had him climb on my back. We got home but it seemed that almost everyone was still sleeping, so we had time.

"What do you mean we overslept? No one's awake yet?" I wondered.

"It was just before, and now it's noon. Something's up, either they're really tired or something happened while we were away. I'll get Kareen and we can meet in the Willow." Dox seemed half dazed, and probably still tired himself. But I nodded anyway and climbed the tree to find Rogue. Maybe I was still asleep but she looked almost as if she had passed away in her sleep. I thought I was crazy until I heard Dox's screams from the cliffside, and I knew I wasn't dreaming. Dox's screams turned to howls and as I knelt beside Rogue.

"How could I let this happen? I promised I'd protect her," Dox whispered. "I'm going to find who did this." The rest of the group woke at our screams and joined at the Willow. Kalo and Jillian rushed to the tree out of breath. They stopped dead in their tracks, and neither of them said anything for a moment.

"Are they-" Jillian couldn't finish.

"What does it look like to you?! Huh?! They're dead!" Dox barked at him and the fear in his eyes disappeared, he was expressionless. They both left and joined the others. Fangs, Ex and Vess came next.

"…No, she can't be...You can save her! You can save her can't you?" Fangs pleaded, tears in his eyes.

"I would but-" I sighed.

"No. Phoenix don't. If you save her you'll die too," Dox snapped.

"She can't die!" Fangs screamed, and ran for Rogue but I grabbed him and pulled him away.

"Fangs, she's gone!" I pleaded, and I yanked him out of reach. He stopped fighting me, and we all fell silent.

"... YOUR QUEENS ARE GONE!" We stood at the top of the tree, shouting over the crowd. There were screams and murmurs amongst the groups, and they all turned back to us.

"OUR PEACETIME WITH THE HUMANS IS OVER! AND THOSE WHO DENY THE ORDERS WILL FACE THE CONSEQUENCES," I explained. The people no longer spoke but looked to us in fear.

"From now on, you're only goal is to stay alive and know your place in our rein!" Dox added, and no one moved. Suddenly there were gasps in the crowd, and the color from my wings faded to black. There were screams from my people as their wings faded to black. The wolves too, their fur, now black as night.

Since then, everything had changed. The people were more violent with each other, fights broke out between everyone. Some fighting against their own, but one fight took it too far.

Two wolves were fighting against each other, and a swarm of people broke them apart. I rushed to the commotion, and there were shouts all over.

"...Leave then! But I would rather die here than out there all alone!" One wolf yelled.

"Then don't come begging to me for forgiveness!" the other shouted back. Kalo, amongst the people tore the wolf away, who then turned and punched him in the face.

"Get your hands off me!" The wolf barked.

"ENOUGH!" I shouted over them over all and they fell to silence. Dox peered down at the fight from the cliffside and caught my gaze. He came to join us himself.

"What's going?" He asked.

"Tell him needs to go! Said he'd rather leave the Groves then be involved in chaos! Because if he doesn't I will! I can't spend another day with hi,=m!" The wolf explained accusing the other one.

"I don't need to tell me what to do, I'll decide for myself." Dox said calmly, "In fact, Ryan, if it makes you both feel better, I could the two of you thrown in a ditch to fend for yourselves overnight. I know you're not that good with hand-to-hand combat, so it'll be an easy death."

Ryan was speechless and said nothing. I was shocked at my friend's reply, Dox was usually calm about these kind of things. Ryan turned and left without another word, and the crowd faded away. I slunk back to the Willow, and leaned against the trunk.

"Not you Thomas," Dox added. Thomas, who had turned to leave himself, turned back.

"Yes?" He nodded respectfully.

"I should expect it from Ryan, but not you. Ryan likes to be a total pain in the neck, but you're not. What I don't get, is that you'd leave. Where are you going to go?" Dox wondered.

"I'm originally from the mountains, I'm used to harsh things, but this feels wrong. We're not so sure that you're alright. You seem...Different," Thomas explained. Dox looked him over for a moment and grabbed him up. Thomas didn't budge, and didn't struggle.

"I don't need anyone looking out for me. But I can't lose my group, understand? You and the others know about as much as I do. Now, I'm going to give you a choice. You can either go back to your cave and follow my orders, or leave and be banished, understand?" Dox let him go, and Thomas ran back toward the Willow Forest. Dox looked back at me, and climbed up the cliffside without another word.

"...Phoenix, are you and Dox alright? I mean...I know what happened, but you guys are tough." Fangs smiled a bit and nudged me on the shoulder. I felt pretty happy that my own son would consider me as tough, but I didn't feel so tough then. I looked at him and then back out at the view from the Willow.

"What does it look like? They're gone, and I can move on with that. But he can't. He's a real tough guy, so now he's finally learning to be nice. She showed him how to do that, but now that she's gone, he's all messed up," I explained.

"Phoenix, you can't move on either, and we both know that," Fangs sighed.

"I loved her. And at least she didn't see me as who I was meant to be, or I would've scared her," I whispered.

"As you were meant to be? What does that have to do with it?" He asked.

"I can kill an average human being in a matter of seconds. If I had kept up with the program, and stayed at the Agency. I could destroy an entire…," I didn't know the word exactly. "I could destroy an entire planet. An entire planet, wiped from existence, all because of me. Rogue, and Kareen, they fixed that, and now I can be myself. But, I'm worried about him," I looked toward the cliffside, where Dox sat by himself, with his eyes closed, and his ears twitching.

"What is he doing?" Fangs wondered.

"He's trying to keep himself from getting upset," I groaned, and left Fangs in the tree. Dox didn't look at me, but kept his eyes forward.

"You okay?" I asked.

"I'm fine. I still have you," Dox looked up at me, and I sat down with him.

"You really miss her don't you?" I sighed.

"Of course, but I'm just struggling to let go," Dox tensed, and paused for a second. He started barking loudly, filling the silence in the Groves. He stopped and there an uprising of barking, a ways away. He had told Mori, I thought it was sweet.

"What did you say?" I wondered.

"I told him I needed some advice. He knows loss really well. Said to just forget. But I'll never forget her. I'll remember her forever," Dox smiled a bit, but it faded as quickly as it came.

"What is it?" I asked joining him at looking out at the view.

"My people are fighting, against each other, against the phoenixes. I don't want to go into war again. Especially against my best friend. I'm sick of fighting people, I've been fighting people my whole life, and I finally had a chance to settle down with a family when I got married. That was one of the best times of my life, I could finally stop fighting. Now that it's back, it might be different then. I won't fight the same way," Dox explained.

"We'll get through it like we always have. But I have to cheer you up first," I added.

"How are you going to do that?" Dox finally looked at me.

"Get the group together, we've got a bit of stealing to do," I explained partly. Dox smiled and nodded. We rounded up everyone, and at sundown emerged from the border, and there were still cars on the road. This was odd, but I guess everyone went back to driving since our attacks had stopped. Humans stepped out of their cars slowly and stood in awe.

"Should we do something?" Kalo whispered to me.

"Clear the street, they shouldn't be here," I ordered and pointed toward the road. Kalo signaled his group and they advanced forward, and the people ran inside. Kalo and his group picked up the cars and shoved them aside.

"Take them out!" Dox barked, and the entire army burst from the trees and into the city. Dox and I stayed behind, and stood in silence.

"Go enjoy yourself, and kill whoever gets in your way," I nodded, and Dox walked off in one direction, and I went the other way. I wanted to have a little fun myself and I for one, enjoyed the markets. I strolled through the streets silently, and stopped in front of a stand. I bit into a piece of fruit, and the juice dripped from my chin, and my teeth were all red from the juice. My ears perked up suddenly, and I stared through the stand, to see an old man, quivering behind it.

"I'm not going to hurt you, no worries. I'm just hungry," I sighed. I held an empty sack in my hand, I had taken it from another store. I filled the sack with the fruits, and left, but stopped.

"I'm letting you go, as a thank you," I added, before flipping my hood back over my head and strolling through the streets. I decided to sit at the top of the glass building, the highest point in the city, a perfect view of everything. Dox came and joined me a while later.

"Did it cheer you up or what?" I laughed. Dox's fangs were red, and I knew he hadn't been eating any of the fruits.

"This definitely cheered me up, thanks, Phoenix." Dox swung his arm around my shoulders, and I did the same to him. I slid over the bag and we feasted on the sweet fruits, watching the sunset. The door behind us burst open and Kalo and Jillian rushed onto the roof.

"This building's been cleared. The others have everything being taken out in chests, they're taking it home," Kalo pointed out, and we all peered down at the phoenixes and the wolves, working together, and taking the chests away.

"Those chests are filled with food, money, clothing, everything we could possibly need," Jillian nodded, and both of them smiled.

"Perfect," Dox smiled back and tossed them each a fruit. After eating the entire bag we all set back to work. Jillian and Kalo left us on the roof by ourselves, while Dox and I watched over everything. I stood back up again, and looked at the sky, before standing on the edge.

"You're jumping again?" Dox wondered.

"Exactly. You want in?" I asked.

"No I'm all set," he shrugged and pushed me off the roof. I loved to dive from high heights, it was fun for me. I formed and turned back around, flying over the roof. Dox ran to the edge and jumped on my back, and we flew around town together, we had done a lot of damage. Houses were trashed, and our chests lined the streets, ready to be taken away. There were shouts from down below, and I landed without being told to.

A wolf and a phoenix had cornered Evian and Ford against their house.

"Leave us be! Take whatever you want honestly!" Ford exclaimed.

"Exactly, and we want the human," the wolf shrugged.

"That shouldn't be the way you treat your own people, should it?" Dox grabbed the wolf up by his shirt, and she seemed panicked.

"They're family?" The girl asked shockingly.

"Leave that to me. Go take another family, and tell the others this house goes untouched. Understand?" Dox hissed. The wolf ran off, and the phoenix seemed frightened, and didn't budge. "I suggest you better get going before I strip those wings of yours too," he barked, and phoenix flew off, without a word.

We gathered up the chests and carried them home. Then we went back to the city and sat up on the rooftops, and strolled through the markets feasting on the foods left out. While the others sat on the rooftops, laughing and having fun, Dox and I strolled through the abandoned streets, quietly.

"Where do you think all the Humans went?" I wondered, scanning the empty streets. This seemed to interest Dox too, and we both looked up and down the long road, but no one was there.

"It feels really different without the people, it's really quiet. A little too quiet…" Dox's ears started twitching, and he paused for a bit.

"You sense something?" I asked cautiously.

"Someone's close, and it's not one of ours," Dox looked at me, and I formed in an instant, and he climbed on. I turned the corner, to see a small crackling fire glowing from the street.

"Drop on the roof of that house over there," Dox instructed, and I hovered over the small structure and went back to being human, dropping on the roof. Up close, the fire was very small, and hidden by houses and apartment buildings along the street. Standing by the fire, was a man and a woman, two girls, and a young boy. They crowded around to keep warm, in the little clothing they had. The family huddled by the fire, sitting in front a house. They were a poor family, and Dox and I looked at each in an instant.

"Should we attack them?" I whispered.

"I don't know, maybe we should check for a Bridge before attacking. I'd attack an average human, but I wouldn't attack children, I'm not that cruel," Dox shrugged. He had a point, it seemed wrong to go after innocent people, even if they weren't one of us. I peered down at the family from the roof, and getting control of the fire, made it disappear.

"I could've sworn I put more wood than that," the woman stared at the burnt wood, puzzled.

"It's alright, I'll see what else I can get to burn," the man sighed and turned toward the house, which I was guessing was theirs. As the man reached for the door, I brought back the fire, burning twice as bright.

"George look!" The woman gasped, and the man looked back at the blazing fire in astonishment.

"It's a miracle," she whispered, and a smile grew across her face.

"Wait...It couldn't be, those animals, they're playing with us Sarah." The man looked up at the rooftops with fear.

"Papa, are those animal people going to hurt us?" A girl asked.

"It's alright, so long as they don't know we're here, we're safe," the man nodded reassuringly and the child must've believed him and his stupidity. Humans were oddly clueless and believed in so much hope, I was shocked. Dox looked at me in astonishment, we were both surprised by this, thinking the same thing. We didn't attack. and we left.

28

We gathered the group and started home, with the wolves riding on the phoenixes, as they carried the chests. Dox and I led the group, with him on my back, as I carried a chest in my claws.

"Are we going for the Agency today, or are we waiting it out?" Dox asked, looking back at the city.

"I don't know, maybe we should wait. Let the others be happy while it lasts. They really had a good time, I'd hate to make them go into a fight right away," I shrugged, glancing back the tribe.

"We'll have to do it sooner or later," Dox pursed his lips in thought.

"I know," I sighed.

"You're worried too, I'm guessing?" He wondered.

"I don't know why, but I feel like it would be wrong to take them out with the entire group. I feel like there's something we're not seeing," I explained.

"You have a point," Dox nodded.

"You want to go, don't you?" I groaned.

"I can't lose the rest of my people. Now my brothers are after my people now that I have no queen. Either I find another queen, or lose them all, but I won't find anyone else. Now that she's gone, I could lose everything," Dox put his face in his hands, and I could tell he was really worried.

"You won't lose Ex and Vess," I added.

"Yes I will. They don't consider me as family because I'm never around. If I lose them, I'm done for. No other rulers, no queen and I lose them to the Traders. I'm already an outcast, how worse can it get?" He groaned.

"Do you want me to answer?" I asked.

"Of course not, that'd be stupid.." Dox looked up and back at the group. He must've been checking for his sons.

"Oh no," Dox sighed.

"Is it bad news?" I asked.

"Yes."

"Then I don't want to hear it. You get all worked up over nothing."

"Well that's rude," Dox snapped.

"What? It's the truth," I shrugged.

"The boys are gone," he added.

"How many?" I sighed, stopping, and looking back.

"All three." He pointed toward the back of the group where he had seen them last. Kalo and Jillian came up beside me looking in the same direction.

"They're gone aren't they?" Jillian asked.

"Yeah. Keep the group heading in the same direction and take them back. We'll get them ourselves," I ordered, and Kalo flew off in the other direction.

We flew above the city, using the X-ray vision to look out for them.

"Do you see them?" I asked.

"Yeah, but….You're not going to like this any more than I do," he sighed, and pointed at a house, and we dropped on the roof. I pulled out my dagger, and he pulled out his gun. I grabbed the edge of the roof, and hanging from the edge, banged at the window. It cracked open, and we slipped inside…To a girl's room?

"You don't think?" Dox looked at me in shock.

"Oh they're going to be real sorry they left after this."

We went down the steps, to find all three of them, with a two girls and a boy. They ducked behind the table, but we didn't care to attack them right away.

"I know this looks bad but I can explain!" Fangs threw his arms in the air as if he were being robbed, and so did Ex but Vess just took a step backwards.

"You're not a part of this?" Dox asked him, and he shook his head.

"No, I just know their brother, I thought he was a Bridge so I thought you'd be okay with it," Vess explained so quickly the words just fell out of his mouth.

"Anything else you want to tell me?" Dox added.

"Ex and Fangs are dating human girls!" he added quickly.

"I'm going to kill you," Ex growled at him.

I glowered at Fangs and he and Ex looked to Vess.

"Who are these people?" One of the girls asked, peeking up from behind the table.

"This is-" Vess was going to introduce us but Dox made him stop dead in his tracks.

"Get over here!" Dox growled, and Vess stood at his side. Fangs and Ex followed without a word, and we slipped out the window without a word.

The trip home was quiet, and all of us exchanged looks on the long walk back.

"We couldn't fly back?" Dox snapped at me, probably still mad at his sons.

"What am I your slave? I do the hard part carrying you on my back," I growled back. I was angry at Fangs and my anger suddenly was redirected at Dox, but I sure did mean it. So I spread my wings and left them.

"Get back here! Phoenix, wait!" Dox shouted behind me, but I kept flying. I landed on the cliffside, and didn't look back once, and this time I felt no regret in leaving them.

"I should've seen it from the start. Letting him ride on my back was a mistake," I grumbled. But I sat down and waited for them to return, just because I was mad, didn't mean I'd change my mind about being sure they got back safely. Sure enough, they came and none of them were too happy.

"What was that for?! You left us!" Fangs shouted.

"You have wings, why didn't you use them?' I scoffed.

"I stayed behind for my friends unlike you. I'm surprised you left Dox," he protested.

"Serves him right for being friends with a phoenix. I'm not going to be nice forever," I shrugged.

"What's up with you? You're attacking weird," Fangs wondered suspiciously.

"I just noticed how his group is a group full of backstabbers. Mori and Edgar, said they'd help me out, then they made me lose my money, paying every week. See what I mean? Wolves can be backstabbers. Dox will get used to ordering me around, and I'll turn on him," I explained.

"More like I'll turn on you," I turned to Dox who stood only a few feet away, feeling at his pocket, "So we're a group full of backstabbers, nice to know."

"Not my fault you ruined me. Could've let your brothers sell me at the auction. Then you could've lived the life you wanted. You know, getting forced to hold a gun your hand and shoot people for the rest of your life. Who knows, maybe you've would've killed me in one of your sessions," I shrugged again.

"What did you just say to me, Fire Boy? If I could live the life I wanted, you'd still be back there, hoping for a sky full of stars. You know how you got here? Me. I saved you, I signed that contract that meant I owned you, and I still do. I'm not like my brothers, I give people their freedom, and a choice. If my brothers had you, you wouldn't have your wife, you wouldn't have your son. Most importantly, you wouldn't have your group, and you wouldn't have your rein. I got you here, remember that?" Dox growled.

"I remember getting robbed, being broke, and treated like I don't matter. In fact, I think you were treated the same way. Isn't that right? You know, being the glitch in the system," I glowered back.

"You didn't."

"I did. Hurts doesn't it? In fact, I remember people thinking I was the glitch. Being the only one of my kind. But I could tell it was you the moment I saw you. You were messed up, no wonder you're an outcast," I added. I must've got him all ticked off, because he didn't look calm anymore.

"You take that back! We all know that isn't true!" Dox barked.

"Really? Or is it? How else were you treated the way you were. Why didn't they love you, huh?" I readied myself for his attack, but it didn't come. Fangs, who stood there in silence, grabbed my arm tightly.

"Phoenix stop," he whispered.

"I guess it makes sense why you grew up in solitary confinement. Why no ever taught you how to feel anything. Without me, you'd be nothing, you'd be ruthless, and live your entire life that way. Seems fitted for you, doesn't it?" I pressed angrily.

"Phoenix quit it," Fangs snapped. I turned leading my son with me, and Dox jumped on my back, and I was pinned to the cliffside. I kicked him off me and he didn't come at me again. Fangs and I rushed off the cliffside, and he led me inside the cave and I had given him. All his books were closed and stacked in one corner, and his odd contraptions were placed in another.

"Are you okay?" he asked.

"Yeah, I'm-" I felt pain in my wings again and I assumed they were broken again.

"No," Fangs breathed.

"What?" I wondered. He led me to a mirror, and I looked at my wings. My wing was ripped, and slit, up to my back where it connected with my body.

"I told you to stop, what is wrong with you?"

"I meant that, and there's no shame in it. He's a glitch and he knows it better than anyone. He's the only wolf I know that can't be bad or good. Bad is what he's meant to be, but he's not, and there's the glitch I was talking about. I may be a total idiot, but he's a glitch, I know that I'm good, and he just can't choose. He's had the decision for years now, but he just plans on not making the decision at all," I explained.

"Oh, so I'm the glitch now. I spared your life back there, I saved you from being a slave to someone who wouldn't even care about you!" Dox stood in the mouth of the cave glowering at me.

"Yeah, I don't care what you did. I think I would've been better off being sold like I didn't matter," I growled.

"I am bad, I let anger get the best of me, but I can be good too. Why, do I have to decide so your life can be straight? I mean, what would you do if I chose to be bad, huh? What are you going to do? You couldn't kill me because you'd remember when we were friends, and remember that bad can't be friends with good. I was meant to be bad, but I chose to be good because I saw how much better it was. Where people cared no matter who you were. I can't be assigned anywhere, so you have to do your job and live with it. Just because I'm a wolf I'm meant to be bad, but what if I wanted to be good? Your people would ban us. But I can see why you would. Wolves are bad, it's our nature, right?" Dox explained. He didn't say anything else, and left the cave. I heard him howl orderly, and there was a rumble of footsteps. I stepped outside to see his group burst through the barrier and disappear. With a wave of my hand, the barrier closed, and I turned to leave when Fangs stepped out after me.

"What-What happened?" He asked. I didn't reply.

"Phoenix?" He asked again.

"Wolves are no longer united with our group. I need you to help me so I can tell the others. They might want to hear it from you more than me. I'm going to talk with Kalo before I talk the others," I explained before walking off.

29

"...You can't be serious," Kalo whispered in shock.

"I know it's difficult...But I can't let you see Jillian anymore. I'm setting out new orders, and denial...I'll find something to do then," I sighed.

"Alright. Should we tell the Council?" He suggested.

"They don't need to know. They'll find out soon enough," I shook my head. Kalo disappeared, and Fangs came back.

"I told them...But they're pretty upset, and they wanted to hear it from you," he nodded.

"They won't be upset once Kalo explains the new set of orders," I shrugged.

"You don't seem that well yourself. Phoenix, you didn't have to make them leave, you know that don't you?" He looked up at me worriedly.

"I never told him to leave, that was his idea," I snapped. There was a screech from the border, and I groaned and formed, and Fangs followed. We flew over to find two wolves barking at Kalo and his men. I screeched as they all looked up. We dropped in, to see Mori and Edgar.

"Leave us," I ordered, and the phoenixes flew off, "What are you doing here?"

"Not the invitation we were expecting, considering we've never thought to come to your place for this. But Edgar suggested we take a walk away from chaos. So if this goes bad, it's all your fault," Mori glanced at Edgar.

"Answer the question!" I barked.

"Well, since you guys split, we're specifically targeting you two for not paying up for the past few years. Ever since you guys got together, we stopped charging you, but now that there's that split, you have to pay up," Edgar explained.

"What?! No. What about 'no worries we'll take care of it'?" I exclaimed.

"Oh, we never said that. Dox said he'd take care of it, but he's broke too. So either you pay up now or we'll be expecting your visits every week. You're a good client, so we're dropping the price by a bit, but that doesn't mean you're off the hook. Get the money and bring it to us, the only thing we need is the money now. This time, we'll pay you back in whatever you need, anytime," Mori explained.

"Well you're not getting it from me, so go steal from some other stubborn idiot," I growled. Edgar shrugged, they both walked away.

"You might want to get that wing fixed, Phoenix. You'll want to be strong enough when that glitch comes back for another fight. We can treat that for you. That is if you still trust us," Mori added.

"Oh believe me, I never thought to trust you even when I met you two. You better not come back here, and tell that glitch brother of yours that he's no exception," I glowered at the two wolves as they walked through the border and disappeared.

"What are they making you pay for?" Fangs asked.

"That doesn't matter, I need to get a group together, and we're going to the city. Put this in your pocket too, I have a feeling we won't be the only ones." I handed him a dagger, while disregarding his question, and called for Kalo. He came when called already with his warriors.

"City?" Kalo suggested.

"Exactly. No more people than us," I nodded. We grouped together and took off.

"What exactly are we looking for?" One of the warriors asked as we neared the city.

"That's classified, I just need you to watch my back, and be sure no one follows us," I explained.

We touched down in the city, and I led the group to a back alley. I took Fangs with me, and the guards stood around the entrance. I felt at the wall for a certain brick and pulled it out. Suddenly the bricks in the wall rearranged themselves to make a door.

"What is this place?" Kalo asked.

"Its location is classified," I snapped, and started down a trail of stairs as the door closed behind us. I flipped up my hood, and motioned to my son to do the same.

"These guys don't know who we are, say nothing about yourselves, and hide your wings," I added.

We came to an open room where there were a bunch of wolves, playing board games, talking, and trading. Two wolves stepped in front of us, and looked me over.

"Who are you?" One of them asked.

"That's classified." I shoved them out of my way, and went down a back hallway. There was another room, with a table and a wolf waiting there.

"No one knows?" The wolf glanced at me interestingly.

"No one knows," I nodded.

"Take the hood off, man, no one's going to hurt you here, Fire Boy," the wolf grinned. "Who's the kid?"

"Not up for sale," I snapped and pulled off my hood.

"What do you need?"

"Money."

"How much?"

"Enough to pay my rent. The groups split, and they dropped the price," I explained.

"HQ can't always pay your rent, you know that," the wolf nodded.

"I am loyal, aren't I?" I placed a sack of coins on the table.

"Stolen?"

"Stolen from the glitch," I nodded.

"Better pay it off quick before he finds out or he's going to kill you," the wolf snickered.

"I don't have to worry about that dog," I groaned and walked back down the hallway when one of the wolves stopped me again.

"Give it back, Fire Boy," the wolf growled, "You know the rules, no magic." At the word "magic" the wolves crowded around.

"You said 'magic' but you never said black magic," I shrugged and pushed past them.

"You don't use black magic, unless you stole it," another snapped and I turned around.

"Okay, I stole it, but I need it, please," I begged.

"For what?" One looked at me suspiciously.

"None of your business." I pulled Fangs close to me and wrapped my cloak around us. In a flash we were gone and outside, the warriors looked at us in shock.

"Teleportation? But that's…-" Kalo didn't finish too amazed to say.

"You don't tell anyone and that goes for all of you. Don't tell the wolves and especially don't tell Dox," I snapped. We took off and luckily made it back home without any trouble from the wolves. But I had a feeling I'd be banned from Trader HQ.

30

I got out of trouble with HQ but not with Dox and his group. He came a day later with four guards at his side.

"I never like playing these games with you," he sighed.

"Why, because I always win?" I scoffed.

"No, because you cheat, you did something with my money and I need it back before they come looking for me," Dox explained.

"Well, I'm not cheating this time, and I can't get back something I gave away," I shrugged.

"Where is it?" Dox groaned.

"I would tell you to check HQ, but I think you're banned from there," I replied randomly. Dox shoved me to the ground, and motioned to the Willow Forest.

"Uproot the trees in back," Dox ordered. The wolves formed and disappeared into the trees. I turned back to Dox worriedly, and got to my feet.

"I'm not looking for a fight, I needed the money. Only wolves can pay with their own money. I have to pay with stolen money and, they don't really like you, so...-" I explained.

"I got it, we're not very close, but why couldn't you take it from someone else?" Dox growled.

"They won't let me take loans, and I can't call favors from HQ to pay my rent," I pleaded. "You have to let me borrow your money, I'll pay you back I promise."

"I'll let you off the hook, if you do me a favor," Dox nodded.

"Anything," I breathed a sigh of relief.

"I need you to go back there and pull me a transfer loan," Dox added.

"Can I do anything else? Because, I'm sort of banned from HQ," I hung my head.

"What?! What did you do?!" Dox exclaimed. I grabbed him by the wrist and put my palm in his hand. I went to pull my hand away, and a pile of black dust lay in his hand. It magically traced out the veins on his arm, and disappeared into his skin.

"You stole black magic from Head Quarters?" Dox smiled amusedly.

"I don't know why I took it, I just thought we could use the extra powers," I shrugged.

"Wait, did you say 'banned'?" His smile faded.

"Yeah, why?" I looked to him worriedly, I had a feeling this was bad.

"Phoenix, if you're banned from Headquarters, your payments won't get through. I'm banned too, so now neither of our payments get-"

There was a scream from the Willows, and there were thundering howls and barks.

"No, no, no. Not yet, I'm not ready," Dox mumbled under his breath. There was a short silence and suddenly two wolves appeared through the trees. At first I thought they were Dox's wolves, when I noticed they were bigger than them...It was his brothers.

"I thought you said you separating?" Edgar seemed puzzled.

"He took my money, and it turns out we're both banned from HQ. None of our payments are getting in," Dox groaned. "And it's all his fault." He glowered at me, and I held his gaze. It was back to being enemies like the first time.

"I don't care whose fault it is, we need your payments," Mori snapped.

"Did you not just hear what I said? None of our payments are getting in," Dox repeated himself.

"We can fix that. So long as we get your payments, and time's up. We can get the money to HQ by putting you under our list of anonymous clients. They won't know a thing, hopefully," Mori explained

"But you still need to give us the money," Edgar added.

"I don't have it, but he does." All three of them looked at me.

"I took his money and payed my rent. That's what you wanted, isn't it?" I explained.

"Yeah, you did it right. But you shouldn't be stealing from another Trader. It's the new set of rules since other clients are also stealing from us. We also need you to pay us back for that black magic you stole. It's probably already in your blood, so we can't get it out of you now, so you have to pay us back in the amount it's worth." Mori nodded. then he looked at Dox. "You need to pay it off, whether it's stolen or not."

"Come on Mori, cut me some slack, I pay it all the time it's only once," Dox groaned.

"Yeah, we're tired of you and your complaints. Just give us the money and we'll cut you some slack after," Edgar added. With that they left us alone, which was odd because I thought we were going to get beat up, or charged more than usually. But with Mori and Edgar, it was all for the money.

"Will you stop trying to ruin my life?!" Dox barked.

"Okay, look, I didn't know! They expect money, they don't say how!" I shouted back. We both fell silent, I looked at Dox and he caught my gaze and we both turned away.

"I do miss you-" We both started at the same time and then suddenly turned away.

"We need to bring the groups back together, don't we?" Dox sighed.

"If we do, it'll stop the problems with your brothers, our families can be back together," I shrugged.

"Ex and Vess did say they missed playing Fangs," Dox bit his lip, he didn't seem so sure about it. Suddenly there was a rumbling noise coming from outside the border.

"What's that?" Dox seemed alerted, and his ears starting twitching again.

"I don't know." I spread my wings and hovered above the barrier, overlooking the Woods. There was the rumble again, and the trees shook wildly. Suddenly there was a loud crash, and far off in the distance near the border, one of the trees fell. I focused in to see a construction crew, with big machines, with the lab logo on each of them.

"DOX, THE AGENCY!" I shouted at the top of my lungs, as screams erupted through the woods. We met up on the cliffside. Fangs must've noticed because he came and met us there too.

"What's going on? I heard the noise," Fangs rushed up behind us, and stopped dead in his tracks.

"We can fix it, no worries," I nodded reassuringly, but both Dox and Fangs looked at me as if I were crazy. I actually thought I had plan.

"You have a plan?" Dox asked.

"Make it up as we go," I shrugged.

Suddenly there were barks and howls, coming from the Caverns.

"No, we're too late." Dox's skin turned pale with shock and fright, and I knew what he was thinking. They had already gotten to the wolves, that meant we had no time for a plan. I raised my arms in the air and the border started to shift.

"We can't stop them from getting here, but we can protect ourselves. Get the group into those underground bunkers you had built, call for any of your tribe that's left too. We can save as many as we can. The border walls are shifting, and growing thicker, that should be enough to hold them off for now." We told the groups our instructions, and in a few minutes, both of our groups were below ground in the underground bunkers.

"Are you sure this will hold them off?" Dox asked worriedly.

"No," I shook my head.

"You're going to tell them the truth, right?" Dox sighed.

"No. It'd be too much for them to handle. I don't want anyone to worry Are you going to tell them?" I asked him next.

"No. The less they know the better-" Suddenly there were voices up above, and we all fell quiet.

"Cowards. Pull them out, this whole thing is stupid," a guard scoffed. Suddenly the whole ground above our heads began to crumble, and shake. Shouts of orders and commands coming from above. Everyone screamed, and suddenly our screams turned to resistance, as we were dragged from the bunker and thrown into nets. The Guards were able to tear down the bunker and jump inside, they grabbed Dox and I and pulled us out, and threw us to the ground. I felt hands grab me, and put me in handcuffs. They dragged everyone away, and threw us into trucks and vans. I pulled at the handcuffs, but the guard was much stronger than me and pulled me toward the van anyways. They shoved me in a van with Fangs, Dox, Ex, Vess,, Kalo and Jillian. Countless more of us packed into the other cars, and driven away. We were all quiet for a moment, and glanced at each other, then I met Dox's gaze and we glared at each other coldly.

"So that was your idea of holding them off?" Dox scoffed.

"Like you had a better plan shoving us in the dirt?" I snapped.

"Never would've happened in the first place if you weren't fighting with each other!" Vess barked. We both looked at him then back at each other.

"Fire Boy," Dox glared at me.

"Glitch," I snarled back.

"Idiots, both of you." Fangs glanced at both of us with a cold stare.

"I don't think I've ever seen you two not in a fight. You just can't be happy with each other," Ex added.

"If you hadn't called me a glitch in the first place, you could've kept your wing," Dox looked back at me.

"Maybe if you could pick which side you're on, I wouldn't have," I shrugged.

"I hate your stupid conversations," Dox sighed.

"How is this stupid?" I scoffed.

"Because you started it," he snapped.

"How about a game?" Ex suggested.

"If it's getting a chance to kill your best friend, I'm totally playing," I nodded, and both Dox and I seemed to agree on that.

"No, not that. You have to get us out of this van, without fighting," Vess explained.

"Can I just say, that's going to be impossible for them," Kalo pointed out, joining in the conversation.

"Exactly," Jillian shrugged. We glanced at each other, and snapped the chains around our wrists.

"Let's make this easy where you don't bother me," I groaned.

"I never bother you, it's the other way around," Dox pointed out. I went to the back doors of the van and went to search for the lock.

"Lock's on the outside dummy," Dox added.

"And what are you going to do, take out the driver?"

Suddenly the car swerved off the path, and flipped over. The window glass shattered, the back doors rattled as they began to come loose. Dox kicked at the metal doors until they were unlocked and wide open. I looked back at Dox in shock. He got out of the van and we all went out right after him. The others and I went toward the Woods, but Dox stayed where he was and looked at the van.

"What are you doing? Let's go," I snapped.

"We can't go back there, and if I know them, they're already coming." Dox put his hand on the tire of the car, and soon the whole car was black, it was fixed.

"How did you do that?" Jillian asked.

"Black magic. Phoenix help me move it back on the trail." Dox and I lifted the van and got it back on the trails, then we hopped in.

"...Who knows how to drive?" I asked.

"I can drive," Dox suggested.

"You said you didn't know how to," I pointed out.

"I know how to make the car turn and stuff like that. I don't know anything else," Dox added.

"Good enough for me," I shrugged. Dox actually meant the truth that he didn't know how to drive. None of us knew how to get it started.

"Which one's the break?" I wondered, looking around at all the levers and buttons on the radio.

"I think it's that one, or it might be another one," Kalo suggested.

"I've seen it in a movie, there's usually some kind of manual," Dox overlooked everything, but he still didn't seem sure.

"When on earth have you had time to watch a movie?" It was the only thing that interested me in the moment.

"Mori watches a lot of old movies, you get used to it. He's got them all on tapes. But you know, they never had anything about cars," Dox explained.

"You people are hopeless! Let me drive," Fangs groaned, so we gave him a shot. He really knew how to drive and we got going. Dox and I jumped in the back, and Vess climbed up front.

"I found a map," Dox picked up a thickly folded piece of paper and I sat next to him, as we spread it out.

"Where are we going?" I asked.

"Through the city. I have a plan this time," Dox nodded, "We pass through the city and hide out there for a while, then when everything's clear we head home," we all agreed to go and sped through the city all day and all night.

We finally pulled over and all of us stopped to rest. We were pretty deep in the city, and exhausted. Since Dox and I liked to stay up all night, we sat up front to give more space to the others who were sleeping. But late through the night I felt really tired and fell asleep. I woke up soon in the dark to see red and blue flashing lights in the small mirror. I looked at Dox but he was asleep too. I shook him awake and he looked at me in alarm.

"Dox, the police. Hurry, drive," I snapped. He quickly started up the car and sped forward at top speed. The wind rushed through our faces as the car bounced along the cracked pavement. The sirens buzzed loudly, and it woke everyone in the back.

"What did you do?!" Fangs groaned.

"We'll explain later. We have to go!" I looked out the mirror on the side of the car, it wasn't just the police but, the Agency too.

"Okay, we really have to get have to get going. Can we go any faster?" I suggested.

"We can only go as fast as the vehicle," Vess added. I groaned and slipped out the window of the car, up onto the roof. I formed and flew low over the roof of the car. One by one all of them climbed from the car and climbed on my back. Dox lastly did something different. He jumped from the car as it swerved off the road and onto the sidewalk. The cars behind him stopped and they all ran toward the van. They couldn't see him, he was invisible.

"Where did he go?" Ex asked worriedly.

"You can't see him?" I was a little lost.

"Of course not," Vess added.

"I guess it's the program," I shrugged when I heard him whistling from the street. I dove for the street and got real close. He ran alongside me and hoisted himself up. He pulled off his hood and everyone looked at him in shock.

"How are you invisible?" Fangs asked.

"It's just a little something I picked up from an old friend," he shrugged holding a glowing ring in his hand.

"You stole it from Edgar," I corrected him.

"How did you know?" Dox sighed.

"Because he's the nice one that keeps his mouth shut when he needs to, unlike you and Mori. Plus, he works with magic, Mori works with objects, it's all in the certain department," I explained.

"Where are we going again?" I asked changing the subject.

"Far off from here. We can hide out there and lay low for a while until they give up the hunt and go home," Dox explained.

"And what if this chase, never ends? What if they keep looking for us?" Fangs added.

"Always rely on the phoenix to ask more questions," Dox groaned.

"Always rely on the wolves to get you into trouble," I snapped.

"They'll give up eventually. It's not like they'll chase us forever," Dox shrugged and I groaned. I called to the rest of the group and an eruption of screeches and howls came from behind us.

"They'll meet up with us soon," I added.

31

We kept flying for hours on end, and I was starting to get tired. My muscles ached, and I was low on energy, so I turned to the city to find a place to land. It was pretty early in the morning and there was no movements out in the streets so it gave me some time to rest anywhere I wanted. With the city not being so hidden from view, it would be difficult to find a place to go. I luckily found a spot, on the rooftop of another building that was covered by the other structures around it. So I landed as silently as I could to not wake the others, and went to sleep.

"Get up, we have to go." Someone shook me awake, and I looked up at Dox.

"Why?" I asked, getting to my feet.

"We need to keep going, we can't stay in the city. With this many people, it'll be too easy to get spotted by someone," he explained, and I shook my head and sat back down.

"Yeah, I'm not going anywhere until I'm ready to leave," I wouldn't leave, I was tired, and wanted to rest just a bit longer.

"Please, Phoenix, not now," Dox groaned.

"I don't get why you're so upset. Everyone rides me and not you. Look, I like your plan, but I'm not going anywhere until I get a chance to have a break. I haven't slept once through this trip, and I'm exhausted," Dox was starting to get on my nerves, which didn't happen much, but I tried my best to stay calm.

"I really don't want to push you around, but we really have to get going. We can stop and rest later," Dox growled.

"Actually, we can take a break, and pause for a minute. You ride me, I choose when we stop. I'm not a machine, I get tired. If you want a machine, go talk to Saube, maybe he can make you into one," I snapped.

"I get that you're tired, but we need to keep going, and I thought you followed the orders of your rider?" Dox pointed out. He had a point.

"That changes when there's this many people. You're really pushing my limits, so don't come yelling at me when we're stuck walking the rest of the way!" I tried to relax again but it was getting difficult. Dox groaned and turned away from me.

"I wouldn't stand so close to the edge if I were you," I added.

"Why? I'm not going to fall," Dox scoffed.

"But you might," I pointed out.

"What are you talking about?-" Dox turned back to me and I shoved him off the side of the building with a rush of flames. He just luckily grabbed the side of the building.

"Are you insane!? Help me!" Dox barked.

"I thought wolves could fly?" I shrugged.

"Not everyone's half bird, idiot! Now help me!" Dox groaned.

"Yeah, I'm all set. I'd rather watch," I shrugged and sat down beside him just out of his reach. "You know, this could've all been avoided, if you had listened to me!"

"I see that now. But really, if you wanted to speak your mind you could've done that earlier and not have pushed me off to explain." He glared up at me and tried to grip harder at the cement. "You can have it your way alright? On one condition, you have a plan to follow," he added. I held out my hand and helped him up.

"Fair enough," I agreed to the terms partially. I had a tough time following plans. "Maybe I should come clean now while we're still here. But we may or may not be heading in the right direction," I confessed.

"What?! How did you not know where we were going?" Fangs asked.

"I did, but I don't know which way is north, or south, actually I don't really know where we are, exactly," I explained.

"That's actually my fault. I don't know where it is either," Dox added.

"So none of you where we are?" Vess groaned. "What about the compass I gave you?"

"I kept it in my pocket." Dox pulled the little trinket out of his pocket and handed it to his son.

"All I know is that it's somewhere towards the northwest," He shrugged.

"Wait a minute, how would you know that if you don't what north and south is?" Ex asked.

"Oh simple. Ask Edgar. He know a lot of stuff about hideouts and getaways. They're meant for hiding from the law, so they're pretty useful in our family," he explained

.

"Actually speaking of family, there's something you should see," Jillian added staring out at the city. Dox and I stood and followed his gazes to the edge of the city. White vans gathered outside the city, with what looked like wolves.

"Why is the Agency using Traders?" Kalo wondered.

"Natural instincts, we're meant for using instinct which makes us good trackers," Dox explained.

"Wait so you can track people?" Vess asked.

"I can, I just need something to pick up the scent," he nodded totally unaware that his son was plotting a plan.

"What if we found someone far off? We could throw them off," he suggested.

"I don't know. That's difficult," Dox shook his head.

"It's not difficult if you're hunting a lynx," I added.

"Do have anything of hers?" Dox asked.

"No but it should be easier once we get into the Arctic-" Fangs explained. Dox wasn't paying attention, he had caught something.

"I found her! She's close." He sprinted down the side of the building and disappeared into the streets. I followed him just to be safe that he didn't get caught. I followed from up above as he found Lynx, sitting on the side of the street licking her paw. She noticed him quickly and took off. The chase wasn't long at all. Dox closed in on her and grabbed the back of her neck and took her down before she even got to the end of the street. Lynx struggled and pleaded to be let go. I returned to the roof with the others, and waited for him to come back. Sure enough he came back with the scruff of her neck in his teeth.

"Let me go! You don't understand, its coming!" She pleaded.

"That's a lie," Dox growled, still holding on to her.

"No, no, the serum! It's coming! They'll kill us all! The Agency hired the Traders to do their bidding in exchange for the Agency to save them. You have to believe me!" She cried.

"I wouldn't believe a Lynx if it was the last thing I did. Even if this is true, why are you coming through the city?" I asked.

"Why else?! We're afraid, it's the only way to go. I saw it with my own eyes. One of my troops was attacked by the Agency. They grabbed a hold of her and cupped this plastic mask to her face, like an oxygen mask, I watched her inhale this kind of gas, and she dropped to the ground," Lynx explained, I saw the fear in her eyes, and I knew she wasn't lying. Dox saw it too and let her go, he backed away in shock.

"They're killing them with a serum?" Fangs asked.

"Yeah, yeah, it's the truth. Come on you look like a nice kid, help would mean the world to me right now. They won't believe but I promise I'm telling the truth. Tell him to let me go," Lynx pleaded.

"Let's leave her alone guys, let her go. We can tell the others," Fangs nodded.

"Thank you, thank you…" Lynx stammered.

"Get out of here before I change my mind," Dox growled. Lynx jumped from rooftop to rooftop and disappeared from view.

"I don't trust her, I bet she'll be back," Dox stared after her.

"Yeah, back with a whole lot of trouble," I scoffed.

"What now? We don't have any troops our group was captured and we're not safe ourselves," Fangs wondered.

"Well maybe if you hadn't let her go we wouldn't have her to worry about!" Dox barked.

"She's slick, she'll cause us some problems, for both of us especially," I added.

"Sorry, I'm sensitive, what can I do about?!" Fangs protested.

"Maybe try not to say anything and let us handle it. Now we lost our one chance at figuring this out. She's either lying or using us in one of her schemes," Dox snapped.

"Or she could be telling the truth," Fangs suggested. "She was probably trying to escape with the others-"

"No, he's probably right," I cut in.

"You're being paranoid, you don't know what she's trying to do," Fangs explained.

"We're keeping the remainders of us safe. Sadly Phoenix, Kalo and Jillian are the only ones including myself," Dox pointed out.

"What about me, Ex and Vess?" Fangs asked.

"We're going to protect you," he added.

Fangs was confused about the plan.

"What he's trying to say is you will be of no help to us what so ever," I explained. "We're just saying we want you to be safe." "Fine," Fangs groaned.

We looked over at Ex and Vess who sat quietly doing nothing.

"Are you done yet? This plan better be good. And it should involve food, because I'm starving," Ex sighed.

"I'll deal with that later, and you're not going to do anything. We'll get you to higher ground, you'll be safe there," Dox explained.

"What!? Wait, so we just sit there and do nothing?" Vess exclaimed.

"It keeps you safe, doing nothing. It saves you from getting into danger," Dox snapped. So he led his sons off down into the streets. I formed and Fangs climbed on my back. We followed from up above and Dox led us all to the Agency. We landed on the roof and Fangs climbed down. I turned human, and looked around. The skyscrapers seemed to have higher ground than that.

"It's less noticeable, we're not in plain sight that way," Dox explained, exactly reading my thoughts.

"I'm still hungry," Ex whimpered.

"Alright, alright," Dox groaned, "Phoenix can you find some stuff from the kitchen?"

"Sure," I nodded and swooped down to one of the shaded windows. I picked the lock with my claw, and slipped inside the office. I pulled the door open a crack and the hallway was empty. So I rushed through the hallways to the employee's room, and got into the kitchen. I grabbed a bag from the cabinet and rummaged through all the shelves and drawers and stuff the bag with food. Meat, fish, fruit, cans, I had pretty much robbed them clean.

I pried open the grate and climbed into the ducts. The vents were the safest way to get around the building without getting caught. As I crawled through on my way out I noticed one of the lights was on. I looked down below to see Saube talking to a girl tied up in a chair. It was Lynx's soldier.

"Is there anything I can do to make you more comfortable before we talk?" Saube asked. The girl looked away and said nothing.

"Where's your leader?" He asked.

"Actually I could use some peace and quiet to think it over," the girl shrugged.

"But there's nothing to think about," Saube chuckled.

"Whether or not I want to tear your heart out is something," the girl snapped.

"Fine, five minutes," Saube nodded and stepped out of the room.

"Psst!" The girl looked up at me and cocked her head. I nodded and left the bag where it was. I pulled open the grate and hung from my feet holding out my hands. She clawed the ropes to shreds and jumped up grabbing my hands. I pulled her up and got up myself. Just then I heard Saube shout. He had probably found the mess in the kitchen.

"Go, come on," I nudged her and we rushed out on the roof. All the guards were gone so he wouldn't leave to catch me. We got up onto the roof and the others looked at me.

"How did you know she was there?" Fangs asked.

"Ducts," I shrugged.

"Thank you, thank you so much," the girl smiled and nodded thankfully. Then she formed and disappeared over the rooftops.

I dropped the bag of food on the ground. We all sat down and ate through the fish, meats, fruits and canned vegetables. Dox and I sat on the ledge and surveyed the city while the boys sat quietly. Kalo and Jillian joined us and fetched some food for themselves.

"Are you sure this plan will work?" Vess asked Dox.

"Do you not trust me?" Dox seemed puzzled.

"I just don't want anything bad to happen and you're not there," Vess explained.

"I'm always going to be there. I've never missed-" Dox's ears started twitching. He stood, formed, and raced off.

"It's probably Ford," I nodded.

Sure enough he came back with his cousin trailing behind him, with Evian on his back.

"Nice going, Ford," Dox sighed and climbed onto the ledge. "Like I said Vess, I never miss."

"Okay it's not my fault I ran into one of their traps," Ford snapped.

"Well it's your fault your sister is of no help to me whatsoever," Dox glared at Evian.

"What do you want a thank you card?!" Evian snapped, "Greedy."

"Don't push me, kid, I saved you, the least you could do is stop complaining to me," Dox growled. We all fell quiet and remained in silence for a while.

"Did you see any of our own back there, in the building?" Dox asked.

"No. The toxin doesn't kill you, it just knocks you out," I shrugged.

“Well, that’s less for us to worry about,” Dox glanced back at his sons, “We have to keep them safe, and if Saube is here, they’re in danger.” I nodded, understanding his concern. Suddenly there was a shout from far off, a distress call, cut short.

“What was that?” The boys looked at us worriedly.

“It was nothing,” I assured them but they didn’t seem convinced.

“We’re not stupid, that was a distress call...Wasn’t it?” Vess snapped.

Dox sighed, “One down, some billions more to go.”

“What’ your problem?” Ex asked.

“One rule, and that’s trust no one,” Dox growled, and they stopped asking. Everyone looked from one another.

“But that means we can’t trust you?” Evian added. Dox and I glanced at each other.

“We’ll be fine,” I whispered and he smiled.

32

I woke up the next morning and found Dox already awake. We had decided to spend the night and move to another location the next day. I sat down with him as he looked out over the city.

"Can they trust us? Most of all can we trust ourselves?" Dox wondered.

"You're not seriously thinking about it, are you? Now's not a good time to go away and think about life problems," I looked at him worriedly. He'd done it before, he'd leave for weeks and then come back and say that nothing happened and that he just went for a walk to clear his mind.

"I already did this morning, and picked up a few things from HQ. No one was there so I wouldn't have to worry about getting caught," Dox added. He handed me a watch, and I slipped it on my wrist. It lit up showing a map of the city, and a red dot where we were.

"Wait, but it's tracking me?" I didn't know what was happening but I had a feeling he understood and would explain.

"No, I set it to track me, now you can find me anywhere. I set mine to track you. We can find each other." He turned to look at the others who were still asleep. They all had the watches strapped to their wrists. "Each person's is set to find one of us. So I did a little work while you were asleep."

"Well, should we get moving?" I asked.

"Maybe we should wait for them to wake up, plus I thought you should get some energy. So picked up some stuff from the market," Dox shrugged. He pulled a loaf of bread from a bag and his dagger. He sliced a few pieces of bread for the both of us. Then he put the rest of the loaf back in the bag. But of course we were still hungry and split and ate the rest of the bread.

The others woke up and we packed up to leave. Ford and Evian stood and watched.

"Aren't you coming?" Dox asked.

"We're going home. He just wants to see you go safely," Evian shook her head, looking at Ford with a smile.

"If it's dangerous I'm just being sure you're safe. That's why I brought a few more friends that are going with you." Ford sounded a little commanding. Mori and Edgar climbed onto the roof. Mori looked at Ford in shock.

"You tricked me, into going with him? I'm not going anywhere with him!" Mori growled.

"Oh you're going, you're safer with them," Ford snapped.

"Fine," Mori groaned, and didn't argue with him.

"That means you follow our rules. That includes helping people," Dox added. He showed them the watch on his wrist, and they had the same ones.

"Oh by the way," I added, the ring on my finger glowed and circled around the three of them, before forming handcuffs on their wrists, "I don't trust you together," I glanced at each of them suspiciously.

"He has a point," the three of them replied simultaneously before glaring at each other.

I formed and we loaded on and took off.

We moved around the city and got further towards the outskirts of town. When I landed on a nearby apartment to rest, white vans were parked below.

"What's up?" Dox asked.

"They're here, right below us," I sighed.

"If they're here we can just go home," Fangs groaned.

"I'd love to, but we can't, we'll be cornered. It's best to keep going," I explained.

We waited for a bit giving each other silent glares. Mori glanced at Edgar who looked back at him, and they both turned away. Then Mori stared at Dox, who caught him staring and glared back angrily. Then Dox looked at me and I looked at Mori. Our glares and glances were passed around, and around, and back again until it was night fall and the guards had left but the vans were still there. We took off again but I hovered over the vans for a moment. Seven white vans with the lab logo plastered on the side, parked in a circle.

"We should get going," Dox reminded me.

"Hold on." I looked around at the buildings for a second, each covered by the shadow of another.

I felt Dox shift on my back, and I knew what he was thinking.

"Phoenix, go," Dox snapped.

"Get off, I need to look at this," I called over my shoulder.

"Look dummy, we need to go now. We don't have time for you to investigate," Mori barked.

"No, he's…He's got a point," Dox's ears twitched rapidly.

"And this is why you never trust Black Cloaks. Always pausing at a sign of danger," Edgar muttered to himself. I ignored him and inched closer to vans. I ducked my head and scanned the area, I had a feeling they were close.

"Look out for airships. They could be close behind," I called over my shoulder before taking off. We got further and further towards the outskirts of town and after hours of flying, we paused to rest again. I rested my head down and dozed off for a bit.

"Phoenix. Phoenix wake up!" I felt someone nudge me continuously, and woke up to find Dox nudging me in the back.

"We got captured again, didn't we?" I groaned.

"Do you think you can get me out of these?" Dox asked.

"Yeah why?" I had not the slightest clue what he was planning but I was willing to help.

"If I can reach that panel on the ceiling, I can reverse the polarity, attach myself to the ceilings crawl through the vents and…" Dox continued to ramble about some complicated plan of his, meanwhile I went to snap the ropes, until I realized our wrists were tied separately, linked by titanium.

"I can get you out, but I'll have trouble seeing so I won't be of much help."

"That'll be fine, I can get the rest done myself."

I focused on the titanium binding, as my vision clouded a bright orange and I heard the binds snap. My vision continued to stay clouded, and when it cleared Dox was on his feet staring at the panel on the ceiling.

"Get to it genius, you've been talking about polarity for the past hour," Mori snapped. Dox jumped for the panel and pulled off the cover. He looked down at the chains around his ankles. He pulled a laser pen from his pocket and used it to cut the chains.

"You have a laser pen on you?" Ex asked.

"Yeah, I build things in my spare time," he nodded and clicked a dial on the back of his left boot. I was in shock to notice he was hovering below the panel.

"I just have to cut the wire and-" Dox's boots suddenly clung to the ceiling as he hung upside, and I felt the binds around my wrists suddenly jerk me against the wall. Suddenly the door came open. He cut everyone loose and led us down the hall.

"What did you do?" Edgar asked staring one of the guards in the face. Each guard we passed was stuck to the wall like a magnet, and couldn't move.

"The one downside to metal walls," Dox knocked his fist against the wall, "I turned on the magnetic field, so when the door opened, it spread everywhere throughout the building. We'll split up, cover more ground, and search for any of our own."

Mori, Edgar, Kalo, and Jillian went one way, Dox, Fangs, Ex, Vess and I went the other way. Both Dox and I were concerned for our sons. We passed through hundreds of hallways, and stopped.

"Can you see further ahead?" Dox asked me. I focused my X-ray vision and stared down the winding hallways.

"The control room's empty except for one. And they're not against the wall," I explained. We continued forward, and burst into the control room. Saube threw his hands in the air and clapped.

"Bravo! I didn't know you were an inventor? I could use your knowledge...If you'd be willing to?" Saube tossed something into the air and Dox snatched it. I watched him hold it in his hand and inspect it. We all peered over his shoulders to see. A gold coin. I turned away, I couldn't watch him be corrupted by gold.

"You like it? It's all yours, if you work for me. You'll get that one and many more," Saube added.

"Fine, but you're going to hate me after this," Dox replied, throwing the coin the air, and I was surprised to hear the snapping noise of solid gold beneath his foot.

"I bet you twenty bucks I can kill him with one hand."

"I'd like to see that. Quite a show," I snickered. I watched as he brought Saube off his feet. I found it to be entertaining until I realized he was strangling him. After a few seconds I came to be terribly bored, grabbed Dox's dagger out of his pocket and lunged forward thrusting out the dagger and just as it pierced Saube's chest I felt a strange piercing of my own. It was a glowing gold dagger the same one Ferdinand had used on me before. Saube thrust out the weapon, and although it didn't stab me, I was jerked back with an alarming blast and thrown against the doors. Dox threw Saube into thrown into the pillar behind him and ran to me. I rose to my feet, and there was a sudden jerk in the floor beneath us. It felt like an earthquake, until I realized we had taken down a main pillar and that the building was caving in around us. Suddenly everything began to crumble and chunks of the ceiling and roof began to fall over us. I held up my hands and formed a shield around the five of us. As pieces began to fall, they burned to nothing as they hit the shield.

"Phoenix behind you!" Dox shouted, but I hadn't noticed and all of a sudden I was hit in the back of the head by a chunk of cement. I fell to the floor in an instant.

33

I woke up and looked all around. There was no longer an exit, just piled high walls of cement and wiring. And in the corner was Saube's lifeless body. We were trapped and there was no way of getting out. The others were also unconscious. Fangs, Vess, and Ex, lying on the ground, and Dox further away from us on the ground, bruised and dripping with blood. I was covered in a heap of cement, wires and titanium. The second I started to move it weakened my body. Suddenly there were shouts and a siren, loud barks, more shouts, and sirens could be heard as they got closer.

"Help. Help, please…," I rasped. Fangs suddenly woke at the noise. He shook Ex and Vess awake quickly and sent them to grab Dox. He came towards me and shifted the weight over me and grabbed my arm. Fangs grabbed me, and Ex and Vess dragged Dox, and at the next blast of sirens, they began shouting for help. I could do nothing. I couldn't move, and felt paralyzed. The wall in front of us broke down and crumbled as it wreckage was pulled away. There was a rush of sirens, and...Humans. They were helping us? They pulled Dox and I into an ambulance and drove away immediately. They gave us no stretchers, only left us in the bed of the truck with nothing but each other. So we were still enemies. Dox leaned against me, and I leaned against him. He held out his hand and I reached out and held it. We were going to be okay…

EPILOGUE

And we were okay. Dox and I spent six months in the hospital. I only needed three months to recover but Dox needed another three, and I stayed the whole six months. When we left we were greeted by Dox's brothers, our groups and most importantly, Kareen and Rogue.

"How?" I asked, hugging Rogue tight.

"I have the Traders to thank for that," Rogue whispered back and hugged me.

Later on we'd learn that the Traders themselves had sacrificed two of their saves, and used their last stored syndrome. The best part of returning home, was watching my best friend see his brothers again. They were quiet and said nothing, but hugged each other.

"Thank you," Dox whispered.

"Hey, I can't watch my only married brother lose the love of his life. We were mourning her ourselves. We care," Mori shrugged.

Dox climbed on my back and we rode off to the skyscraper with Rogue and Kareen. We arrived just as the sun set. We were home, and like I said, everything was okay. Or at least...I thought it was.

THE END

ABOUT THE AUTHOR

Mya Lampley is 13 years old, and currently lives in Massachusetts, with her mother and father. She enjoys using her imagination to create stories that allow her readers to escape the bonds of reality. *Phoenix* is her first book and she hopes readers will enjoy discovering more about the characters she has created.

Made in the USA
Middletown, DE
30 August 2017